SPLIT

THE

EASTERN

SKY

To "Joel
God Bless,
Wm Eyer

Lawrence E. Jerome

SPLIT THE EASTERN SKY

WILLIAM J. EYER
LAWRENCE E. JERALDS

A&L Enterprises
Ava, IL

The Scripture quotations in this publication are from the King James Version of the Bible.

This is a fictional work. The names, characters, places, and incidents (other than Biblical references) used herein are from the imagination of the authors or are used fictitiously and are not to be construed as actual. Any similarity to actual events, organizations, locales, or persons, living or dead, is completely coincidental.

Split The Eastern Sky by William J. Eyer
Lawrence E. Jeralds

ISBN-10: **0-9745359-4-X**
ISBN-13: **978-0-9745359-4-4**
Copyright © 1997 by William J. Eyer
Copyright © 2006 by A&L Enterprises

Cover Art by **Jarrett Eyer**
Edited by **Ann B. Jeralds**

Published by:
A&L Enterprises
1531 Hwy 151
Ava, IL 62907

Printed in the United States of America by
BookMasters, Inc.

TABLE OF CONTENTS

DEDICATION and ACKNOWLEDGEMENT

DEDICATION:

We wish to dedicate the entire Covenant Trilogy and especially this the third book of the Trilogy, **Split The Eastern Sky**, to **Jesus** our **Lord** and to the following people:

Bill- My parents who took this orphan in and gave him a chance in life. My wife Jan who has stuck by me for 35 years now in marriage and has put up with much for me to write this Trilogy over the past 15 or so years. To Terra, my daughter and her family and my son, Jarrett, and his family.

Larry- My wife, Ann, and my son, Joseph, for their support and enduring long hours of my attention glued to the computer screen

Lastly to our fans who have made the completion of this Trilogy possible.

....

ACKNOWLEDGMENTS:

We want to thank our Publisher, A&L Enterprises and especially one of our Editor, Ann. Without your eye for detail, well this just wouldn't be as good a work.

Bill would like to thank Pastor Terry Jackson for his friendship, for holding me accountable and for reading every last word of our manuscripts, both the first and subsequent rewrites. Thanks Terry for the help, the ideas, the Biblical expertise and the encouragement.

Finally, we thank You Jesus for the inspiration that started this project and carried it and us to this point in our lives; we can't wait to enjoy our place in Your Kingdom.

CHAPTER ONE

UNHOLY NIGHT

"And it was given unto him to make
war with the saints, and to overcome
them: and power was given him over
all kindreds, and tongues and nations.
And all that dwell upon the earth
shall worship him, whose names are
not written in the book of life of the
Lamb slain from the foundation of the world."
Revelation 13:7-8

GENERAL WORL'S CONSTANT BATTLE:

General Worl stood high on the hill watching the battle that was raging below. He was surrounded by a haze of reddish yellow sulfuric smoke, which was threatening to block his view. It was caused by the hundreds of demons who had been charging Worl's position for the last hour. Worl's faithful guards, Left and Right, had been slashing, blocking, and spending the entire hour killing one demon after another in protection of Worl allowing him to direct his men in this mighty warfare.

Worl so trusted his guards that he ignored the fierce battle at his own feet and watched instead the largest build-up of demons that he had seen in years. Worl saw the Demon of Darkness, Satan himself; rise up from the nether world below to personally direct his troops. Shrieks of pain, which could be heard even above the din of battle, came from a large group of demons located behind the front lines of Satan's attack force. They were painfully molded and melded together to form large brightly lit Demon Ships. Worl had seen these ships many times; Satan had used them to deceive mankind for centuries. What Worl had never seen before was this large a build-up of ships. The ships rose into the air and were full of light and power. It was only Worl's trained angelic eye that could discern the darkness within. Individual demons were also painfully transformed into smaller ships as they too rose into the air and then flew straight for the larger ships. Millions upon millions of these smaller ships were formed and then flown into the larger ships until they were filled to a copious capacity.

Meanwhile on the front lines, Worl's men fought to reach and stop these ships from forming. Just as they broke through Satan's defenses and began storming the newly formed ships, the order came to Worl from Michael, the Archangel, that he and his men were to pull back! They were to allow the demons full access to the earth. When Worl's men heard this news, they instantly stopped their attack, but began shouting in protest until Worl raised his hand and all became silent. Even the demons stopped their fighting to listen to this mighty General.

Worl smiled a broad happy smile and spoke in a powerful, even joyful voice, "My friends! We've been ordered to return to Heaven! Our Lord has agreed to a meeting between himself and that Demon of Darkness, Satan. This meeting will take place very soon and will loose such power, as the world has never seen. Satan is to be given free reign to devour earth and everyone on it!"

The Angels' and Demons' collective mouths dropped open! This meant only one thing! They had all anticipated its arrival but now that it was here, none could believe that it was true. If the Lord were going to allow Satan free reign on the earth, then that could only mean that Jesus was about to remove "The Body of Christ" from the world. The long awaited Rapture was finally at hand!

Satan watched, as the Angels departed and his own Demons celebrated the news. A knot formed, with mixed feelings of triumph and dread, in the pit of his stomach. This had all been too easy. True he had petitioned the Lord Jesus for an audience to discuss the dispersion of property and of the humans on the Earth; and he had been granted the meeting; and now it appeared that in his very moment of triumph, Jesus had recalled his men in honor of that meeting. Still, it had been too easy. Satan laughed uneasily at his fears and at the predictability of his enemy, the supposed Christ of the World, the Savior of the human race. Satan knew that Jesus would follow the rules and that has always given Satan the upper hand.

Satan shook off his doubts and reveled in his victory, dreaming of the final battle and his final victory, once and for all, over this Lamb of God, this so-called Jesus the Christ!

C/K West Outpost (code name: Secret Eye One) August 31st, 2---: 0558 HOURS:

On the border where Colorado joins the state of Kansas, in a newly built, well hidden Air Force bunker, a defense group lay in wait for any enemy who dared to cross this position on it's way to attack Scott Air Force Base. This was Secret Eye One, the west defense outpost for the newly formed Response Section of Scott Air Force Base. Scott had been mostly a search and rescue type of operation. Now it had a fully operational section, named "Sting", that could give a complete military response to any threat making it this far in-land.

Sting had thirty newly built F-117A stealth fighters. They were sleek, black, and looked like bats in flight. They were fast and deadly with both machine gun and missile capability. Sting also had six F-15 and F-16 squads as well as forty new F-35 response fighters. But the eyes and ears of the defense were these "Secret Eyes" which were located one hundred miles apart and usually one state away from SAFB in all directions. Nothing could get by them undetected, or so it was boasted!

These outposts were manned by two Air Force personnel, working in twelve-hour shifts, assigned to the highly secret "Sting" operation. The two operators of Secret Eye One, were buried alive some forty feet below the surface and could only hear the sounds from above through the speakers over their heads and see through the lenses of the many cameras, which were well hidden around the "Tree". There was only one access to this bunker and that was through the door, which was hidden in what looked like a large tree.

If a person could get past the electrified fence which surrounded this 70 acre game reserve of Secret Eye One, and if they followed the rock road leading up to the parking area just outside of the "Tree" they would only find a large plaque which read:

GAME PRESERVE OF THE UNITED STATES
GOVERNMENT
"For the preservation of our most sacred resources."

Only the knowledgeable were aware that the plaque meant people not animals. But it didn't lie! This place would help preserve life and freedom with its early alert warning system.

This 70 acres was filled with all sorts of wild life, including deer, owls, raccoons, and beaver. As a matter of fact the two bored operators of Secret Eye One were watching a deer on their monitor screen at this very moment. It was not that they really expected anyone to break into this secret facility, but security protocol called for external "seeing and hearing" devices. Psychologists also insisted that these devices would lessen the claustrophobic tendencies of personnel locked in the bunkers for twelve hours at a time. Thus the sensors and cameras in the immediate area of the "Tree" had a two-fold function and were coupled with occasional aerial reconnaissance planes from Scott. These planes were fitted with special infrared cameras to catch any would-be trespasser. They had in fact caught a team of poachers in this manner. Poachers, who were shocked, when the large, very fast black attack helicopters landed near them and even more shocked when several security personnel stormed out of the helicopters and arrested them, confiscated their truck, left outside the compound, and fined them heavily. The citizens of Hale, Colorado, were shocked when they saw just how serious the Government was about these protected animals, and no one dared to enter the reserve again.

The deer the operators were watching on the infrared raised its head as if to test the air for enemies. Its nose and ears twitching and turning like radar found no enemy, so it returned to it's early morning grazing.

"Hey Sarge! Pass me a smoke, would you, I just ran out!"

Sgt. Carlyn, a thirty year professional, looked up from the radar screen he was monitoring, sighed heavily and threw the pack to Winston. Lt. Oliver Winston caught the pack gratefully and lit one of the cigarettes. While Winston was watching the smoke of his cigarette rise upward and then spill into the vent, the monitor showed the deer jump suddenly and then bolt out of sight. This was unseen by either of the operators. All of these Secret Eye posts were, for the time being, operated only by personnel with the rank of Sergeant or above. Later, after the system had been tried, tested and deemed ready, lower ranking personnel would be trained and brought on duty, but that was at least two years down the road.

Lt. Winston slowly turned his head to continue watching the deer and groaned, "Oh shoot! The deer is gone! I was hoping that he would wait until 0800 so I could bag him. My freezer is getting mighty low!"

The Sergeant laughed, "Sure, kill your promising career for a hundred pounds of deer meat. I..."

Lt. Winston interrupted Sgt. Carlyn and asked, "What's the forecast like today?"

Sgt. Carlyn looked at his notes and said, "Clear and sunny. Why?"

Lt. Winston sat forward in his seat and said, "Because a tree just fell and knocked out camera three. Look at this!"

The Sergeant looked at his own screen and whistled. What few trees there were here in the plains, were being bent almost in half. Some were breaking and some of the broken ones were actually rolling on the ground, making a roaring rumbling sound, which was feeding into their loudspeaker system. They had to turn it down; it was beginning to hurt their ears. Then came the flare of light that burned out all of their cameras and set off every alarm in the compound.

As the ground shook and the bunker cracked Lt. Winston reached for the red phone.

Scott Air Force Base: (New Response Section-OPS) August 31st, 2---: 0600 HOURS:

Had she been asked for her preference, Sgt. Jackson, a 22-year-old female who loved her new assignment, would have wished for day shift instead of midnights. As it was, though, she was told which shift to work and that was all right. She had decided to make a career of the Air Force and, therefore; knew that her life would be full of others telling her what to do. The hardest part of her job came at about this time of the morning and she wasn't the only person affected. Everyone in the room had trouble staying awake between 0600 and 0800. Their bodies screamed for sleep at about this time every morning, no matter how much sleep they might have had during the day. The only thing that helped was when they were busy and currently, they were not! Sgt. Jackson would talk to the other First Response Operators as they were called in the OPS room and they would joke around and share stories, anything to cut the boredom.

For now though, she had just poured her tenth cup of coffee for the night and was just taking a sip when her board lit up like a Christmas tree! Alarm lights lit up, buzzers went off and the red phone rang. Sgt. Jackson spit out her coffee, dropped the cup that shattered on the floor, and yelled for Captain Yelders to get his tail over here.

The Captain was there in three seconds, but Sgt. Jackson had already answered the red phone, switching it to "hands free" and said, "Code name?"

An agitated voice came over the loud speakers in OPS, "Secret Eye One-Code 6-niner-Alpha-6.

Sgt. Jackson opened the sealed red codebook, the codes are updated weekly, and she looked up Secret Eye One, today's date and said, "Confirmed! What's the nature of your report Lt. Winston?"

Lt. Winston yelled nervously, "They're gone OPS! It's all gone!"

"What's gone Winston? Make sense man!"

"The trees around us, they're all gone! Blown away by some kind of gale force wind. Radar shows contact with an object that's at least two football fields across at the center. It's east bound at an airspeed of 300 mph, and it's on a direct intercept course for Scott. The object has refused to identify itself to us and must be considered hostile."

"All right Winston! Stay put and we'll send a team out to you to check on damage and pick you up." It was Capt. Yelders, Operations Officer in control of "Sting", who yelled that last order, right before he hit the red alarm button, which would alert the pilots to man their planes, and then he picked up the phone to call Base Commander Pips.

Barracks for First Response Pilots:
August 31, 2---: 0600 HOURS:

Glang! Glang! Glang!

Flight Leader Derecks was ripped from his warm dreams, as he leaped from his even warmer bed. The air conditioner had the floor cold and goose bumps played over the pilot's body as he slid into his flight suit.

The incessant alert Glang! Glang! Glang! continued to blare in his ears clearing any stubborn cobwebs from his brain. Then something happened that turned this from a dull routine drill to a thrilling, yet terrifying reality.

"All flight leaders report to OPS! This is not a drill! I repeat, all flight leaders report to OPS! This is not a drill! Blue flight cleared for immediate take off! Authorized Capt. Yelders, Alpha 88 Omega!"

Derecks was Blue Flight Leader! Here it was! This was what he had been trained for all of these years, and now it was time to show what his squad had.

Possibilities rolled through his mind as he and his pilots ran for their planes.

He loved the sight of those sleek, black jets! The very quiet sounds of their "whisper" engines warming up, the smell of burned fuel! Derecks didn't know who the enemy was but he was ready to take them on.

As he climbed into the cockpit, he refused to think of his wife, Debbie, or their newborn son, Jeffrey. It would only serve to slow him down, or cause him to take his mind off of his duty. No, from this point on he had the single-minded purpose of finding this unknown enemy, turning him back if he could, or destroying him if he could not!

"Blue Leader to Flight Control."

"Go ahead Blue Leader."

"We are five for five rolling out."

"You're verified and cleared for take off. Good hunting, Blue Leader. Flight Control out."

The five jets quietly slipped into the early morning sky like ghosts fleeing the first light of day and headed west toward the intended target.

The OPS room was quiet with anticipation as everyone watched the large radar screen at the south end of the room. Suddenly, the single, unidentified Bogie was joined by the five friendlies, which had left their identification beacons on so they could be seen by OPS. The two targets raced toward each other with one inevitable outcome. One of them had to leave this air space!

The speakers came to life as Blue Leader's voice exploded from them with the excitement of anticipated battle but covered with just a little static, "Flight Control this is Blue Leader, we have a visual on the bogie. It appears to be metal-{garbled}. Its round and {unintelligible} diameter is about two football fields across. It appears flat on the bottom and rises toward a smaller dome on the top. It's - typ {garbled}--al U. F. -. sh..."{lost contact}.

The static had been slowly increasing until his last words had been all but covered over. The men and women in the room had to strain to hear his final words.

{contact reestablished} "Flight Com-{static}, I think...Oh my God it's {static}-ing it's...Code name Mother Sh--!{static fades over} - repeat C... name Mother Ship!" Loud static was all that filled the speakers after that.

On the large screen, they saw the larger blip swallow first flight leader, then each of the other jets, until only the large blip was left. Then the larger blip stopped much too suddenly and impossibly shot straight up and out of the Earth's atmosphere before anyone could react and disappeared off of all screens.

Everyone just stood in shock for a moment. There was no other noise in the room other than the incessant static coming from the speakers.

The Base Commander, who had just arrived, still wearing his pajamas, face gray, hair disheveled, snapped, "Turn that thing off!" The static abruptly stopped, leaving a silence that was more deafening than the noise.

He turned to his communications officer, Sgt. Jackson and said, "Get me the President on the red phone and patch it through to my office."

He walked silently out of the room barely able to carry the weight of command on his shoulders this particular morning. In less than fifteen minutes, he had lost five pilots, and five jets, to an unseen and unknown enemy. Each Jet would cost two million dollars to replace and of course the pilots were irreplaceable. This wasn't the first squadron that the Air Force had lost to this enemy, but it was the first that he had lost. As he approached his door Capt. Yelders said, "Sir? I..."

Pips turned and said in a very tired, strained voice, "Don't worry Stan, there was nothing you could do."

Commander Pips entered his office, opened his bookcase and removed a bottle of Scotch. He poured a stiff glass and then walked over to his desk. He had just taken his first mouthful and was choking on the bitter liquid when the red phone rang.

His stomach knotted as he coughed and choked and then reached for the phone.

He picked it up and a stern male voice said, "Commander, the President will be with you in a moment."

Commander Pips had practiced this scene many times in his mind as part of his job, but he had never really believed that he would ever have to do it.

"Commander Pips this is President Place. How can I help you?"

"Mad.." Pips coughed loudly and slobbered on the phone. He cleared his throat, wiped off the receiver and repeated, "Madam President, excuse me! We've had a situation here. At exactly 6:14 this morning, we lost five jets. Blue Flight Leader Derecks gave the code word Mother Ship just before he was swallowed up by the blip. According to regulations, I'm instructed to inform you,

Madam President that this code word means that he saw many other ships within the one ship and that it could be an invasion force. The blip is gone for now, but I suggest we go to yellow alert Nation wide."

"Thank you, Commander, we'll take it under advisement. In the mean time, get in a jet and report to my office at 0900 tomorrow morning. That's all."

The phone line went dead and Commander Pips finished his drink, as he thought, *"That's not part of the plan that I was taught!"* Commander Pips was really nervous now because this summons to Washington could only mean one thing, *"Oh my God! This wasn't the only incident this morning! That's got to be it!"* He poured another drink.

Covenant's Warehouse District:
August 31st, 2---: 2200 HOURS:

The dark recesses of Warehouse #6, held its own secrets. Here was the site of the Temple of the newly revived Brotherhood of Faith. These people were a combination of Satan Worshipers, Witches, and other Occult groups. They had joined together for one purpose and one purpose only; namely, the revival of the ancient practice of human sacrifice, in exchange for the power promised by the Lord of Darkness, Satan, himself!

*　　　　*　　　　*

The blade of the ceremonial knife caught and reflected the candlelight as the Master of the Temple raised it above his head.

He cried out, "To your honor and glory Lord Satan!"

He then brought the knife down slowly toward the bound and gagged woman tied helplessly to the altar of sacrifice. She was paralyzed with fear and didn't even scream as the razor sharp blade cut into her carotid artery spraying her life's blood upon the altar, the Master of the Temple and all the worshipers.

As her life slipped away with every drop of blood that pulsed from her artery into the ceremonial chalice, the woman thought, *"Oh God forgive me in Jesus' name. I'm sorry if I offended you please don't desert me now!"*

Maria was becoming dizzy and cold as she thought, *"Why is this happening God? I'm just a poor homeless girl, why did they pick me to offer to Satan? I assure you God that I love you and not Satan. Please sweet Jesus come to my aide..."*

As these final thoughts flashed through Maria's mind, and she eased into death, a bright flash of light caught her attention. The most beautiful being that she had ever seen appeared before her. The light seemed to come from within the being. As the light dimmed slightly a woman appeared. It was then that Maria noticed the wings unfurling to their full seven-foot wingspan.

The Angel smiled down at Maria and said, "You've been heard my child, and our gracious God has summoned you to appear before him this very day. Come!"

The Angel bent down and took Maria's hand and she found herself suddenly engulfed in a warm, loving, and very peaceful light. Gone were the memories of the terrifying experience that had just taken her life. The dissection of her heart for the consumption of the witches present was hidden from Maria. She was forever out of reach of Satan's evil deeds and all of his evil servants.

Maria felt the wings wrap around her, and she sensed rather than felt their movement through the veils that separate this world from the next. When the wings opened again, Maria was lost in the magnificence of God. For the first time in her life, Maria had a home.

Covenant Business District:
August 31st, 2---: 2100 HOURS (One Hour Earlier):

Officer John T. Stone and Officer Frank P. Winslow were more than mid-way in their shift and they needed a break. Since 1600 hours, they had handled five burglary reports, three lost dog reports, and one skunk, which had some how found its way into the City of Covenant. They had also stopped three bar fights that had broken out among the workers, who had filed into the many bars of the factory sector immediately after work.

Now, however, the officers had left the factories and bars behind and were in the main business area of Covenant. The city had grown from thirty thousand people to over sixty thousand people in just over a year, bringing many opportunities to the community along with a lot of crime, drugs, gambling, and the occult.

Officer Stone, a five-year veteran of Covenant and a self-proclaimed "Ace" driver, was behind the wheel of the squad car. He pulled up to their favorite restaurant as Winslow, a first year rookie, reached for the mike of the radio.

15

Winslow said, "C-50 to Central."

"Go ahead 50."

"Show us out for lunch at Eadie's on 23rd."

"10-4, 50. Hey, bring me a ham and cheese on wheat would you?"

"Sure Martha, want chips too?"

"No, I'm watching my girlish figure, but thanks anyways."

The officers laughed because Martha weighed 300 pounds if she weighed an ounce.

Winslow said, "10-4 Central. We'll be out on PAC Radio."

Each officer turned on his PAC Radio they carried on their duty belts along with the 9mm, pepper mace, clips, handcuffs and other tools used in the performance of their patrol duties.

Eadie's Eats was a quaint little family restaurant that was clean, had excellent food and reasonable prices. Stone had been eating lunch here for the past five years, and Winslow didn't argue about his choice when he became Stone's partner almost a year ago. Eadie's was nestled between Luke's Bakery on the one side and Sam's liquor store on the other. This small shopping mall also was home to the A & P Finances, Mohr's Travel Agency, and Kim's Video/Arcade, a favorite kids hangout.

It was to Sam's Liquor store that the officers went first, however. It was Stone's second wedding anniversary tomorrow night and Winslow wanted to buy him a present. Winslow knew that neither Stone nor his wife Nancy drank, so he went to the non-alcohol section and picked the fancy, bubbly, grape juice that tasted and looked like champagne without the alcohol.

He looked at the bottle and thought, *"You would think that since they don't put the alcohol in that it would be cheaper than this!"* Winslow took his $20.00 present to the counter and told Stone, "My present to you and Nancy."

Stone picked up the bottle, looked at it, then smiled and said, "I'm really touched. I know how hard it is for you to buy the non-alcoholic beverages."

Winslow smiled. They had agreed to disagree on this point. Stone had preached the evils of drinking and had tried to "win" Winslow over to Jesus Christ the whole time they had worked together. Winslow had finally blown up and told Stone to leave him alone about it. He didn't believe in God and that was the end of it. It had been about a week before they could even talk to each other after that, but slowly their friendship healed, and they agreed not to talk about it anymore. Stone had been sad but resigned himself to the fact that not everyone wanted to be saved.

Winslow smiled and said, "It's the least I can do after all those free meals that you and Nancy have fed me."

Sam, a bald, over weight, Italian man in his sixties, had been watching the two officers. Sam liked these two, and he smiled at them as they approached the register.

Winslow set the bottle down and reached for his wallet.

Sam protested with his usual Italian flair and many hand gestures, "No, no! You-a-no pay here! You good-a-boys. You take-a-good care of Sam."

17

Winslow laid the twenty dollars on the counter as he said, "Sam, the Chief would kill me if I didn't pay, besides it's a gift. Thanks for the offer, Sam, but please take the money."

Sam frowned good naturedly, took the money, and then with his usual smile said, "Well, I-a-thank-a-you boys very much!"

The last thing that Winslow and Stone saw as they left his store was Sam's face, which shone with the child-like radiance as found only in the innocent. They could not remember ever seeing Sam that he wasn't full of happiness and joy. He helped many people in this neighborhood and probably far beyond it. As a matter of fact, he had just won Citizen of the Year for his help in setting up a shelter for the homeless. The food, shelter, and clothes had kept many a body and soul together in the past year.

Winslow deposited the bottle in the trunk of the squad car, closed the lid and then joined Stone as he walked toward Eadie's. As they opened the door, the most wonderful sights and smells met them. There were several happy families eating at the many tables and booths that filled the restaurant. To their left, Eadie was sitting behind her register. She was the first to greet her customers when they came in and the last to wait on them as they left. She liked it that way.

As the officers entered, Eadie looked up, smiled, and said, "Good evening John, Frank, how are you two this fine evening?"

John rubbed his hands together to indicate just how hungry he was and said, "We're ready for a hot meal and some iced coffee, Eadie."

"Well, You've come to the right place, I have both here as well as the best desserts in the county." She pointed to the large glass case which held the most tempting pies the men had ever seen, at least since the last time they were in here.

Winslow said, "Eadie if I keep eating here, I'm going to have to order a larger uniform, and soon!"

The officers had continued toward their table and were getting a bit far away for this conversation with Eadie, but she had already accomplished her purpose. She had made them feel welcome and like one of the family. It was her belief that people enjoyed their meal better if they were at peace with their surroundings, and she had lifted most of the tension from the officers' shoulders and made it possible for them to relax.

The officers had looked at other people's plates and had pretty well decided on the meat loaf by the time they sat down.

When the waitress came, Stone said, "Jane, I'll have the meat loaf dinner, some iced coffee, and apple pie."

Winslow said, "I'll have the same, Jane, but make mine pumpkin pie."

Jane wrote down their orders and went to get their coffee. When she had placed the coffee in front of them, the men sat back and sighed with the relief that comes from finally being able to relax for a moment.

Winslow smiled and said, "You and Nancy got all your anniversary shopping finished yet?"

Stone said, "Just about, actually. We're still waiting for you to get married or something, so we can get you a present"

"Not much chance of that my friend, I..."

Just then Jane brought two plates of steaming hot food and placed one in front of each officer, and said, "You want to wait for you're pie till after?"

Both officers nodded, their mouths were already full of food.

Just then their PAC radios went off together and they heard Martha's voice in stereo, "Attention all units Code 46 at Sam's Liquor on 23rd!"

Stone jumped up first, took one last bite of his hardly touched meal, and reluctantly headed for the door. Winslow followed suit. They both ran through the restaurant toward the exit.

Stone yelled, "Sorry Eadie! Someone's robbing Sam next door. We'll try to come back, but..." he shrugged his shoulders and then opened the door.

As they ran out Eadie yelled, "Don't worry about the bill, boys. You don't have to pay for food you don't get to eat!"

They had to smile at her patience with them. They had lost count of how many times they had repeated this very scene. As the hot August air blasted them instantly bringing sweat to their brows, the officers drew their weapons.

Winslow took cover behind the squad car and covered the car, which was parked in front of Sam's with its motor running. The driver turned white as a sheet when he saw the officers' weapons. The man was thinking of how to react when a gun shot from inside the liquor store decided it for him. He threw the car in gear and spun out of the parking lot.

Stone yelled, "Winslow you go get him, I'll cover the store!"

Just as Winslow slid behind the wheel of the squad, a man came out of the store and Winslow watched in horror as the man shot at Stone, with Stone returning fire. Both men went down simultaneously, in slow motion. Winslow was tempted to get back out, but he knew his orders were to catch the car and that was what he was going to do.

Winslow had backed out, spun out, turned on his lights and siren, reached for the radio mike and yelling, "Martha this is Winslow, Stone and one suspect are down in front of Sam's, and Sam may be down too. I'll need three ambulances! I'm in pursuit of the second suspect who's driving a red Lincoln Town Car, which looks to be an old '98 or '99 model. We're heading west on 23rd toward the warehouse district."

When he let up on the mike button he instantly heard the tones for his ambulances, which were already in progress on another channel. Winslow watched as the Lincoln fish tailed around the corner onto Horner St. and sped off to the North.

Winslow spoke again to Martha, "We are now north bound on Horner St., speeds reaching 80 to 90 miles per hour."

He listened distantly as Martha relayed his information to all units in the area.

Martha spoke to him, "Units 4 and 5 are setting up a road block at Horner and Ninth St."

Winslow couldn't answer for a moment because he was about to loose control of his squad as he fish-tailed around the corner of Eleventh St."

He found the mike, which had fallen on the floor and yelled, "This guy has a scanner. He just turned west on Eleventh, straight into the warehouse district."

Winslow had lost some ground on that last turn and had to really floor it to catch up.

As they approached Workers St. where eleventh dead-ended at a railing above a railroad yard and a warehouse just 300 yards beyond, Winslow watched with a mixture of terror and excitement as the Lincoln tried to avoid the two squad cars which had just pulled into view from opposite directions and stopped right in his path.

What Winslow saw next looked as though it were happening in slow motion.

The Lincoln veered left hitting a row of over stuffed garbage cans spewing both tin and garbage high into the air like a putrid geyser in some weird park. He then hit a mailbox and a fire hydrant, which caused an instant mixture of letters and water to fill the air. An instant later, the Lincoln hit the first squad car. Since the Lincoln had become air born it skipped off the roof of the squad car like a stone skipping across a lake. The Lincoln soared higher, cleared the guardrail and flew through the space between it and the warehouse just across the tracks. As the Lincoln crashed through the warehouse windows, a million shards of shattered glass reflected the red and blue lights of the squad cars high above. It would have made for one spectacular show if it hadn't also meant the loss of life and property.

*   *   *

The Master of the Temple and his followers had just finished their "meal" at Maria's expense when they noticed two bright lights flying toward their Temple window. The Master at first thought of the Demon Ships of his Master but then their world exploded in a sea of glass, fuel, and screaming metal, as the Lincoln crashed through the window into their world of sin and corruption! The Master threw himself under the Altar as the car and debris crushed many of his followers.

*   *   *

Winslow had started to brake even before the Lincoln had left the ground but he watched helplessly as his squad continued to skid toward the second squad car. With all the water and debris on the pavement he just couldn't stop. He felt a little better when he saw the officer jump out of the squad car as it was about to become scrap metal, and jump clear of the accident site. He felt the impact of the passenger side of his squad against the driver's side of the other squad. He heard the ear-piercing squeal of metal being torn apart in some places and fused together in others. Winslow also felt the slow motion and almost weightless drop as the two newly joined vehicles shattered the guardrail and slowly dropped over the edge into the railroad yard below.

CHAPTER TWO
THE FACE OF SATAN EXPOSED

COVENANT'S WAREHOUSE DISTRICT:
August 31st, 2---: 2215 HOURS:

Winslow smelled the smoke first! He was dreaming of barbecues of the past and of all the pleasant memories that go with them. He was laughing as he picked up the fire extinguisher and doused the blazing fire covering the grill. The steaks sizzling happily on the grill, even though not affected by the chemicals of the extinguisher, exploded suddenly causing a great crater to open up under Winslow's feet and he began to fall into a dark, bottomless, pit...

Winslow jumped awake in time to hear his own screams of pain and fear. In an instant, he was aware that he was lying on his back half in and half out of his squad car. The hard rocks of the railroad yard were digging into his flesh as he looked up into the night sky now filled with billowing smoke. The eerie lights from the many squad cars danced wildly on the smoke making a bizarre backdrop for Winslow's nightmare, which was only slowly fading from his tortured mind. The sound of the train whistle brought Winslow back to his present danger. He turned his head to the right and was blinded by the bright headlight of the train engine that was bearing down on his squad car.

As soon as his mind cleared enough for him to understand the danger he was in, he made his body move. He pushed himself out of the squad and half crawled, half ran toward the warehouse. Winslow heard the explosion caused by the train hitting his squad car, and then felt the concussion wave lift him off of his feet. He somersaulted head over heels and then landed on his back. He was gasping for air as the Master of the Temple came stumbling out of the hole in the wall, which was created by the Lincoln. The Master of the Temple was wearing a black robe covered in blood. He had a gash on his forehead but Winslow didn't think that the head wound was the only source of that amount of blood. The man's eyes reflected hatred, and it was all being directed at Winslow. The Master screamed wildly and stumbled toward Winslow. There was the squealing of steel train wheels on the track behind Winslow as the train derailed seconds after destroying his squad car. As the wheels of the train dug deeply into the ground behind him they showered him with dirt and debris. The sounds they made, as loud as they were, became lost in the screams of pain emitting from Winslow's own mouth as he tried to get up. His arms and legs would just not hold him, and he again fell onto his back. Winslow heard the other officers shouting at the Master to freeze. The Master stopped momentarily, looked up toward the officers who lined the torn guard railing above them and then looked over at the others who were running for all they were worth, hoping to stop the Master before he could reach Winslow.

Then the Master looked down at Winslow who lay helpless a mere five feet away and made his decision.

With speed that caught them all by surprise, the Master flipped the knife into the air catching the point and then threw it straight at Winslow before anyone could stop him. Winslow rose up; trying to dodge the incoming knife but it struck his side piercing a lung. Winslow tensed and gasped as an incredibly sharp pain wracked his body. Time seemed to freeze, while Winslow watched, with no little satisfaction, as every other officer there opened fire on the Master of the Temple of the local witch Coven. The man just stood there shaking from the impact of the many bullets, which struck him from every direction at once, depriving him of his life. He stood, frozen in death, for a time after the officers' ceased firing and then with the slowness of a tree just cut through, he fell stiffly forward with a sickening thud onto his face.

The world around Winslow exploded into a kaleidoscope of colors, sounds, and smells. He smelled fresh bread baking, reminding him of his mother's kitchen on a frosty snow covered afternoon. Suddenly, his mother was standing there shaking her finger at him.

She said, "Son, I told you to go to church every Sunday, stay away from alcohol, and those kind of women, but you wouldn't listen. Watch what happens when you disobey God!"

Frank Winslow jumped when he was again confronted by the Master of the Temple, a man he knew to be dead. The Master was running hard toward him, screaming at the top of his lungs, but before he could reach Frank, three shadowy figures appeared in front of the Master, caught him by the shoulders and they all four dissolved slowly out of sight into a dark pool of blood amid the terrified screams of the damned Master.

Frank looked back toward his mother, but found John Stone standing next to him instead. John's uniform was covered in the blood that the armor piercing bullets had caused as they ripped through his bulletproof vest and into his body.

John smiled at him and said, "Like I've always tried to tell you Frank, there is a God, and he does love you. Tell Nancy, that the Lord is coming for the Christians soon. Tell her to keep the faith alive and to spread the word, Our Lord Jesus will soon return! Tell her that I love her Frank, please don't forget." John turned and walked away into the light.

"No, don't go John!" Frank reached for him, but John was already engulfed by the light and his form was lost in the glare.

Just as he was about to disappear all together, John turned and spoke one last time on this side of Heaven, "Frank, a man named Rev. Smith will be coming to see you. Listen to him. Your time is very short." With that, he was gone.

Explosions of light, singing, warmth, love...Frank found himself floating over his own body. It was lying on an Emergency Room table, and doctors and nurses were working frantically on his bloody side.

"Let's shock him again!" A nurse charged the machine and then yelled, "Charged!"

The doctor yelled, "Clear," then zapped him again.

Frank watched in fascination as his body jumped off of the table, then slammed back down again. He watched as the flat line on the machine began to beat sporadically, then flat lined again.

The doctor yelled, "Again!"

Frank watched as they repeated this three more times, and then the beat became regular. He felt a pressure pulling him toward his body. Just as he was sinking back into the bloody mass of flesh, a beautiful being of light appeared before him.

The Being smiled and said, "Frank Winslow, you are being given another chance. Use it wisely! John will be fine with us, but you will not be with us unless you accept Jesus Christ as your Savior. Your time grows short. Don't delay."

With that Frank was engulfed by darkness, and he was once again at the mercy of terrifying nightmares.

IN A DEMONSHIP SOMEWHERE OVER THE NORTH POLE:
August 31st, 2---: 2300 HOURS:

Lt. Derecks reached for his wife, Debbie. She smiled at him but stepped back out of his reach. The faster he ran forward, the faster she slid backward, smiling all the way. Then she was gone, and Lt. Derecks stopped. He saw one of those creatures with his son, Jeffrey. The being was holding him tenderly enough, but something was warning Derecks to be alert. The being bent his head toward the baby as if to kiss his forehead, but suddenly the black line that was the creature's mouth opened wide exposing large teeth. The monster closed its mouth over the baby's head biting hard causing a spray of blood...

Derecks jumped into the world of reality and found that he was still restrained by his seat straps within the cockpit of his jet. Outside his jet was a world of light that shone so brightly that he couldn't see anything. He tried to call the others on his radio but there was nothing but static. Unstrapping himself, Derecks popped the canopy of his jet, which obediently hissed open. He had left his oxygen mask on just in case. He sat tensely still as cool air rushed into the jet. After a few minutes of waiting, he decided that there was no ill effects so he slowly removed his mask. He took a tentative breath and was met with fresh, perfumed air. It was very pleasant so he took his chances, removed his helmet and climbed down the ladder onto the floor below. The floor was covered with some sort of a fog, which was about knee deep. Stomping on the floor to be sure just where it was, Derecks finally let go of his death grip on the ladder. He determined that the floor was some type of plastic or maybe thin metal and that it would support his weight.

As Flight Leader, his duty was clear. Find his pilots, determine their condition, then find and destroy the enemy. As an after thought he pulled his 9mm and popped the clip out to check that it was full. He snapped it back in place and stepped into the cloud of light, or whatever this haze was that surrounded him.

As he fumbled his way through the haze, he thought of the other four humans who had entered this mission with him. There were two men and two women all with about five years of experience; Tom Pierson, Julie Henderson, and Joyce and Robert Flemming, the first married couple to be allowed to fly together in the same squad. They had no children as yet and had decided to get married after they had worked together for three years. After some arguments, meetings with the brass, and a lot of press, the Air Force had caved and let them both stay active, at least until any children come along. Thinking of his fellow officers helped to make the situation seem a little more real. He kept thinking that any minute now he would wake up from this bad dream, or he would find that he was playing a part on an old X-Files rerun and he had just taken his part so seriously that he had forgot he was acting. Somehow, though, he knew that this was very real, and that he was about to see something that not too many humans had lived to tell about. Of course he wasn't sure that he would live to tell about it either.

Derecks thought, *"Daniel get a hold of yourself! Remember what you were always taught! You are named after Daniel, who faced the hungry lions. Pray Daniel! Pray!"*

No sooner had he thought this than the fog began to clear and he heard Tom Pierson calling his name.

"Lt. Derecks, where are you?"

Then he saw Tom and the others walking toward him. He was glad to see that they were all well. None looked hurt in the slightest way. As a matter of fact they were laughing as though they were on a picnic. This made Daniel angry although he couldn't put his finger on why.

He yelled, "Attention aviators!"

They stopped and stared at him, and then slowly, reluctantly, they came to attention.

Walking up to them, Daniel came to attention in front of them and stared them down.

He finally said, "I don't know if you're just happy you're alive, or if you're in a state of shock, but obviously you have forgotten that you are on a mission here. One in which you are still responsible for the safety of the United States of America. Now I understand..."

He was interrupted by a voice from behind him, "Excuse me Lieutenant..."

Daniel swung around and aimed his 9mm, which he still held in his right hand and pointed it at the creature that had just spoken to him, in English!

Pulling the trigger and expecting to see the creature die, it was rather disappointing to hear a "click" and nothing more. Daniel pulled the slide back on his 9mm and let it slam home, hopefully freeing the "jammed" round. He pulled the trigger again with the same loud "click" result. It gave Daniel a frustrated and hopeless feeling to realize that he had no other functional weapon. It was also very anti-climatic to find not a creature standing before him but a rather handsome looking human male instead. The man's eyes were black as coal and had a slightly oval shape to them. He looked to be in his thirties, stood six feet with a slender muscular build. His brown hair was streaked with gray and he had a whimsical smile on his face.

The man didn't react to the gun, which had just misfired for the second time. Instead, as Daniel watched, the man's eyes changed from black to a deep emerald green with yellowish pupils. It gave Daniel the creeps to watch those deep eyes stare into his very soul. A chill ran down his spine as the man spoke.

He said, "Daniel, it's useless to try to shoot me, nothing of that sort will work while you're on my ship."

Daniel put the gun away slowly as he said, "Your ship? What do you mean your ship? This didn't come from Earth."

"You're right of course Daniel, but as I have already explained to your friends over there, I'm not from this Earth either. Not only that, you're also alien to the Earth. We put you on this planet thousands of years ago just as we have populated many other worlds in several different universes. The creation story that you are so familiar with is true, Daniel, but it wasn't a story about your world but rather it was a story about mine.

"But we have time for explanations later. For now, let me introduce myself. My name is Alfred Canards, at least on my world. On your world, which I visited last about two thousand years ago, I was called Jesus of Nazareth, or Jesus the Christ. As I promised, Daniel, I have returned. The time of my arrival has come."

Daniel couldn't believe his ears. He stared at his friends and could tell instantly from their expressions of awe that they believed the man totally. He looked at the man's hands and sure enough there were white scars on the front and back of both wrists. The man had held them up and was turning them over, daring Daniel to deny the evidence before him.

Daniel, however, was the only person in the group that was both a Jew and a Christian and he had his doubts. Something just didn't fit and Daniel was going to find out just what it was that was bothering him.

COVENANT; CHIEF GRADY O'LEARY'S HOUSE: September 1st, 2---: 0010 HOURS:

Grady O'Leary was the Chief of Police of Covenant. He was hard working, fair, and everyone liked working for him. He worked so hard and his hours were so long that no one wanted to bother him at home at this hour. They also knew his wife Marla had just flown in from a story in Florida and she was scheduled for an early flight in the morning for Washington. As a news anchor she traveled all over the United States, and the world for that matter, chasing one big story after another. They had spent hours discussing their plans and making contracts with each other to cover every contingency for the next twenty years.

They decided that Marla would work at her career before they had children. After children, she would lay off work until they were in school and then she would go back to work. It made them feel like they had control over their lives, which they both knew they did not. Grady missed Marla so much when she was away, but he seldom complained about it because he could see how happy it made her. They had spent the day catching each other up on their careers. Grady was trying to solve a series of serial killings affecting his city for the last three weeks, but they were no closer to the killer now, than they had been after the first murder. In those three long weeks, five women had been found murdered and mutilated, and Grady feared that the witches were back in town!

Marla told Grady about the story she was going to cover in Washington. She expected the President to announce tomorrow the withdrawal of the United States from the United Nations early next month.

They had talked for hours, eaten the pizza they'd had delivered, and then had gone to bed early. They had not slept, of course, but had become reacquainted, as only a married couple should.

Grady turned over and held Marla from behind and whispered, "It was a great day, honey!"

Marla sighed with pleasure and whispered back, "It sure was honey. It will be great to have you to cuddle with tonight. I sure miss you when I'm on the road."

"I miss you too, sweetheart."

They cuddled closer and slipped into a very contented sleep.

Grady jumped and scared Marla nearly to death. There it was again, the phone! Grady jumped out of bed and stubbed his toe. He bit his tongue before the expletives that came to mind could escape his lips and snapped up the phone where it was ringing for the seventh time.

"Hello!" he yelled into the phone.

"S-Sorry Chief, but Jimmy said it was urgent."

Grady recognized Mandy's voice instantly and he knew his people never bothered him with trifles. He said, a little calmer, "What do you have Mandy?"

"It's pretty involved Chief, but the thumb nail is that Stone got in a shoot-out with a robber and both he and the robber are dead, sir! Winslow got in a chase, a wreck and then was stabbed by a witch. He's in critical but stable condition at the hospital. All this has really brought back some bad memories, sir.

"I'm sure it has Mandy. I'll be right down and you can fill me in on all the details."

Grady started to hang up but he heard Mandy yelling on the phone, "No, Chief, don't hang up! There's more that Jimmy wants you to know before you come." Grady put the phone back to his ear and Mandy continued, "They found him, sir! Big as life, they know it's him! He's dead sir but it's him all right."

Grady interrupted her, impatiently, "Who'd they find Mandy?"

"Starvas Creen, sir! They weren't sure but Jimmy faxed his prints to the CIA and got an immediate response to the affirmative."

Grady didn't hear the next few sentences. He was just too stunned. He sat on the bed as his body went rigid, his jaws tensed and even though it was too dark to see it, his face was red with rage!

Marla sat up and whispered, "Who did they find Grady, what's happened?"

Grady hung up the phone, without a word, turned on the light, and started to put on his uniform.

He just stared straight ahead as he whispered, "They found Starvas Creen! He was caught tonight with undeniable evidence that he and his Coven are the ones who have been kidnapping homeless women and ceremonially killing them in their pagan rituals. We better get ready, honey. You'll want to cover this story." Grady then turned and walked into the bathroom for a quick shower, knowing as he did that he would not be back for quite awhile.

Marla called Michael Pro, her cameraman, and asked him to meet her at the warehouse district in thirty minutes. She wasn't going to miss this story. They had found and killed the rogue CIA agent, Starvas Creen, who had shot and killed the kindest man that Marla had ever met. Joshua White, retired police officer, healer, preacher, and just an all around good guy. Starvas had shot Joshua and wounded his brother Jarrett White at the same time. Jarrett White, whom they had discovered, was a CIA agent, deep under cover in the Demon Slayer's motorcycle gang. He had survived the many plastic surgeries, which had changed his looks totally. The President had given both he and Angela Boner, another undercover agent the Medal of Honor for their participation in the largest sting operation, ever, of its kind. The President had been so pleased, that she had given them both a year's paid leave, so they could rest. Jarrett had moved into Jesus Park to try to find this faith that Joshua had told him about, while Angela had gone home to her folks to find some peace. Grady reviewed these facts subconsciously in seconds, but now it was time to go.

Grady and Marla hugged one last time, kissed, and Grady whispered, "Sorry about the good night's sleep that we won't get now."

"It's all right Grady. At least we shared a couple of hours of memories."

Grady smiled at those memories and kissed his wife tenderly, "Yes, I suppose we did at that, honey. Be careful, sweetheart, and I'll see you when you get back. Tell President Place I said, hello."

Marla would shoot some coverage of the Creen story and then catch her flight to Washington.

Little did the couple know that this would be the last time they would see each other on this side of Heaven.

*   *   *

When Grady pulled up to the scene, Sgt. Jimmy Hankins came running up with a mixture of grief and excitement. "Good evening, Chief." He handed Grady a cup of coffee, which he always seemed to have right when Grady needed it the most.

Hankins continued, "I guess Mandy told you about Stone and Winslow. Stone was gone when he got to the hospital, but Winslow will pull through. He's not out of the woods yet, but it's hopeful."

Grady bowed his head and wiped a tear from his eye, "I feel so sorry for Nancy. It's their wedding anniversary." Grady looked at the date on his watch, "Yes, today. That's terrible!"

After an awkward moment of silence, Jimmy told Grady the whole morbid story. "We identified this Creen character from the wanted posters and then verified his identity through his fingerprint records at the C.I.A. With the evidence we found in his Temple, we had no trouble deducing that he and his Coven had been committing all of the rapes, murders, and mutilations of the homeless girls in the area. He also, told Grady how the robber had led Winslow on a terrifying chase which ended in several cars being totaled, and the robber's car exploding through the warehouse window, interrupting Creen and his Coven's progress in one of their unholy rituals."

Hankins continued, "Chief, after we took Creen out, we entered the Temple area. It was awful! That sweet young girl was lying there with her heart ripped from her young chest. There was a chalice of blood, which had fallen and spilt its contents on the floor. We even found a few bits of uneaten heart on the floor. What was even worse though was that poor sap that drove the get away car. The car had crashed through the windows of the warehouse upside down, and we found the man hanging half out of the car, head down, with his throat cut from ear to ear and a pool of blood on the floor beneath. The look of horror on the man's face...well it was just terrible, Chief! Forensics says he was cut with Creen's Ceremonial knife, the same one Creen used to pierce Winslow's lung, barely missing his heart.

"And one more thing Chief; these witches were interrupted so fast and with such violence; they didn't have a chance to destroy their computer records like the last time. We have them all and I have locked them up in a safe place. As soon as we can break the codes, we'll know everything about them."

Grady had stopped listening. It was just too much all at once. He would study the reports later. For now, he had to deal with Mrs. Stone.

"Thanks Hankins! You've done exceptionally well as usual. Stay with the scene, if you don't mind, and make sure everything is done right. No short cuts of any kind. I'll be at the hospital speaking to Mrs. Stone."

Grady drained the coffee from the cup, handed it back to Hankins and then walked toward his car.

CHAPTER THREE
THE VISITATION

WASHINGTON-OVAL OFFICE:
September 1st, 2---: 0600 HOURS:

General Worl, Angel of the Almighty God, stood behind President Roberta Place with his hand on her shoulder giving her support and comfort. He knew that the President was in for the hardest day of her life and she needed all the help she could get to make it through.

General Worl had been assigned to protect President Place immediately after the Battle of Covenant in which he had defeated Capt. Tumult. The human didn't know it, of course, but when she got General Worl, she also got his two bodyguards, Left and Right, who were always at his side watching his back. This General, who had fought innumerable battles for the Lord, was about to lead this human into the last battle of her life on this Earth. The human race was about to enter the next stage of God's plan; a stage that would be frightening in it's scope, but one that would bring them happiness and joy as soon as they were transformed into full membership in the Body of Christ.

Worl smiled as he prayed, "Lord Jesus bring peace to this troubled soul and give her the strength to stand during this final battle..."

As Worl prayed on, the President felt the power, the peace, the joy, and yes, even the approach of a new experience, as she continued to kneel in prayer to her God. It hadn't always been like this, however. She had turned away from God for years, but a man named Joshua White had brought a message back from the grave. He had told her that God had healed her son, Patrick, of his brain tumor and after doctors ran a few tests, she found it to be true. From that time on, she had turned back to God and His ways.

Just last November, under the guidance of the Holy Spirit, she had been re-elected to the Presidency by the largest margin ever enjoyed by a Presidential candidate. She had the highest "popularity rating" of any President and she had selected as her new running mate Senator Thomas Holstrum, who had added his followers to hers. Her old Vice-President, Phillip Huggens, had been arrested for treason and had made a lengthy confession. On the first day of his trial, however, he had been murdered; the elevator in which he and the federal agents had been riding, exploded, thus saving the tax payers millions in lawyer fees.

Now it was September and the President didn't have the luxury of thinking about these things, but instead must think about the upcoming meeting with the Congress of the United States. She had all but obtained a sufficient vote to remove the United States of America from the United Nations. She had fought hard for its removal. She believed that the U.N. would be used to form a One World Government, which would swallow up the United States and the freedoms that she and many Presidents before her had spent their lives defending. To insure that this wouldn't happen, President Place had made a formal request to the Congress just before the election last November. They had stated that they would take a vote upon the issue, if after the election; President Place was still in the White House. That vote was to come later today, after ten months in which she had fought for every possible vote. She had done every earthly thing that she could do, and now it was the subject of the President's prayers.

"...Lord that's why I've come to you today with this project. I've tried to do your will on these and many other important issues of our day. Help me Lord! I just don't know which way the Congress will go with this new threat. Should I withhold the information until after the vote, so they will go ahead or should I do the right thing and tell them, so they can make a better informed decision?"

She stopped praying for a moment and thought about what she had said, then continued, "Well, Lord, I guess I just answered my own question there, didn't I? If it's the right thing to do, I must do it even if it means losing the vote. With this new threat, Lord, I'm not sure that the better idea might not be to stay united as a world through the U.N. and it's forces. After all we are now up against an unknown alien force from who knows where. This is too much for me Lord, please guide me. Surround me with your guardian angels and let them keep the demons away from my decisions. You know..."

"Roberta, don't take it so seriously." The familiar voice had come from behind her. She jumped up, turned around, and then fainted, falling back down to the floor.

When she came around she looked through the haze of her semi-consciousness and saw the friendly face of Joshua White smiling down at her. She knew that she had to be dreaming this, because Joshua had been murdered a year ago, as he saved his brother from an assassin's bullet. Yet his touch was firm and warm as he helped her to her feet and then into a nearby chair.

Roberta whispered, "You're dead Joshua!"

Joshua smiled, "Thanks for telling me, Roberta."

Roberta smiled back feebly, "That was a stupid thing to say, wasn't it?"

He smiled even broader and said, "Stupid but understandable." He helped her up off of the floor and into a nearby chair, as he continued, "I really didn't mean to scare you so much, Roberta. I'm the answer to your prayer, if you can believe it. God has allowed me to come back to talk to certain friends and guide them in these last days. You asked for clarification and I can offer you some, though I must withhold certain details from you."

Roberta began to question Joshua but he held up his hand and said, "My time is short and I have a lot to tell you, so please just listen!"

Roberta thought, *"Why is their time always so short?"*

Joshua looked at the President and said, "All right I'll tell you that one. Our time is always short, because it is a precious gift that we are allowed to be here at all, and we are never given much time. We must use it wisely. Unfortunately, it takes so long for people to get over the initial shock that there is never much time left for the message.

"Now, Roberta, you must believe that it is me. I'm here to warn you of Satan's plot to overthrow the world's governments and to take over the world through his Anti-Christ, just as warned in the scriptures. These U.F.O. sightings and abductions are part of that plot. The ships and the vile creatures in them are all manifestations of Satan himself. He also has a few humans lined up in high positions. At just the right moment, he and his highest demon generals will possess them and set up the One World Order for the good of all people. He'll trick millions into believing that he is the true Messiah and many souls will be lost forever."

Roberta interrupted, "Look, Joshua, I know you were always a level headed man and not given to flights of fancy or illusion, but a Spaceship, which is really a demon? Come on!"

Joshua pulled up a chair and sat down across from the President. He took her hands in his, looked her right in the eyes and said, "I'm very serious, Roberta. You must try to get the U.S.A. to pull out of the United Nations, but I must tell you that it won't happen. It's not meant to happen. God has given the United States over to Satan because of its failure to follow God's ways. For a time, the World will fall under the spell of Satan's mad man, the Anti-Christ, and all will be peaceful in the world; even though it will be a forced peace. Then the beast's true nature will be exposed, and he will devour the innocent and the guilty alike.

"The only way to defeat the Beast is through prayer. God sent me here to ask you to call for prayer around the world. Go on international television, while you're at the UN vote today, the world will be watching that vote and warn them of the things I have told you. You must do this no matter what it costs you. Do you understand me, Roberta?"

"Yes, of course Joshua, but..."

The phone rang. Roberta turned toward the phone and when she looked back, Joshua was gone. The phone rang again. The President got up, tiredly, from the chair in which she had been sitting, walked over to the phone and picked up the receiver, experiencing the loss of Joshua's departure. She put the phone to her ear and simply said, "Place."

Her secretary, Jon Holder, said, "Madam President, President Gordi Vochi is on hold for you."

Gordi Vochi was President of The New United Russia and wouldn't be calling unless he had either heard of yesterday's incident or had a few of his own to report. It turned out to be a little of both.

Roberta took a deep breath. Her head was still spinning from Joshua's visit as she picked up the receiver from the red phone and said, "President Place here, how are you Gordi?"

A tired strained voice answered, "I've been better Roberta. I've called because of some events that have happened here in my territory and about something that has also happened in yours as I understand?"

His sources had always intrigued Roberta, but she said, "I won't pretend I don't have troubles over here but I really haven't heard about yours."

"Well Roberta, to start with, yesterday, my son, Jochoyish, was flying his first mission when he and the other six jets in his group disappeared from the screen."

Roberta closed her eyes, tears finding their way down her face and dripping onto the hand that held the receiver to her ear.

Gordi continued, "If that were not bad enough, the same UFO that they had been chasing until *it* caught them, shot some kind of power beam at several of our nuclear power plants, instantly and irrevocably taking them off-line, which of course cut the power to half our cities.

"Roberta, I beg of you to hold off on this vote to withdraw from the United Nations. We're facing an unknown foe, of an unknown strength and I believe that we need to stick together on this issue. So, what do you say? Will you stay in, for now at least?"

There was silence and Roberta felt the pressure of that silence. She decided, however, that she would not be forced into any action, so she said, "Gordi, I can appreciate the problem and this new threat will certainly be weighed in the decision. I cannot, however, commit to a yes or no answer at this time. I am meeting with the Congress later this morning. After I speak to them and they vote, I'll announce our decision at my UN speech this afternoon."

The silence continued and when Gordi did speak, the disappointment was very evident in his voice, "Well, I guess that'll have to do for now, Roberta, but please let me know the outcome just as soon as you know. We'll all have to work together on this one.

"Well, Madam President, as usual, it has been a pleasure speaking to you."

"Yes, and to you Mr. President. I do hope they find your son and I hope he is well."

47

"I thank you. Until later then? Oh, Roberta when does your flight get into New York this afternoon?"

"I should be there by two. My speech is at three. That's when I'll announce to the world what's going on."

"Well Madam President, all the leaders of the World are here in New York, just waiting for your support. Please don't let us down." With that he hung up.

President Place spent the next three hours on the phone with the Heads of State, Presidents, Kings, Sheiks and Rulers of more countries than she could count, and they all wanted the same thing, namely for the United States to remain with the U.N. She had told them the same thing she had told Gordi, but to others she had told of her intent to call for worldwide prayer against Satan and the call to turn back to God.

Bzzzz! The President reached for the button and said, "Yes?"

"Madam President, they're ready for you in the conference room."

"Okay, thanks Jon, I'll be right there."

She looked at her watch and thought, "*It's 0900 already! What am I going to tell them? What can I tell them to do?*"

She whispered, "Oh God, give us all the benefit of your wisdom. Tell us what to do."

Roberta picked up her brief case, took a deep breath, and tried not to vomit as she left her office. She opened the door and was still looking down trying to snap her brief case closed when she ran into someone. She looked up and saw that she had run into CIA Director Richard Aires who was now bending down to help pick up the papers that had just fallen out of Roberta's briefcase due to the impact.

Roberta bent down to pick up the stray papers at the same moment that the Director stood up and they hit heads. Roberta grabbed her forehead and the Director grabbed the back of his head and they both yelled, "Ouch!"

Aires, still holding his head said, "I'm so sorry Madam President! Here let me get the rest for you!"

As he picked up the papers Roberta laughed and said, "That's what I get for not watching where I'm going and getting there late"

With a more serious tone, she said, "If you need to talk to me, Director, you'll need to walk me to the conference room. Okay?"

"Certainly, Madam President", Aires said as he passed her the last of the fallen papers.

She laughed again, "I guess I'll have to sort these out when I get to the meeting."

As they entered the hallway and turned toward the conference room, Roberta asked, "Now, what can I do for you today, Richard?"

"Well, first of all Madam President..."

"Please call me Roberta when we're alone."

"All right Roberta, first off, Special Agent George Jones is waiting down stairs where he will join you on your flight to New York and also on your ride over to the UN, I want him to be there as an added precaution for your safety during your speech."

The President nodded and Aires continued, "Secondly, Dr. Kamerman has been spotted in the Covenant area. We have an agent deep under cover with the homeless in Covenant and he has been keeping us informed for a couple of days now that the good doctor is active again in the area. This has now been verified by Chief Grady O'Leary, who called and reported that by some fluke accident that ended a high-speed chase, a car crashed into the warehouse where Creen was actively offering up another homeless girl, murdered just like several others had been. When Creen attacked the officer he was shot down by several other officers, who were there as backup.

"Madam...I mean Roberta, I would like to reactivate Eagle who is already in Covenant. He can make sure that Dr. Kamerman doesn't get away again. I know that he has another month or so left on his year vacation but we need him now! Our agent on site is not good at physical conflicts, but as you know Jarrett White is."

Roberta thought about how she had rewarded Eagle and Hawk, for their last assignment. Hawk, Angela Boner, had infiltrated Dr. Kamerman's organization by allowing herself to be captured as a slave and then ended up saving Roberta's life when she was in turn captured by Kamerman. At the same time Eagle, Jarrett White, had collected fifty of the meanest, most violent and notorious outlaws that this country has ever seen and started the "Demon Slayer" motorcycle gang. He had then sent his men to rob and damage stores in Covenant but had set an elaborate trap for them instead. They were all captured or killed in one night.

Roberta had given them both a year off with pay so they could rest. Hawk was visiting her parents in Indiana while Eagle was staying in Covenant getting over his brother's murder and learning more about this Jesus Christ.

Roberta came out of her reverie as they arrived at the conference room.

She ordered, "Ask him to take the assignment and allow him to refuse. If he does take it, then reinstate him with full powers and authority. Give the same offer to Hawk. This is just too important to trust to one agent."

Director Aires said, "I'll call my assistant, Bob Swaggert, right away. He's in Covenant now and will approach White for us. I have Agent Kevin Sievert on the way to speak to Hawk."

He looked toward the door of the conference room and said, "Good luck in there, Roberta, and may your God Bless You."

"Thanks, Richard." They shook hands and she watched as Richard walked away to handle the next problem on his list. She had a strange feeling that she would not see him again and she was correct. At least, she wouldn't see him in this world again; this world was about to be changed forever.

Roberta took a deep breath, opened the door, and walked into the conference room. She walked to the head of the table, pulled out her chair and sat down. She looked around the table at the men and women who were the highest-ranking officers of each of the Armed Forces. The room had been abuzz with the whispering, laughing and arguing of those present but had gone abruptly silent as the officers stopped talking and watched the President take her seat.

Roberta always got the feeling that they were just watching to see if she would crack under the pressure.

She ignored these high-ranking officers and addressed Commander Pips, who was sitting in the corner looking very intimidated, "Commander Pips!"

He jumped to attention; his face turning red as he realized that he should have done that when she walked in, he stammered, "Y-Yes Madam!"

"I've just spent the last three hours on the phone to leaders around the world and we are not alone. Besides our five jets, there have been a total of sixty-five others, that have just vanished."

She watched the reactions of those seated at the table. First, there was shock and then they began whispering urgently to each other.

As her gaze passed over the last of the officers, she said, "We have a world-wide crisis on our hands, ladies and gentleman, and the world is looking to us for the answers. Before we begin to sort this out, however, we'd best go to the Lord in prayer and then I'll share what Joshua White had to say on the subject, just this morning."

She watched with satisfaction as the color drained from each face in turn. Their expressions of curiosity turned to sadness and horror as they each remembered that Joshua White had been murdered almost a year ago.

NEW HOPE MEMORIAL HOSPITAL:
September 1st, 2---: 0800 HOURS:

Nancy Stone's shoes echoed down the hall as she walked slowly toward the morgue. She had to collect John's things and it was the hardest thing that she had ever had to do. Rev. Smith walked beside her. In fact he had to hold her up to keep her moving forward.

It broke his heart to see Nancy like this. She was normally a very strong and forceful woman, but now she just looked like a crushed and sobbing child. Her eyes had temporarily lost their gleam and were as dead and expressionless as John's, who lay on the table before them. Nancy whispered something that Rev. Smith did not catch.

He said, "What is it Nancy?"

Nancy repeated, "Why Pastor? Why did God take John now, on our anniversary no less?"

He just hugged her to him as she cried against his shoulder.

John and Nancy had been members of Rev. Smith's church for a long time and they had followed him out to Jesus Park when he had moved his church. They were great helpers and an important part of his extended family. For the most part, Covenant had accepted his leadership and hadn't minded that he was black. The first day he arrived in town some rough young men had beaten him, but a young police officer named Joshua White had saved him. From that day to this there had been no more trouble with his color. There had, however, been a lot of prejudice against his Christianity. They had fought many battles already and had buried many friends and now another had gone to the Lord.

Nancy's sobbing had eased some, and Rev. Smith asked, "Do you feel up to seeing Frank now? I really think that I should stop in to see him and I'm sure a visit from you would help. What do you say?"

Nancy blew her nose and nodded her agreement.

When they walked in, they saw Frank lying on his back in bed. Tubes were hooked into every part of his body and he was hooked up to oxygen. He appeared to be asleep and Nancy asked Rev. Smith, "Perhaps we should come back later?"

Before Rev. Smith could answer, however, Frank opened his eyes and spoke hoarsely, "Nancy could you give me an ice chip please?" He pointed painfully toward the nightstand.

She walked over, spooned a small cube out and put it in Frank's mouth. As the ice melted in his mouth, she just stood there and stared at him. His eyes were black and blue and a bit swollen besides. There was a bandage on his head, and his hands were wrapped to cover the very bad burns that he had received. Nancy couldn't see them, but the doctors had told her that Frank's legs had been burned as well. They had told her that he was very lucky to be alive.

Frank coughed painfully and then he motioned Nancy to come closer. She bent down, put her ear close to his mouth, and held her long hair out of the way so Frank could whisper, "Nancy! I was dead for a while and I saw John!"

Nancy stood straight up, gasped, and put her hand over her mouth. After she had rallied enough courage, she bent down again, so that Frank could continue, "You have to believe me Nancy! John asked me to tell you that he is very happy where he is, and that Jesus would be coming back for the Christians very soon! Nancy, he really emphasized the very soon part and said that you should spread the word." Frank stared into eternity as he whispered, "Be ready for Jesus will come back very soon!" Nancy shivered involuntarily as Frank continued, "I don't understand it all but he was very happy about the news and seemed to want everyone ready when it happened. He also told me that Rev. Smith would come and that I should listen to him. After all that has happened to me, I'm now ready to listen. Would you ask him if he would talk to me now?"

Tears were streaming down Nancy's face, but she felt a little lighter with the news that Jesus was coming soon and that she would then be reunited with John. She turned her head, kissed Frank on the forehead, very gently of course, and then stood up. She knew that Frank wouldn't have mentioned Jesus unless what he had just told her was true. She believed it instantly!

She turned to Rev. Smith and said, "John told Frank in a vision that Jesus would return for the Christians very soon. Frank would like to be saved for that occasion and has asked that you bring him to the Lord. Could you do it now?"

Rev. Smith smiled and said, "Of course I can! Why don't you go get some coffee and I'll meet you in the cafeteria when I'm finished here."

Nancy looked a little better when she walked from the room and that made Rev. Smith feel a whole lot better as well.

He pulled a chair over to the bed, sat down and said, "Well Frank let's start in the beginning and see if we can't get you to the Lord before lunch." Rev. Smith opened his Bible to John 3:16 and read, "For God so loved the world, that he gave his only begotten Son, that whosoever believeth in him should not perish, but have everlasting life..."

*   *   *

Emerson, mighty Angel of God, and the newly assigned guardian angel for Frank Winslow, arrived causing Murphy, the angel who had protected and guided Frank during his lost years, to look up from her post where she sat in the corner of the hospital room. From the moment that Frank had accepted Jesus, Murphy had been expecting her replacement. She stood then and gave the right hand to left shoulder salute of respect to Emerson as she said, "It's been a long time coming, but he has finally accepted Jesus Christ as his Savior. Guard him well Emerson, while I go attend to another stubborn soul. I would certainly like to see a few more souls saved before the Lord returns!"

Emerson returned the salute and said, "Well done Murphy! Don't worry about Frank; I'll protect him with my very life. I wish you as much success on your next assignment."

With that Murphy extended her wings to their full seven foot wing-span and soared into the air, quickly fading from sight, while Emerson settled in for a long watchful vigil over Frank Winslow, a newly washed in the blood soul, who was now guaranteed eternal life through Jesus Christ.

The three terrified demons, the ones who had just lost their hold over Frank, cowered in the corner. They were arguing about which one of them would have to go and tell Satan of yet another loss to his kingdom.

Satan squirmed, feeling the sharp pain that accompanies the loss of each and every soul that his enemy steals from him! He looked up and immediately began to think of punishments that would suit the three fools that had failed him yet again! His evil smile broadened as he summoned the three before him.

COHEN HOUSEHOLD; NEW YORK:
September 1st, 2---: 1200 HOURS:

It was finally Rosh Hashanah, the Jewish New Year. It was a time for gentleness, for reflection and a time for taking personal stock. It was a time, too, for religious rededication and a time for reconciliation with your enemies. It was also a time for opening new pages in the life of your family. In the case of the Cohen family, this particular New Year was a time for very dramatic changes.

These changes were in the forefront of Nathan's mind as he sat in his comfortable armchair and reviewed these last thirty days of preparation for this New Year. He was thirty years old and could now hold the office of Priest. Rabbi Shorisk had approached him just two months ago with the proposal that at first had caused Nathan to laugh. When he realized that the Rabbi was serious he began to get nervous with excitement. There was currently a big movement of Jews back to Jerusalem and there was a spot open on the next flight out, which was tomorrow. The Rabbi wanted Nathan and his family to be on that flight so Nathan could take up his apprenticeship in Jerusalem under the great High Priest Tzvi Cohen, the man after whom Nathan had named his youngest son! The High Priest was also a distant cousin.

He couldn't believe his luck! To be offered this position was a great honor. One that brought honor not only to him and his family, but also fulfilled the great tradition of families that could trace their roots back to the Tribe of Levi, the Tribe of Priests. Nathan was such a man, a pure blooded Jewish first-born male and a documented descendant of the Tribe of Levi.

His wife, Eva, had accepted the news better than his children, who like most children didn't want to leave their friends. They were too young to feel the pull of the ancient city, but now they would have time to learn to love it.

Nathan could smell the lamb as it baked in it's own juices, with the potatoes, carrots, and onions sharing the roaster with it, and all covered with his wife's secret savory spiced gravy. His stomach grumbled at the thought, he was getting very hungry. He had two hours yet, however, before the assigned time for dinner would arrive. They had invited several family members over and after the meal Rabbi Shorisk would make the proud announcement to the rest of the family. It had been hard not to tell anyone, but this was the day for such announcements and most of Nathan's early lessons had been on patience.

For some reason, Nathan's thoughts turned to his baby brother. This was a day of family and yet he might never see his brother again. His brother had converted to Christianity and the thought still brought sickness to Nathan's heart. They had argued! Nathan had tried to explain the scriptures. He had brought Daniel to Rabbi Shorisk, but nothing would deter Daniel from making this grave mistake. Daniel had left two years earlier to join the Air Force and changed his name to Derecks. He had told Nathan, "If I'm to be disowned by my own brother, then I won't carry the family name!" Nathan had yelled back, "If you insist on shaming such a proud name then you shouldn't carry it ever again!" That had been the last time that the two brothers had seen each other.

A tear ran down Nathan's cheek as he remembered disowning Daniel and because he could no longer treat him as a brother, he had missed his wedding. He had married a nice woman named Debbie and now they had their first born, a baby boy, Jeffrey, but Nathan wouldn't get to hold him in his arms. Worse, the boy wouldn't get to learn about his heritage.

"Enough! This train of thought will get you no where!" Nathan got up and walked over to the bookshelf intending to get his scriptures but instead stared at the picture of his brother. A picture that he just couldn't bring himself to destroy. In it Daniel knelt down on one knee. He was holding a large football trophy, and wearing his football uniform, number 36. He was quarterback in his last year of high school and his team had won the State Championship. It was a proud time. It was only two months after this picture was taken that Daniel had come to Nathan and told him of his intentions of becoming Christian and marrying Debbie. He had also dropped the news that instead of studying for the Priesthood or joining the accounting trade with his brother, he was going to join the Air Force as a career officer.

Nathan regretted his harsh treatment toward his brother. He whispered, "May God keep you safe my brother, wherever your are. And may you be inscribed in the Book of Life."

CHAPTER FOUR
CHRIST MEETS ANTI-CHRIST

ON BOARD THE DEMON SHIP:
SEPTEMBER 1ST, 2---: 1215 HOURS:

Lt. Derecks had been on board this ship for hours now and he still knew nothing about it. Mr. Canards had separated him from the other officers and had locked him in a comfortable room. It had white walls, which emitted a slight glow and served as the only light in the room. There was a bed, a desk with a hard plastic chair and one recliner. A second meal had just appeared on the table right next to the first, but Daniel had eaten neither. After all, they could be laced with poison or drugs. Daniel was getting very hungry, however, and he was beginning to give in to depression. Between the shock of getting kidnapped by aliens, being separated from his family and starving himself, he was weakening. His thirst was making his tongue grow thick and the only water in the room that he could trust were his own tears. Unfortunately they did nothing for his thirst. Oh, how he wished that his brother Nathan were here.

Daniel prayed an old blessing, "May all Thy children unite in one fellowship to do Thy will with all their heart..."

As Daniel prayed, Satan watched the tortured Christian with satisfaction. He knew that he wouldn't eat and was all too happy to provide him with tempting meals to worsen his torture. He had isolated him from the others to prevent Derecks from spreading his Christian propaganda. He had hoped not to have to deal with Christians on this part of the mission, but it appeared that he couldn't get away from them anywhere. This thought angered him and he yelled, "This infestation of Christians must stop!"

The ship shook with Satan's fury. Lights flickered, wind howled through the entire ship and all the human captives could hear the eerie screams of the damned. The officers who had been in Daniel's squad were filled with terror. Surprisingly, however, Daniel knelt down in prayer with a smile on his face. He had just been given the last piece of the puzzle that had been bugging him since his arrival. He now knew who Alfred Canards was and he would fight him the best way he knew how.

He prayed, "Jesus I ask you to bless Alfred Canards and all of his demons. I forgive them for what they have done to the others, and me and I ask that you guide them. I forgive my brother for his rude behavior toward me and ask that you keep him in your Book of Life. And Lord, if possible, please lead him to a belief in Jesus Christ as Lord and Savior..."

As Daniel prayed, Satan's angry tantrum turned to desperation and pain as the prayers for Daniel's enemies heaped literal coals of fire upon their heads. Satan and his Demons writhed in pain, and this ship, as well as many others was in danger of dissolving. Satan had to act fast, before this Christian could single handily bring down all of his well-laid plans.

The Satan possessed Canards faded out of existence, racing toward the gate of Heaven. It was now time that he face Jesus down!

Heaven: Date and time irrelevant.

Joshua White arrived back in Heaven, from his visit with President Place, to find people running down the golden streets of New Jerusalem. Some were shouting orders and all was confusion. Joshua soon found Moses, staff in hand, walking at a fast pace.

Joshua matched his pace and asked, "Moses what's all the excitement?"

Moses smiled, "Oh! Hello Joshua! You haven't heard? Oh that's right you're still active in World affairs! Well, I just heard that Satan is coming to meet with Jesus, and we all get to watch and listen as they confront each other, directly, face to face, for the first time since Jesus was a man on earth. Come along, Joshua, and we'll watch together."

Joshua felt both excitement and revulsion at the news. Excitement, that this meeting had to mean something big, perhaps even the end of the world, but revulsion that Satan would dare to set foot even at the Gate of Heaven!

They arrived just in time to see Jesus walking out of the Glory of his Father's presence. Light seemed to flow from every pore of Jesus' skin. Jesus stood at the top of a flight of stairs, looking down at the immense crowd of Saints forming below him. Joshua was filled with awe every time he saw Jesus in person. There could be no doubt that Jesus was one with his Father.

The usual applause cheers and praise where absent as the crowd stood in silent anticipation waiting to see what this meeting was all about. Everyone felt that something big was about to happen, but no one dared hope that the end had finally arrived.

Jesus looked to His right and He seemed to darken somewhat, as a disturbance erupted at the edge of the crowd.

*   *   *

As the form of Alfred Canards walked toward to outer edge of the crowd brilliant points of light began bursting forth from every pour of his body. As he continued the crowd watched as Canards body dematerialized into the form of Satan, in his original angelic existence.

*   *   *

As Jesus walked to the edge of the Glory that was his Father, he looked down on the immense crowd below him. He felt total love for these people for whom he had suffered. As he scanned the crowd, he saw Abraham, all of his sons, grandsons and many other generations of Abraham himself. He saw Moses, Joshua White and Abraham Lincoln all standing together with the same expectant looks as the rest of the crowd. His thoughts raced back across the generations of spiritual warfare that these Saints had endured to arrive at this day.

He thought of the millions of people who were not famous by worldly standards, but who upon arriving in Heaven, had been surprised at not only the welcome they had received but also the rewards they were given for their invaluable service to God. Their lives had been filled with selfless prayers, sacrifice and love for their fellow humans and they soon found out that it was their service on earth that gave them their new stature in heaven. Jesus allowed himself to drink in the love that was filling this place and then it happened. First he felt the presence of evil; then he heard the disturbance at the edge of the crowd and finally, he saw his old enemy walking toward him.

*   *   *

Joshua White watched as Satan walked toward Jesus. He had expected to see some horrible monster on the order of Satan's demons, Tumult or Rumpus. Instead he watched Lucifer, whose name actually meant Morning Star or Light Bearer. He watched as this beautiful Angel of Light walked proudly toward Jesus. He stood six feet tall, a slender build, brown hair which was graying at the temples and he had a pleasant looking face which almost looked kind, except for the underlying shadow of evil which hung at the edge of his smile. As the man passed Joshua, he turned his head and looked directly into Joshua's eyes. Joshua felt as if he had been struck by lightening, as hatred shot from the deep emerald green eyes of this man Joshua knew as Satan. Joshua also knew him now as Iblis, as the Islamic people call him. Then there's Malic, the Overseer of Hell, or Malaku'l-

Maut the Angel of Death, or Canards, impostor to the Lord Jesus himself, but no matter what he was called, the evil that emitted from this powerful being was unmistakable.

Joshua broke out in a cold sweat as fear gripped his heart and he repeated in his thoughts, the prayer that he had prayed on the day of his death, *"Oh Lord! I lie helpless before the ravenous fangs of my enemy. I watch in despair as he tears at my throat, his fangs ripping muscle and tendon, freeing my life's blood from its body. But! Even in this the hour of my death I am loyal to you, Lord Jesus. I trust that you will make use of my death and that you will give me everlasting life as my reward."*

The Lord had blessed Joshua beyond all expectation, but for just a fleeting moment as this powerful being passed and focused all of his evil attentions on Joshua, all was forgotten and Joshua nearly fainted dead away. Moses reached out and steadied Joshua and a second later it was over, the being of evil had gone on, walking ever closer to Jesus.

As Patricia, Joshua's earthly wife arrived and supported him from the other side; Joshua absent-mindedly compared the body of Satan to the body of Jesus and was surprised to find that Jesus' body was full of flaws. Flaws that no doubt had caused some problems for him on earth. His features were plain. He was shorter than Satan and maybe even a little over weight in comparison. It wasn't the body of a god, and that was as Jesus had planned. What made Jesus beautiful and pleasing to the eye was not his body but the Godliness, which radiated from every pore. If one missed His Godliness, one missed His beauty as well.

Satan on the other hand, had a seductively beautiful body, with no flaws whatever, unless like Joshua, one looked too deeply into those emerald green eyes which exposed the evil lurking within.

The Souls and Angels closest to Jesus backed up and parted, making way for Satan to pass and then closed in behind him forming a large circle around the two adversaries. They stood face to face, one glaring with arrogance and hatred, the other offering love and understanding.

The untold multitude, which had now gathered to witness this meeting, first, saw the light as it rose up between the two foes and then a low rumbling sound began to shake Heaven to its foundation. At first everyone feared that Satan was about to attack Jesus and they shouted as if of one mind, "Jesus!" The sound of their shout and their combined concern for Jesus contained such power as to knock Satan to his knees and to cause blood to trickle from his ears, nose and mouth. Satan wiped at his wounds and then looking up toward Jesus with much hatred, he held up his blood stained hands, which had begun to shake with the rage and humiliation at having to kneel before Jesus. Lightening flashed, thunder rolled, the ground outside New Jerusalem shook with the demands of a righteous God. All present bowed low to their God and fear gripped even the strongest angel, as they too, knelt before God, who is Jesus.

Satan yelled out in pain, "Is this why you invited me here, to humiliate me in front of your slaves?"

67

Jesus' face darkened, as he looked at this pitiful fallen Angel who was once considered God's most perfect creation. He spoke softly so only Satan could hear, "You've fallen so far my friend, what am I to do with you?"

Satan gasped through his pain, "You could stop fighting so unfairly! Remove your followers from the earth and admit that you have lost the war. I've taken the earth away from you and I've gotten back all but a few of your so-called Christians. Give me a free hand on earth and I'll prove to you that I can get all the remaining humans to follow me. They'll reject you and your Father-God." He watched as Jesus shook his head sympathetically and Satan taking that as a "no", yelled, "I thought not! You've always been too cowardly to fight for what you want. You know that if you give me what I ask that I'll tear your precious kingdom apart and expose your Father's true weakness!"

A wall of fire swept across heaven and raced toward the two men. The crowd of Angels and Saints gasped and jumped to free themselves from any contact with the fierce fire. They had never seen the Holy Spirit so angry. The wall of fire passed within inches of Joshua and he felt the heat of the purifying fire as it singed the hair on the back of his hands, which he was using to cover his head. The fire fully engulfed and surrounded Jesus causing a rotating wall of fire to hide Jesus from view.

Satan was thrown face down into a pool of his own blood, which was still flowing freely from his wounds. Every being in Heaven joined him as they prostrated themselves before their fierce and wonderful God. The wall of fire that now engulfed Jesus slowly descended to the ground exposing Jesus' head. All present gasped at His Glory! His hair had turned white as snow and light shot from the ends of each hair. The skin of his face and body had turned the color of bronze! He glowed with the golden presence of his Godliness and fire churned in his eyes, only hinting at the power contained within. As the wall of fire moved further into the ground, it exposed Christ's golden breastplate and a cloak of pure white as radiant as his hair. The cloak blew in the wind, which was the Holy Spirit. Just below his breastplate, Jesus' white robe was bound around the waist by a blue sash. Jesus was dressed as a mighty warrior, garbed in the heavenly power of God Himself. His appearance left no doubt in the minds of the gathered Saints and Angels, nor even in the mind of Satan, that Jesus was accepting Satan's declaration of war!

The crowd was overcome with awe and respect as they watched Jesus in all of His glory. It had been a long time since the Angels had seen Jesus in His Glory and they had forgotten just how magnificent he was. The human souls present had never seen him this way and they felt privileged and fearful to be witness.

Jesus Christ, the King of Heaven and Earth spoke. The sound of his voice rumbled through heaven with such power that it shook the gates of New Jerusalem and threatened to split Satan's body in two.

The echo reemphasized each word as Jesus declared, "Lucifer! Angel of Light! You've turned from the purpose for which I created you, in order to follow your own selfish and evil goals. You've meddled in the affairs of men and in so doing you've caused mankind to fall. You've condemned them to an eternity of Hell and have never ceased to condemn them for performing your deeds. You've asked me to turn the earth over to you, so that you can turn it totally against my Father and me. SO BE IT!"

The Angels and Saints present all gasped as if they were one person!

Satan, who had just climbed to his knees, was knocked flat on his back by the combination of Jesus' proclamation and the gasp from the assembled crowd. The deep rolling thunderclap still vibrated throughout heaven as Satan, painfully sat up.

Jesus continued, "I'll come and take my church from amidst the world's earthly kingdoms. I'll free you for a time to do what you will to win souls to your cause. My faithful Angels and the Holy Spirit will continue to walk the earth and minister to the humans that you can't sway or those you push toward us with your ever obsessive and evil purpose. Mark my words, Satan!" Satan covered his head with his arms as if to ward off the blow to the head that he expected would soon be delivered.

Jesus continued, "The more you try to crush the Spirit of God, the more you free Him to redeem your kingdom! After seven years, a time set by my Father, Himself, and a time that can't be altered, I will return in the clouds, with my Angels and Saints! I will split the Eastern Sky, ripping it asunder and exposing Heaven in all of its Glory! You will see me riding on the clouds and leading my mighty army!

Then we'll do battle with you Satan and you'll finally fall, as it has always been ordained in God's Holy and living Word! You will then be chained and thrown into the bottomless pit, in which you will stay locked for one thousand years. Before you go, you will see the glory of New Jerusalem as it descends to take it's rightful place amid the ruins of your hated kingdom and all will be renewed and purified at that time. Finally, during those one thousand years, I will rule in peace without your interference! Then again as it is written, you will be set free for a time until I lead my army against you one last time and you are forever locked into the Lake of Fire, which burns yet does not consume! Now! Depart from me and make your plans! You've finally obtained what you've always wanted! Now go! Prepare for your eternal damnation and set foot here no more!"

Tears streamed down Jesus' face as he turned his back on Satan. Just before he disappeared into the Glorious presence of God His Father, Jesus turned around and spoke in a tone that demanded obedience, even from Satan himself, "Oh yes, Satan. I suggest that you release Daniel Derecks and the other Christians that you hold on your various ships at once, before I send my Angels to retrieve them!" with that, he was gone.

Satan slithered to his feet and stood shaking angrily before the empty throne of Christ. He stumbled and staggered as he turned to walk back the way he had come. Every being in Heaven still lay prostrate before the fearful power of their God and they hid their face from Satan as he passed. Satan continued walking away from the crowd as he was forced to re-materialize into that detestable, weak human form of Alfred Canards. It was an unsure, pathetic looking Canards who tried to save face by yelling, "The fool gave in much easier than I thought he would. No matter! I'll use it to my advantage and I'll move swiftly to that end!"

Satan stood trembling, taking stock of Canards' body as he did so. His clothes were torn. There had been too much blood loss. His skin was split open in several places on his face and these were still bleeding. This encounter with Jesus had cost him plenty, but he had what he'd wanted, so it was worth it. Wasn't it? But through this false confidence, cold fear crept up Satan's spine. Doubt entered his mind for the first time; since he had started this rebellion thousands of years before and for a fleeting moment there was a glimmer of regret.

Satan recovered quickly, however, and yelled, as he faded from sight, "If you follow Jesus back to Earth, you follow him to your doom!"

Joshua had peeked up and saw a very different being from the one who had entered this meeting. He evoked not fear, but pity in Joshua's heart. He no longer looked brilliant next to the glory that Jesus had demonstrated. Joshua thought, *"It's just a matter of time now, Satan, before your doomed kingdom falls."*

Satan had gone! The human souls and the Angels, alike, stood shakily to their feet. Joshua smiled as the last of the thunderous echoes fell silent around him, and he said, "This is really it! Can you feel it? Nothing will ever be the same again! A new Heaven and a new Earth are about to be formed. We'll witness the creation of both! Wow!"

Heaven filled with the praise and thanksgiving of Angels and Saints, each worshipping and praising God in his own way. God shone through each being there, whether angel or saint, glorifying Himself in their individual uniqueness. The love and fellowship was immense. Joshua hugged Patty and then Abe and, of course, Moses. They all jumped with joy. Yes! The day of the Rapture was definitely at hand!

*   *   *

Jesus knelt before his Father-God and prayed, "Thank you, Father, for bringing me back to my full Glory in Heaven and Earth. I will carry out your will and bring it to its preordained end. Finally, we will establish our kingdom on earth as it has always been here in Heaven. In just seven short earth years, you will deliver New Jerusalem to the earth and set up a Kingdom of peace run by the Saints of Heaven with the help of our mighty Angels.

"But first must come the great purging of the human race. Oh the suffering to come! This will be their hardest time since being banished from the Garden of Eden. Please, Father, help them to endure and give them the strength to carry out Your Will!"

Father-God reached down and touched the head of Jesus and said, "You've spoken well my Son. Go with my blessings and love. Fulfill your mission and bring real peace to my earth and its people. The end of time is drawing near. The Earth must be purified and the humans given one last chance before the end of time comes and the two sides are separated forever. Go now with my blessings and make your plans for the permanent separation of the Kingdoms of Light and Darkness."

Jesus rose, bowed, and then turned walking toward the waiting crowd, who anxiously awaited the arrival of their newly glorified, Commander and Chief.

*   *   *

Joshua hugged Patricia, and they both continued to jump up and down with excitement. Moses and Abe shook hands and smiled. The Saints and Angels rejoiced throughout Heaven at the news that Jesus had just proclaimed to them. He was sitting again upon his throne and he was still as dazzling as the sun.

Quiet slowly settled over the crowd and Jesus continued, "It'll happen just as the Spirit wrote it in God's word. You'll soon be renewed with glorified bodies and shortly, at least by our standards, you will join me for the last battle, Armageddon."

Thunderous applause spread through the crowd. Singing and celebration took over as everyone, including Jesus himself, praised God for His faithfulness, power, and glory!

CHAPTER FIVE

THE FEAST OF TRUMPETS

COHEN HOUSEHOLD, NEW YORK:
September 1st, 2---: 1400 HOURS:

Eva and Nathan were very nervous. They sat at the head of the table as all of their guests settled into their places. The children sat together at a separate table with a couple of Aunts to watch over them. Eva felt odd being waited on hand and foot, but this was their celebration, and the family wouldn't hear of having her do any work. The news had leaked! Everyone knew the real purpose of this gathering! From the moment they arrived, they had taken over and busied themselves in Eva's kitchen while the men kept Nathan busy sipping wine in the living room.

Rabbi Shorisk passed the slices of apple around the table and each dinner guest took one and held it. This was then followed by a bowl of honey into which they dipped the apple.

When everyone was ready, Rabbi Shorisk held up his own slice of dipped apple and said, "May it be thy will, Oh Lord our God, to renew unto us a happy and pleasant new year." Everyone shouted, "Leshanah tovah", "May it be a good year," and then they ate their slice of apple and applause and laughter filled the room while the joyous meal continued in earnest.

When the meal was finished, Nathan got up and played his favorite CD. It was a recording of the powerful Shofarots (trumpets) of the Jerusalem Temple.

As they played softly in the background for effect, Rabbi Shorisk stood and said, "My friends we are gathered here today for a duel purpose. The first of course is to celebrate Rosh Hashanah, the Feast of Trumpets, and our new year! The other is to celebrate the beginning of a great adventure by our favorite young Priest, Nathan Cohen. As you all know the name Cohen means Priest and one must be a descendant of Aaron himself to be a Priest. Our friend here is of course a direct descendant and a member of the Tribe of Priests, and has been called to serve under the greatest High Priest ever, Tzvi Cohen, himself." Everyone gasped in surprise, as was expected of them. The Rabbi continued, a broad smile appearing on his face, "Nathan and his family are about to embark on a trip to Jerusalem, a trip that will change their lives forever." Everyone applauded and yelled their own congratulatory remark!

Rabbi Shorisk waited till order was restored and then began the ceremony that they all knew must come next, "I have the great privilege and honor of giving this lucky couple and their children their Scriptural, Jewish names! Nathan, please stand."

The Rabbi turned to Nathan and said, "You have been called Nathan, but you will now be known as Natan!" With that he touched Natan's head and blessed him.

Next he turned to Eva and said, "Eva you have been a good wife to Natan and we now call you Chava!" He touched her head. "Now if the children will come up here and I will give you my blessing."

Reluctantly the children came up and Rabbi Shorisk continued, "Moses you will now be called Moshe. You are six years old and need to help your father as much as you can. All right?"

Moshe whined, "Why do I have to be called Moshe?"

The Rabbi laughed, turned to Tzvi and said, "Tzvi you have always carried your proper name, but have you been told what it means?"

The boy shook his head.

"It means Deer with Antlers."

Tzvi complained, 'That's stupid! I don't want to be known as a deer with ants."

The Rabbi joined the crowd in their laughter, "Not ants, antlers."

"Esther and Sara what can I say about you? Grow into fine women like your mother and make your family proud." He blessed them and sent the confused children back to their seats.

Natan's heart swelled with pride as he watched his complaining children take their seats. He stood and said, "Thank you for everything you have done Rabbi. To serve under the High Priest is a great honor, and I will endeavor to make you proud. I have worked for many years as an accountant while I pursued my studies but I have a great desire to devote all my efforts to the Priesthood."

The Rabbi interrupted, smiling and waving his hands in the air, "No my friend, you mustn't think that way. They also need your accountant talents to help with the building of the new Temple. You will be working

77

closely with them on keeping track of the money for the project."

Natan hadn't thought about that. He'd assumed that it was a strictly religious reason that he was chosen. He felt a fleeting stab of disappointment, which must have shown, on his face.

Rabbi Shorisk spoke light-heartedly, "Yours is an honorable trade, my son. Don't worry; you will have a high standing in the Temple some day. You're literally getting in on the ground floor."

Natan had heard about the new Temple idea and how they had agreed to build it on the edge of Jerusalem so as not to disturb Islam's Dome of the Rock that sat on the site of the old Temple. The idea of the new temple excited Natan and his gloom lifted.

"Yes, you're right Rabbi and I'll be as much help as I can be to them. I..."

The ground shook! Everyone's ears popped and the windows of Natan's apartment exploded inward spraying them with wicked shards of sharp glass. Suddenly Natan was covered with the Rabbi's blood as several shards of glass sliced through his neck and back. The room was full of screams and cries of pain. Natan looked quickly around and saw several of his relatives and friends lying dead on the floor of his apartment, all killed by either the flying glass, fire or bricks which were thrown inward by the large explosion. The survivors were crawling toward the door and as Natan tried to join them he realized that he too was on the ground and that a shard of glass was protruding from his own leg. Chava crawled over to him, tears streaming down her cheeks. He feared the worst.

He shouted, "The children!"

Chava said, "They're safe."

It was then that he heard them crying. He pulled the glass from his leg; barely noticing the new cut it caused on the palm of his left hand. Another explosion rocked the building and the outside wall and most of the floor fell outward toward the street. Natan watched helplessly as his wife and children fell with the floor that had only moments ago safely supported them. Before he could register what had happened, they were dead!

The dust, the smell of blood and burnt flesh, fear, and death floated in the air mixed with the shouts of the survivors and dying alike!

Then came the cries from the outside, "Go home Jewish pigs! You're not welcome here anymore! Go home Jewish..."

On top of everything that had just happened here; the death, destruction and pain, the only thing left working in his apartment was Natan's CD player which was still emitting the triumphant sounds of the Shofarot's, heralding in the new year.

*   *   *

Aaron, the mighty Captain of the Angels, charged with the protection of Natan and his family, screamed with rage as the humans died all around him. His men were fighting valiantly but General Rumpus and his army out numbered them three to one.

Aaron's men were in shock as Liberty carried the soul of Chava to the Lord for Judgment. She had been robbed of her chance of Salvation through the Lord Jesus

Christ by being killed before she could be born again in the Spirit of Christ. The angels in charge of the children gently and kindly picked them up and followed Liberty as they transported them all to the Lord for comfort and judgment.

Aaron ducked and barely avoided having his head severed from his body. The attacking demon wasn't as lucky, however, as an angry Aaron sliced upward through the demon's midsection. Pivot! He blocked another attack, kicked out with his right foot as he struck downward cutting the demons throat. There was a reddish "pop" and the demon disappeared. Block! Parry! Pivot! In a series of swift moves Aaron destroyed three more demons and then turned his attention to the men in the streets below which at the direction of these hate filled demons had turned their bigotry into a fatal rage. Aaron pointed his sword at them and lightening flew from its tip. Light surrounded the men and they fell to the ground screaming with the pain that their newly blinded eyes were causing them.

Too late! The third explosion took out the rest of the building, and Natan was falling to his death. Aaron hated loosing people in his charge, but just as he resolved himself to accept the loss, the word came.

Aaron gave the command and Beriak moved faster than light, flashing to a spot just underneath Natan, physically catching him and lowering him gently to the ground.

*   *   *

Natan heard the third explosion and welcomed death with open arms. If he couldn't have his beautiful family, then he didn't want to live. As he fell toward the sharp bars of steel that protruded out of the jagged ruins of his building, he watched with the detachment of a bystander, as death reached for him, and he hoped that it wouldn't hurt too much.

Just as he braced himself for the deadly impact, he watched in utter amazement, as a being of light swooped down, grabbed him, and then lowered him slowly and safely to the ground. The beautiful being knelt down on one knee and lowered Natan's head to the ground and said, "You'll be fine, my friend..."

Natan, in a sudden burst of strength, brought on no doubt by a rush of adrenaline, started pounding on Beriak's chest screaming at the top of his lungs, "Why didn't you save my family? Why didn't you let me die? Why has God abandoned me?"

Beriak took the onslaught until Natan was hoarse and weak and had to lie back, exhausted. Beriak tried to comfort Natan by saying, "Natan, God has always been there for you, but as Daniel tried to point out to you, only Jesus the Christ can save men from their sins. Unless a man is born again of Spirit, he can't see the kingdom of God. You must accept Jesus before He can save you. It's your choice, not his. Jesus has already done all he can do for you, by dying for your sins, but unless you accept his gift you can't be protected by it."

Natan whispered, "My wife! My beautiful wife! What will happen to my wife and children?"

Beriak looked away for a moment, trying to control his emotions, and when he looked back he found that Natan was mercifully unconscious.

He whispered, "If only you had both listened to Daniel." Beriak wiped away a tear as he prayed, "Oh Lord Jesus, make a way to save these good people, who have been ripped from life before their time." He held Natan to his chest and rocked back and forth singing a hymn of comfort until an ambulance could arrive and tend to Natan's many wounds.

Aaron wept as he followed Liberty and the others to heaven, covering their retreat. He was ready for any attack that might come from the proud and bragging demons that wanted to press their advantage.

HEAVEN: NO DATE OR TIME APPLIES:

Jesus wept over the lost souls that mourned before him.

"We didn't know Lord!" they shouted as he told them that they had their chance to come to him.

Abraham shouted over the protests, "Didn't know? Across the ages we prepared you for the coming of the Messiah, and yet when He came, in the person of Jesus, you refused to accept him."

Isaiah shouted, "Did I not tell you plainly the whole story. I told you about Jesus' ministry. How the people who had walked in darkness have seen a great light. I prophesied the Jewish rejection of the Lord, and I even showed you the exact manner in which the Christ would die. You've had the opportunity to read the Scriptures have you not? Did you not believe me?"

The crowd fell silent. They knew he was right. They had clearly made their own choice to reject Jesus as their Savior. As the ground outside of the New Jerusalem began to churn with demons and the screams began to rise up from the condemned crowd, they began to sink into the blackness below them, when someone shouted, "But what about our children?"

Jesus looked up and spotted Chava, holding her four children to her. They all looked terrified, as the demons rose out of the ground around them. Slimy claws grabbed at their ankles and legs and began pulling them down into the ground.

Jesus stood and shouted, "Wait!"

The demons slunk slowly away, mumbling under their breath. Angels drew their swords and the demons began to move a little faster. The churning mass of demon filled blackness was held at bay a mere three yards from the terrified group of damned souls.

Jesus addressed Chava, "What was that woman?"

Chava, shaking with fear, spoke with a quivering voice, through sobs of grief, "I-I asked about our children. They are below the age of reason, surely they can stay with you?"

Jesus held out his arms and said, "Let the children come to me."

Forty-five children ran to the Lord, their tears of grief turning to tears of joy, as he smiled at them asking as they sat down all around him, "Would you like to stay here in Heaven with me?"

Unanimously the children shouted gleefully, "Yes!"

He blessed them and sent them into the city. As they passed through the gates they became full grown adults of about thirty years of age. It was a marvelous sight to behold.

When the children had gone, Jesus turned back to the adults and spoke again to Chava, "I see you still have a great love for your children, and I sense a great faith in you. One that you had hidden in your heart during your lifetime."

Chava nodded and wiped tears from her eyes, *"Odd,"* she thought, *"It's like still having a body, even though I know I'm just a Spirit."*

Jesus interrupted her thoughts, "Do you believe that I'm the Messiah?" he said this to the entire crowd.

Some shouted, "Yes Lord!" but they didn't mean it. Others grumbled, "You serve a hard hearted God! Who can serve such a God?"

All the rest, except Chava, said, "We serve only the one true God, the God of Abraham, Isaac, and Jacob but you are not Yahweh!"

At this Abraham, Isaac and Jacob just shook their heads in disbelief at the stubbornness of their people. They stepped out where they could be seen and said in unison, "We serve the God who is Jesus the Christ!" The crowd finally got the point that had eluded them for so long, but it was too late for most of them.

Some had a hidden faith in Jesus and were spared, happily running into the city of God. Most, however, continued to sink into the darkness, until the last of the lost souls were dragged, kicking and screaming, into the demon infested darkness and the grass once again sealed the gateway to Hell.

When the last of the screams were just distant echoes, Jesus asked Chava, "What is this woman? Did they not take you?"

Chava trembled with fear as she said; "I believe that I made a mistake in not joining Daniel, Natan's brother, when he became a Christian. I can see that you are indeed the Christ, the living God. If only I could have believed sooner."

Jesus smiled and said, "You do have one chance and one chance only Chava."

She looked up hopefully and said, "What Lord, anything at all!"

Go back to your husband and convince him to come to me. I need him in the battle that is brewing in Jerusalem. He's been chosen to be one of the 144,000 prophets who will turn away the tide of The New World Order. Go back and tell him what you have seen here. But know this! Your life will be full of more pain and misery than you would have believed possible. Satan will try to stop you, as he has tried to stop your husband. You will most likely die a second horrible death."

With courage beyond herself, Chava accepted the challenge, "Lord I'll go and do as you say. Will I remember all that has happened here?"

Jesus turned away and spoke over his shoulder, "Yes, my child you will, but it won't be enough by itself. You'll have to rely on your new faith to make it work. Don't hide your faith this time! It is a gift to be shared by all!"

Liberty swooped down and picked Chava up, wrapped her in his wings and raced toward earth. While engulfed by this loving creature, Chava praised God for this second chance. She so was happy! She felt the love, warmth, comfort and strength of this loving being. Just as she was about to lean back into the peace and tranquility of Liberty's company, her fragile world was shattered as she became once again encased in the mass of raw, burnt, tortured flesh, that had once been her rather healthy body. The pain was immense and unbearable; she screamed at the top of her lungs, thinking to herself, *"What have I done?"* She then passed into the blessed oblivion of unconsciousness.

CHAPTER SIX

THE EAGLE TAKES FLIGHT

JESUS PARK: COVENANT:
September 1st, 2---: 1400 HOURS:

Lt. Andy was one confused angel. For months now, there had been tens of thousands of angels coming and going in Jesus Park. Many of them came with the pilgrims as they continued to flock to the Park for healing, peace, or just to see where Joshua White was buried. Now, however, there were a mere two thousand angels. Thousands had been recalled to heaven with very little explanation, leaving their human charges unprotected. He couldn't wait until Capt. Aaron arrived later this afternoon to explain just what was going on!

At the moment, he stood at Joshua White's tomb, the largest monument in Covenant cemetery. The large white building that housed his remains sat in the center of the cemetery and had the statue of a mighty angel standing on top. The artist had done a wonderful job! The angel was represented as a mighty warrior, his wings stretched to their full ten-foot span and his right hand held a beautiful sword. There were thousands of flowers surrounding the monument, cared for by Ellen White herself.

Lt. Andy had been assigned to protect Jarrett White and had walked out here with Lt. Oath, who was assigned to Ellen. The angels listened to their human charges talk as they pulled weeds together in Josh's flower patch.

"Ellen, I'm thinking of leaving Jesus Park."

"Jarrett, you can't be serious!"

"I'm sorry Ellen, but I just don't get it. I've tried for Josh's sake to learn about Jesus, but I just don't feel anything. I can touch people and heal them, but it just happens and I don't feel anything when I do it. It's not me, but some unseen force that flows through me. All I get out of it is exhausted!"

"Don't you see, Jarrett? That's the Holy Spirit working in and through you. Just open your heart to him and he will speak to you."

Jarrett got up suddenly and started pacing as he shouted, "That's just it, Ellen! He doesn't speak to me! I've begged and I've pleaded but there is only silence in reply. There is no love, no comfort, only silence!"

They were both silent for a moment. Then Ellen stood, removed her gloves and walked over to Jarrett. She took his hands in hers and looked into his sad eyes and whispered, "We all love you, Jarrett. At first I cared about you because you were Josh's brother, but I have come to love you as a brother myself and I know that you have a good heart. I, also, know that whether you feel it or not, Jesus loves you very much. I also know that we are surrounded by guardian angels that are here to protect us and to take our prayers straight to God for an answer. Won't you pray with me now, Jarrett?"

Jarrett hugged Ellen to him to hide his tears. He whispered into her ear, "I love you too, Ellen. You're the sister I never had, and I appreciate your love and kind words, but I'm different than you somehow. I just don't fit in here. This isn't what I do well."

He held Ellen out at arms length, looked into her kind, sad eyes and said, "Pray for me if you will, but I just can't accept all this God and Jesus stuff. I never really have. I see that now. I tried as I said I would, but it just didn't take. Maybe some day but not now! I can't lie to myself, to you, or to Rev. Smith, nor the people that come here to find God for that matter. No! I must leave and find the answers for myself!"

Ellen hugged him and said, "I'll pray for you, Jarrett White!"

"I hope you do Ellen, and I hope that I can find the happiness and peace that emits from every pore of your body despite all of the pain that you have endured. You seem to have an arsenal of love and gentleness to give others. I just hope that you can find someone to give you kindness and gentleness in return."

"Don't worry about me, Jarrett. I'll see Joshua again very soon in Heaven. But please don't stop looking for the Lord, Jarrett. I feel your time is short. If the Lord were to decide to come back soon, I'm afraid that you'd be left behind, and I fear what you would have to endure."

"I'm not worried, Ellen. He hasn't come back in over two thousand years. I doubt he'll come back in my lifetime."

Ellen sighed, "I guess you're right, Jarrett, but just don't forget everything that you've learned here."

Jarrett hugged her one last time this side of Heaven and walked back toward the newly completed church building, just a few hundred yards from the cemetery.

As Lt. Andy began to follow Jarrett, he turned to Oath and said, "This isn't looking good for Jarrett is it?"

Lt. Oath just shook his head, and Andy turned sadly away and whispered, "The Lord told me that this assignment wouldn't be a picnic."

*   *   *

Just ten miles out from Jesus Park, the sky swarmed, swirled and churned with slimy, hungry, and very angry demons. Capt. Crygen had been given command of an unprecedented army of 300,000 demons and was told by General Rumpus to attack Jesus Park and Covenant with all the force he could. He explained that this stronghold must fall by tonight at sunset. He had been told that he must be in place by midnight, that was when the Lord Satan would manifest himself in this world, in human form, for the first time since the temptation of Christ in the desert. The thought of Christ sent a chill up Crygen's spine and he quickly changed his thoughts to the task at hand.

He had laid his plans well and had trained his warriors to carry them out. They would hit the puny force that remained in Jesus Park hard and with surprise, which he knew would work in his favor. Then they would wipe out any remaining forces in Covenant itself! The enemy has had control of Covenant for far too long, but that would end tonight! Over the last year, the enemy had allowed Dr. Kamerman to set up shop in Covenant and he had secretly built up quite a following among its citizens. This November would find many new candidates for the various city offices of Covenant, people who were loyal to Dr. Kamerman and thus loyal to Satan himself. Yes, things were about to change for the better.

*   *   *

Rev. Smith entered the chapel and found Jarrett White crying. He was sitting in one of the stage chairs, holding the phone on his lap and crying. When he saw Rev. Smith coming toward him, he quickly dried his eyes and put the phone back in the cabinet.

"What's wrong, Jarrett?"

"Hi, Rev. Smith. Nothing I shouldn't have seen coming. As I told you earlier, I have to leave. I had thought of getting together with Hawk, I mean Angela, so I called her. Not only won't she be going back to work with me, but she's also getting married in a week, to a doctor no less. She has had this crush on the guy all her life and when she got home last year, they renewed their relationship, and now they're getting married."

As Jarrett spoke, Rev. Smith could tell that the hurt and pain he felt was turning to anger and resentment. He said, "Try to be happy for her, Jarrett. There's a woman out there for you. You just have to find her."

Jarrett wanted to yell at Rev. Smith, ""You don't understand! Angela was the woman I wanted, but now she's out of my reach forever! I hate you! I hate this place but most of all, I hate the cruel God that has taken everything from me!"

Instead he smiled a cold smile and said, "Yes, Pastor, you're right. There is a woman out there for me. Her name's Genulata. I should've listened to her months ago, when she warned me not to come to this God forsaken place. Yes, I will find her, and when I do, I'll marry her!"

Jarrett stormed out before Rev. Smith could think of what to say. He really feared for Jarrett's Salvation. Jarrett had told him about Genulata, the psychic, and the encounter they'd had with her demon guide.

Rev. Smith prayed, "Oh dear Lord protect Jarrett White from the enemy. Strengthen his guardian angel to fight for his soul and..."

*   *   *

Thousands of howling, dreadful demons came in hard and without warning. Before he could even pull his sword, Lt. Andy was struck by ten demons at once. Five of the ten blades pierced vital flesh and Andy disappeared from sight, leaving Jarrett helpless before the ravenous demons.

The war cries of the demons filled the chapel. Brock, who had managed to pull his sword out, was now fighting for his life, trying to protect Rev. Smith. There were just too many! Demon upon demon filled the chapel, overwhelmed the struggling angel and then Brock too was cut down.

A few seconds after Andy was killed, he appeared before the Lord Jesus. Andy looked at the Lord and then looked again and bowed low before the glorified Savior of mankind. Jesus sat on his Judge's Bench, his eyes lit with purifying fire and his white hair gleaming with the brightness of a million suns.

Andy had to yell above the worship and joyous singing of a million angels, not to mention the souls of the millions of humans saved by their Lord, "I have failed you, my Lord!"

Jesus stood and walked down the stairs to his wounded servant. He bent down and touched the wounds, which still bled onto the golden floor of Jesus' throne room. As he touched the wounds and healed them, strength and vitality flowed back into Andy's body. He helped Andy stand. As they stood together, Andy began to glow a pure white and his renewed wings folded peacefully onto his back, blending with his garment and disappearing.

Jesus then told Andy, "You haven't failed my friend. Satan will have his day, but the war is still ours. Jarrett has never accepted us and has now turned his back completely on the way to salvation. We must not interfere until he turns back of his own free will.

"Stay with us for awhile Andy and rest. If he does turn back, you'll need your strength to rescue him. Do you understand?"

Andy nodded his agreement, embraced Jesus, and then joined the other beings that were worshipping the Lord.

Jesus smiled at his growing army of true believers. He had recalled most of his angels and he would soon recall many more, leaving just a few of his bravest, most stouthearted angels on earth to patrol the enemy territory until God launched the final battle.

Love, peace and harmony were filling this place. Those present were renewed by their close proximity to God. All was going according to plan.

Just then Oath, Lt. Devok, Warren, Brock and many other angels, who were veterans of Covenant battles, popped into existence at the feet of Jesus. They were burned, bloody and generally in poor condition.

Lt. Devok looked up and said, "It's bad sir! The Christians' prayers just aren't helping and we're losing what few angels we have left to protect Covenant. The Christians are under full attack and will not be able to withstand Satan's forces for long. Never has there been such an intense push of his forces."

Jesus smiled and said, "Yes, there has! On the day I died! But now, as then, Satan is playing right into my hands." Jesus stretched his hand over the angels that kept appearing before him, and healed them all in that single gesture. As his healing power filled the angels with strength, it also brought with it a knowledge that made them all smile knowingly. They bowed to God's wisdom and began to worship with renewed vigor.

*   *   *

Lt. Boliczar was elated at how easy it had been to overcome Andy and take Jarrett White back. He immediately attached himself to Jarrett's back and dug the gnarly, yellow, bloody claws of his left hand into Jarrett's brain and those of his right into Jarrett's spine. It felt good to possess this human's body once again. He'd been away far too long. Boliczar began to pump feelings of hatred, revenge and lust into Jarrett's very soul. He felt Jarrett's need to find Genulata and in due time would help him do just that. First, however, he wanted to ensure Jarrett's damnation by helping him take revenge on Dr. Kamerman. General Rumpus had decided the good Doctor should die and join his many friends in the torture chamber right away. The Committee would just get in the way of Lord Canards, and it was about time to clear the path for the One World Order, which would bring peace and harmony to the earth.

*   *   *

As Jarrett was leaving the Chapel and walking out to his car he literally ran into Special Agent Bob Swaggert. He caught Bob before he could fall and then just stared at him for a moment.

Agent Swaggert looked at Jarrett and for a moment could swear that his eyes had a reddish tint to them.

"Just the sun!" he thought as he noticed the anger that emitted from every pore of Jarrett's body.

"What's wrong, Jarrett?"

"I'm blowing this place. I want to find Dr. Kamerman and bring him in."

"That's why I'm here Jarrett! President Place has authorized your reinstatement, if you want it. You'll have your full powers back, with code name Eagle, as always."

Jarrett was tempted to tell him to shove it but then he realized that this fit well into his plans for revenge on the good doctor. With full powers as a CIA agent, came the license to kill. He liked the idea instantly and said, "I accept! Did you bring my gun?"

"Yes I did. I wanted to be prepared just in case you did agree. To tell you the truth, I had my doubts. I thought you had found this Jesus or something?"

Jarrett laughed, "No, Bob! It was something that my brother talked me into trying, but it just didn't take. Now let's get to your car, get me armed and then tell me what you know about the whereabouts of Dr. Kamerman."

They started walking rather quickly toward Bob's car and Bob said in a surprised voice, "Didn't you now? Dr. Kamerman's right here in Covenant. The police just found and killed Starvas Creen last night and we have a deep under cover agent living among the homeless. He has put out a call for backup and you're it."

They had arrived at Bob's car and he had handed Jarrett his 9mm Beretta, I.D. and a thousand dollars in cash. Then Bob said, "Go find the oldest, dirtiest clothes you can, put them on and then go find this man."

He handed Jarrett a picture. Jarrett looked at it and saw an older man with a baldhead, wire rim glasses and a smile that seemed out of place.

Jarrett said with disgust, "This is your undercover agent? This is Scorpion?"

Bob laughed and said, "Sure he doesn't look like much, but he's the best computer expert the agency has that is willing to go out into the field. You'll find him in jail. He was picked up last night for vagrancy and has spent his "time" going over the computer records that the police confiscated last night from the witch Coven's Temple."

Hope swelled up in Jarrett's heart. He would see Doctor's Kamerman's skinny neck in his hands before the day was out.

*   *   *

Dr. Kamerman shouted, "Hurry up Winter! I've got just one more Committee member to warn and then we're getting out of here!"

Winter was a man who had linked up with Dr. Kamerman right after his escape from prison. He had made a deal to work for Kamerman in exchange for information on Jarrett White, or Spike as he used to call him. Winter was Spike's second in command in the Demon Slayer Gang until one treacherous night Spike had betrayed their entire gang. Winter later found out that Spike was really Jarrett White C.I.A. Agent. Well, his plans were just about complete and he would soon have his revenge on Jarrett White.

Dr. Kamerman made contact with the last of his Committee. They made up a group of twelve of the most powerful people in the world. The real power behind all other power on earth. They ran Governments and individuals alike.

Kamerman spoke quickly, time was short, "Gordi, I'm glad I caught you before you left for the meeting. I have warned all the others and you're the last. By some fluke of an accident, the authorities have captured my Temple, with all of its records in tact and they killed Starvas Creen! This all occurred last night so we still have time to transfer funds and move to our ghost corporations. There is something that can't wait, however, and you've been selected to take care of it."

President Gordi Vochi of the New United Russia asked, "And what would that be my friend?"

Kamerman smiled and said, "President Place must die! And Gordi? She must die today!" Kamerman broke the connection.

Gordi Vochi hung up the phone. It wasn't totally unexpected but it was still a sad task to say the least. He really felt genuine affection and friendship for this brave woman. He would, however, do what was best for the World, and whatever the Committee decided was best was indeed the best thing for this World.

Gordi picked up the phone again, this time to give the orders that would ensure the demise of the most powerful woman in the world, President Roberta Place!

CHAPTER SEVEN
THE UNITED NATIONS

UNITED NATIONS BUILDING:
September 1st, 2---: 1430 HOURS:

President Place was in the back of her car reading over her speech one last time. Except for her secretary, Jon Holder who was sitting across from her, she was alone. Roberta wanted some quiet time before giving the most important speech of her life. In it, she'd outlined the concerns of her staff. She'd incorporated some of the ideas from her meeting this morning with her military advisors who were convinced that a massive invasion force was poised and ready to strike. She'd given them Joshua's message on the subject, but after an uncomfortable silence one of the generals had dismissed the idea of demons and had gone back to the reality of space aliens.

Roberta had to smile at the thought, "*These men would rather believe in invading aliens than demons from Hell. Well, who wouldn't after the years of brain washing that has come through TV and movies about kind and wise aliens coming to solve our problems?*"

She whispered, "God help us!"

Jon looked up from some papers he was sorting, "What was that Madam President?"

Roberta smiled and said, "Sorry, Jon, I was just thinking out loud."

Jon nodded, used to her moods, and returned to his papers.

Roberta continued to look at him. He was young, handsome and very organized. When Jon looked up again, Roberta asked him, "Jon what do you think of this situation?"

"Which one Madam President?"

"This alien incident. Do you believe that demons can be involved, Jon, or is it really aliens?"

"Well, I don't believe in God, so that leaves me out of the demon question all together. I'm even having trouble believing in aliens from another planet, dimension or whatever. However, the evidence for the alien theory far outweighs the evidence for the demon theory."

Roberta nodded. She was disappointed with his answer, but said, "I expected as much and I fear that my message will not be well received today at the UN. I'm still for pulling out..."

Just then the phone rang and Jon answered it. He listened, nodded, and said, "Thank you Congressman." He hung up the phone and said, "Madam President, I'm sorry but the Congress just voted to stay in the UN."

The President fought to hold back the tears, but wasn't quite successful. She pulled a tissue out of her pocket and dabbed her eyes and said through false laughter, "Well, Jon, there goes the first six pages of my speech."

Jon remained silent and allowed the President to grieve in her own way. He was worried about her, because she was making far too many waves for the powers that be. He knew that they would not allow her to disrupt their plans with all this talk about demons. Some had even talked about getting her committed, as mentally incompetent, but they knew that it wouldn't work. He was afraid of the alternative plans that they might have laid instead. Before he got too far into this line of thought; however, the car pulled up to the UN building.

Jon said, "More bad news Madam President, the congressman suggested that you watch the news channel before you go into your speech." As he said this he turned the car's TV monitor on and they were greeted with sirens, shouting and gunshots.

"This is your news reporter, Tom Harshaw. I'm just three blocks from the UN building in New York where the President will speak just moments from now about many world affairs. Madam President, if you're watching please don't leave out this subject of Anti-Semitism. Behind me are the remains of the once high-classed 39th street Jewish neighborhood. Bombs mercilessly set to destroy not only the buildings but to take out as many Jews as possible have destroyed six high-rises. They waited until Rosh Hashanah (The Feast of the Trumpets) also known as the Jewish New Year, knowing that most of the Jews would be in their homes enjoying holiday meals.

"Seven hundred are dead and many more are wounded. Men, women and children slaughtered without mercy. The police, at this very moment, are caught in a raging gun battle with the hate mongers responsible for this slaughter. This must stop!"

Tom looked off camera for a moment, took a piece of paper, and then read, "This just in. It appears that the first of the survivors are being pulled from the wreckage. The first two are identified as Nathan and Eva Cohen. Mr. Cohen is a respected C.P.A. with the Hamerstien

Corporation. Their children, I'm afraid, didn't survive the attack. We'll keep you informed as..."

As Jon switched off the monitor, Roberta dried her eyes and tried to pull herself together. She knew that she'd have to represent the will of the Congress of the United States. She'd announce that the United States would stay in the UN and would face this alien problem head-on with all of the other countries. She also knew that she'd lose face with many, if not all, of the delegates to the UN when she proclaims the message that Joshua had given her to announce to the world. Added to this already huge burden was this new Anti-Semitic attack on the Jewish neighborhood, practically in the shadow of the UN building.

Before Roberta could give it much more thought, the door opened and there was suddenly a wall of security personnel around her door. As she got out of the car, she was instantly pressed from all sides by these special agents and was hustled into the building.

As Roberta obediently followed their lead, she could hear the loud voices of the protesters who were chanting anti-Place slogans. Some began to throw eggs, garbage, tomatoes and even bottles at her, but they would be disappointed at the results. Nothing ever got on her because of the press of agents and the umbrellas they held over her head.

She thought it was a bottle breaking. Then one of the agents in front of her fell. Roberta felt her face hit the sidewalk and the weight of several agents on top of her before she even realized what had happened. She heard the screams of the crowd, the shouted orders of the agents, and then the rapid fire of assault rifles.

The agents got off of her and yanked her to her feet and roughly pushed and pulled her toward the building at a dead run. She tripped over the downed, probably dead agent, scraping both of her knees on the pavement before several urgent pairs of hands could pick her up and hurry her into the building. Once inside, they rushed her to a nearby women's restroom. Several agents burst in and pulled two half-dressed women out of their stalls and threw them roughly out, clearing and securing the room behind them.

President Place yelled to the women as they passed, "I'm sorry about this but..." and then she was in the bathroom with the door closed.

The two women forgot about their own modesty and just stared at the closed door. They had both recognized the President just as the door closed behind her. One of the women whispered, "She must really have to go!"

The other woman just nodded in agreement as they left to find another bathroom.

*　　　*　　　*

General Rumpus slapped Capt. Poe in the face and yelled, "How could you allow him to miss?"

Capt. Poe still had a death grip on the dying sniper's brain. He was waiting for the man to die, so he could take his soul to Hell. The man lay beneath Capt. Poe and was coughing up blood. He had several bullet holes in him and several broken bones to boot. The special agents that surrounded him were just itching to finish him off but instead waited impatiently for the ambulance to arrive.

Capt. Poe asked, "Shouldn't we try to tempt one of these agents to kill the man and thus win another soul?"

General Rumpus slapped him again and yelled, "We have only one mission today, and you would have done well to concentrate on that. I'd like to take the man's soul myself, but I'm not going to leave here until she's dead. It's crucial to our Master's plan and I'll see it finished!"

Just then the man went into a coughing, wheezing fit and finally breathed his last. His soul came out of his body and began to scream at the sight of the two demons that had a hold on him. Capt. Poe grabbed him around the neck and dove through the ground, dragging the kicking, screaming soul with him.

When they'd gone, General Rumpus streaked toward the secret weapon he'd held in reserve. He would succeed! He had to succeed!

*   *   *

President Place looked at herself in the mirror and gasped. Her right cheek was scraped raw and hurt as she dabbed it with a wet paper towel. Her lip was still bleeding and beginning to swell. Her suit was torn and dirty; her hair was a mess, not to mention the bloody scrapes on both knees.

She went toward a booth and asked, "Could you fellas leave me for a couple of minutes please?"

The head agent looked sympathetic but said, "Sorry."

Her face was red when she entered the stall. She came out a few minutes later and keeping her eyes averted, she washed her hands. The door opened and there was a loud crack. She jumped and had visions of bullets flying or a bomb going off, but all she saw when she turned to look was a large chair being brought in. She was about to ask the purpose of it when her hairstylist, Helen, was pushed in right after the chair. The agents searched her bag and then Helen got to work.

She said, "I was so sorry to hear about this attempt on your life Madam President! Oh look what they've done to you! I'll try to apply some makeup for the discoloration around your eye and chin, but that watery wound will have to be bandaged or it will run all over your makeup."

As if on cue, Dr. Lawrence was ushered in and immediately came over to the President and said, "It would appear that your agents are rougher than the attackers."

"They have to be Doc! They're charged with my safety, and they seem to have their hands full today. Now would you be so kind as to bandage this scrape, so Helen can apply some more makeup and fix my hair?"

Dr. Lawrence went to work but continued his speech, "Roberta you need to let me take you to the hospital where I can X-Ray your cheek and make sure you're all right."

Roberta laughed and said, "There are bigger things to worry about here than my cheek bone doctor."

"I know, Roberta, but I'm just worried about you, that's all."

"I know you are Doc, but it can't be helped. I must give this speech today no matter what. The Lord sent Joshua back to me to tell me so."

The doctor began to protest, but Roberta held her hand up to his mouth and continued, "I know that you are uncomfortable with all this talk of angels, demons and visitations from the dead, but you've seen the power of God at work."

Just a few months ago Joshua had announced that her son was healed of his brain tumor and Dr. Lawrence had verified the miracle but had never been swayed. He just didn't believe.

When the doctor finished, Helen took over. While Helen applied makeup to the President's face, Dr. Lawrence cut Roberta's pantyhose away from her knees and cleaned and bandaged those scrapes. Within twenty minutes they had the President looking as good as she could under the circumstances. Roberta looked in the mirror and smiled. The flesh colored bandages hardly showed and the work-over that Helen had done, in addition to the fresh clothes that Roberta had just finished putting on, once again made her look like the leader of the most powerful nation on earth.

THE O'LEARY HOME:
September 1st, 2---: 1440 HOURS:

Marla Brinkle O'Leary had a rough night. She'd covered the warehouse incident last night. They had caught about twelve witches who were still covered in blood. They had discovered three bodies of innocent homeless girls, who'd been abducted and then sacrificed on those rancid altars. This brought back bad memories of the time when Marla, herself, had almost been sacrificed by Governor Bradley now long dead and good riddance!

Grady hadn't come home this morning, so Marla hadn't had the chance to tell him that she had canceled her trip to Washington. She was going to cover the President's speech from right here in Covenant. She had grabbed a couple of hours sleep and was now ready to go back to the station. She wanted to be there for President Place's speech live from the U.N. at 3:00 p.m. Marla taped a note on the refrigerator telling Grady of her love and that she would be at the station for the rest of the day.

Marla was just walking out the door, when the phone rang. She hesitated and almost let the machine get it, but changed her mind.

She picked up the receiver and said, "Hello."

Michael Pro, Marla's cameraman, was on the line and spoke as though he was out of breath, "Marla, get down here now! The President was shot at just a few minutes ago! Reports are sketchy, but I think she's all right. She's still going to speak. She's reported to have minor injuries and her doctor is with her now."

Marla was stunned! She whispered, "Okay, I was just on the way."

Marla hung up and slowly dialed Grady's number, but a woman answered, "Police Department, may I help you?"

Marla recognized Mandy's voice and said, "Oh, I'm sorry Mandy I must have dialed the wrong number I wanted Grady's private line."

"No Marla, right number, it's just that it's crazy around here and the Chief called me in to answer his phone and take the many messages that are coming in after last night. Can I help you, Marla?"

"Just tell Grady that when he gets a chance, turn the television on and watch our news broadcast. There has been an attempt on President Place's life. She's at the UN and at last report, she's still all right."

Mandy whistled, "I'll tell him, and we'll all try to watch."

Marla felt a momentary surge of jealousy. She was jealous that Grady was around all of those other women at the station and they spent more time with him than she did. She even began to envision him being unfaithful to her.

Marla caught herself and prayed, "Oh Lord Jesus, please cast out this demon of jealousy from me!"

At that moment, Marla's Angel, Long Blade, drew his sword and swung at the demon, Jealousy, who was then forced to let go of Marla in order to draw his own puny sword. He actually blocked two of Long Blade's thrusts before being cut in half and disappearing in a puff of reddish yellow sulfuric smoke.

Marla felt much better and mentally apologized to Grady for doubting him even for a second. Her last thoughts of Grady O'Leary this side of Heaven were pleasant thoughts.

UNITED NATIONS BUILDING:
September 1st, 2---: 1500 HOURS:

It had only been a half hour since the attempt on the President's life. Roberta hadn't had time to even get scared.

"Funny how detached I feel from all of this", she thought as she walked toward the podium and everyone in the room stood and applauded her resolve. She'd heard from her sources on the way to the chamber that

even her enemies had great respect for her because of her courage in the face of danger.

Roberta thought, *"Maybe that's God's plan in allowing this to happen. Maybe it will make me more acceptable to these people, and, therefore, pave the way for the message he has charged me to give."*

She'd never become used to the flashes of the cameras or the floodlights of the TV cameras. They still blinded her and caused a momentary disorientation, but Roberta continued to smile as she walked up the steps to the raised podium. The large horseshoe table that held so many distinguished guests looked intimidating from up here. For one terrifying moment, Roberta lost all train of thought. She bowed her head and prayed for help and received it instantly. She felt a surge of the Holy Spirit taking away all fear and doubt. She looked at the assembly through new eyes, eyes filled with hope and love. She truly wanted to help these people understand that something big was about to happen; something that would change the world and it's people forever.

President Place started to open the folder that still held her crumpled speech and she knew that its content was totally off the mark. She'd missed the point entirely. She closed the folder and whispers arose from the audience.

The President leaned forward and the speakers squealed. Technicians rushed to make adjustments and the President began, "Good afternoon, ladies and gentlemen of the world. Most of you know that I stood against The One World Government proposal, which was voted on by Congress today. The Congress of the United States has, however, voted to not only remain in the UN but will support a World Government, if it can be set up properly."

The crowd exploded to their feet, and applauded with pleasure at this unexpected but very welcome news.

President Place continued, "Human rights issues must be met. World hunger must be dealt with and homelessness must be alleviated. It will take a generous government to accomplish this and a government with the proper motivation."

Heads were nodding their agreement throughout the audience, giving Roberta the courage to continue, "I'm here today to announce to the world that several fighter aircraft from the United States, Russia, China and England have been reported missing immediately after encountering alien spacecraft in each of the respective nation's skies."

The audience erupted with cries of disbelief! Several of Canards' spies rushed the President to shut her up, but were turned back by her special agents who had their automatic rifles at the ready.

Several moments passed and it took Roberta several tries to resume, "Please hear me out! What I am about to say will sound fictional, but it's as true as the attempt on my life!"

This reminder of the assassination attempt seemed to calm them down, and Roberta continued, "For years you've watched television, read books and heard stories about aliens from outer space; some friendly, some benevolent, some scary, powerful and cruel. This has been an orchestrated attempt by Satan himself to brainwash you into believing that these aliens have more to offer than our God does. These sightings are not new in our history. Until the last few hundred years;

however, the sightings were called demons and many stories from these encounters filter down to us through mythology and horror stories. Once science came on the scene; however, the demonic sightings diminished and U.F.O. sightings increased. For some reason we can more easily believe, and indeed want to believe, in a race of alien beings that are much more powerful than ourselves; a race that can solve all of our problems; a race to which we would willing give all of our freedoms for the right price.

"My friends, that price is the sale of your very souls to Satan, himself. The Anti-Christ is about to come charging into this world riding on one of these U.F.O.'s. He'll promise you the answer to all of your dreams, and you'll hand over to him full power to take over and to run your kingdoms."

Again the crowd stood this time; however, they were shouting and jeering! After a much longer period of time President Place finally could be heard, "Please! Please! Let me finish!"

The crowd began to sit down again and Roberta spoke for the last time, "My friends, I was wrong about the One World Order! We'll have one and it is indeed on the way. It will be a One World Order run by Jesus Christ, Himself, with His Saints and Angels in positions of power throughout the World. It'll be a truly peaceful time where the lion will lie down with the lamb, and we'll be at peace with our Jewish brothers. Just three blocks from here they have been cruelly attacked today and I publicly denounce such barbaric actions and call for peace with Israel."

The crowd turned ugly in it's anger and surged forward!

*   *   *

Marla, who'd been watching the President's performance with pride, now jumped up in terror and shouted, "No!"

The crowd had mobbed the President, and her Agents had to finally open fire to disperse them, killing several in the process. They started to move the President toward the exit, when a man at the back of the room stood up and yelled, "This is for Allah!" He shouldered the rocket launcher, aimed it in the general direction of the President, and fired.

*   *   *

General Worl began to draw his sword but after a moment of thought he let it drop back into its scabbard. He knelt down, a tear running down his cheek. He watched as the rocket raced toward Roberta "Alex" Place, President of the United States. He waited!

Roberta was frozen in a moment of fear. What would happen to Patrick when she was gone? She knew the arrangements she had made. He would be safe. Besides, if what she was just saying were true, then there was nothing to worry about.

Roberta watched detached as if this were happening to someone else. She felt the rocket as it swished past her. She felt the pain as her head once again hit the ground as her guards tried to cover her with their bodies. The missile exploded just five feet from her throwing its fire and debris across half the room. The initial explosion singed most of Roberta's hair from her head as well as the clothes from her body. It had, after killing and throwing the guards away from her, left her totally conscious and very much alive so that she experienced the first gust of poisonous gas that caused her to choke. Blood oozed from her eyes, nose, and mouth. Roberta died a violent death, as had so many of the peacemakers before her.

The process of death was a transition to her. One moment she was choking and in pain; the next she was sitting up looking into the lovely face of General Worl.

Roberta stood and asked, "You're Capt. Worl aren't you? The Angel I met at the Battle of Covenant?"

Worl smiled, "Well it's General now. Yes, the same at your service." He bowed low out of respect.

Roberta smiled in turn and said, "Well what do we do now?"

Before Worl could answer, Roberta looked down at her body, what was left of her human body anyway, experiencing no feeling of loss. She found it interesting how quickly she had lost interest in her life and the affairs that seemed so important just a few moments ago. Now she looked on from a different angle that showed her the scene from a much clearer vantage point. The room was on fire and there were several dead bodies scattered about. Those who weren't killed by the explosion would soon be dead from the gas and bacteria that had been released by the missile. The demons were having a field day collecting the condemned souls of the many dead in the room. The man, who'd shot the missile at her and who was then summarily shot and killed by the guards even before the missile exploded, was shocked by the demon who came to collect him.

He screamed, "No! I'm to go to Allah! There's been a mistake!"

The demon yelled back, "Yes, there's been a mistake, and you made it by not believing your Christian friends. Now, however, it's too late and you will go with me!"

All the mournful screams disappeared as one by one the demons left with their charges in tow.

Most of the Angels had left as well when Roberta turned to Worl and asked, "Was I finished here General Worl? Did I do everything that God had asked me to do?"

Worl smiled and said, "You did well Madam President. Now if you'll come with me, Jesus has all the information you'll need. We have many preparations to make before the Kingdom arrives."

Satisfied, Roberta turned away from her old life and went with Worl toward her new life. They faded from this existence through the vale to appear in the next and entered the wonderful realm of love, to which Roberta had no objections whatsoever!

CHAPTER EIGHT
UPON DEAF EARS

IN A DEMONSHIP OUTSIDE WASHINGTON DC:
September 1st, 2---: 1600 HOURS:

Daniel had been on this ship for over thirty hours now and he hadn't eaten, drank or slept the entire time. He did this in order to assure that he wouldn't be drugged or harmed through trickery. He was very tired, however, and he wasn't about to believe that this Canards guy was really going to just let him go.

Daniel thought, *"Sure I walk down that plank to the street below and I get it in the back! Well, I'm not playing his game!"*

Alfred Canards was slightly amused by this human, but he had too many things to arrange in a very few hours. Therefore, he simply ordered his demon guards to throw the man out. As they picked Daniel up and carried him down the plank, Canards said, "We'll keep your jet for you, after all you people won't be needing them anymore.

Lt. Daniel Derecks yelled, "Canards I know who you are! You're Satan incarnate! You're the Anti-Christ!"

Alfred Canards frowned and had second thoughts about letting Derecks go. *"After all, I can't have this human running around calling me the Anti-Christ, can I? On the contrary, that's exactly what I want. The more Christians that rant and rave about me being some sort of evil Devil, the more believable I will become."*

115

He yelled down to Derecks, "Daniel! You just go right ahead and try to convince the world that I'm the Anti-Christ, but they won't believe you. I've done too good a job convincing the world that I do not exist! Oh and Daniel, in order to help convince you, I want you to look at me!"

Daniel struggled against the guards as they threw him to the street below. He heard Canards yell at him and when he ordered him to look at him, Daniel fought the impulse to look. In the end, however, he did turn his eyes toward Canards. When he beheld the monster before him, Daniel turned white as a sheet. Standing in the doorway was not Canards, the man of power, but rather Satan as he really looked after generations of being pure evil. After he got over the initial shock, he realized that he wasn't seeing the little red man with a tail and a pitchfork. No this being was ever so much more evil! The monster's head was very large, with dark red eyes and a mouth full of very sharp yellowish teeth. Slobber ran down his chin as he growled at Daniel. His body was reddish in color, but he had scales instead of skin, and his tail was thick and long with a spearhead shaped bone at the end. His hands were empty of a pitchfork but his large, bony hands each had four fingers, no thumb, and at the end of each finger were spearhead shaped nails, each of which looked very sharp and deadly.

Daniel thought, *"I can see where the idea of a pitchfork came from with hands like that."*

Satan, in all of his glory, howled one more time for Derecks, before the door slowly closed and blocked the hideous vision from Daniel's terrified eyes.

Daniel lay on his back, the ground hard and uncomfortable beneath him. He watched in fascination as the demon ship rose into the air and streaked away disappearing as instantly and completely as if it were a forgotten memory. Daniel feared, however, that nothing would block from his memory, the hideous creature he had been forced to witness. He had to warn the world about the real identity of this smooth-talking, peaceful, confident looking man, Alfred Canards!

Daniel was free now. He had a duty to get word to Commander Pips, but he didn't even know were he was. He hadn't seen his squadron members or anyone else since they had locked him in his cell and he hadn't seen the ground until the guards threw him onto it.

Daniel prayed, "Lord Jesus Christ, please give me the strength to complete this mission. No doubt this will be the hardest mission of my life. I place my future in your hands, Lord Jesus!"

He started walking and had only gone about two blocks when he collapsed from exhaustion and his mind was overcome by darkness.

THE WHITE HOUSE:
September 1st, 2---: 1700 HOURS:

Vice President Thomas Holstrum was afraid. He had enjoyed the last few months as Vice President and had even enjoyed working for President Roberta Place. He had become used to her strange Christian ways and she had grown accustomed to his lack of faith. From a mutual healthy respect of each other's opinions, they had developed a good working relationship. He couldn't believe that she was actually dead. Not only President

117

Place, but also almost every major leader in the world was dead. They all had been killed in one horrible afternoon. Less experienced and fearful subordinates were now running the world's governments. There was a lot to fear in this world, which had been thrown into instant chaos, anger and grief.

Holstrum barely had time to be sworn in as President before the avalanche of phone calls, faxes and visits overwhelmed him. There were military skirmishes breaking out across the globe and even threats against the United States specifically for allowing the leaders to be killed on her soil. Some even accused Holstrum of orchestrating the entire plot to gain power. They weren't far from wrong on that score, of course, but they were just guessing. They as yet had no proof.

He looked around the Oval Office and thought how different it looked from this side of the desk. He wasn't ready to be President, but here he was and here he would have to stay and deal with the problems. Problems! Where to start? The space alien problem? The terrorist problem? The Anti-Semite problem? Or the Senate and Congress who wanted to instantly join the One World Order and completely do away with the U.S. Constitution!

Bzzz! Tom jumped up and then realized with embarrassment that it was just the intercom. He reached over, pushed the button and said, "Yes?"

It was his secretary, Tricia, "Mr. President! Director Aires is here to see you."

Tom sat back, took a deep breath, and said unenthusiastically, "Please send him in."

Aires walked in and without preamble, greeting or explanation, walked over to the TV/Recorder unit and popped in a disc that he was carrying.

As the video began, Aires said, "Mr. President, this is important. You remember the pilots that were lost in action yesterday morning?"

Tom nodded and thought, *"Was it only yesterday morning?"*

Aires continued, "One of them was released by this new enemy at about 4:00 p.m. this afternoon. A passing motorist who called police found him just outside of Washington. When they saw the flight suit and all, the police called us from the hospital where they had taken him. They were freaked out by the time they called us and you're about to see why."

Holstrum turned his chair so he could see the image better and while Aires sat down in front of the President's desk, Holstrum thought, *"He's taking all this in stride. You wouldn't even know that he'd lost one of his best friends today, but Richard was a professional. He would grieve later, if there were a later."*

Tom's thoughts were interrupted by screams from the monitor, "I'm not crazy! These aren't alien ships! Not space ships at all! They're demon ships, I tell you! And Satan is coming in the form of a man called Alfred Canards! He's the Anti-Christ! He wants to take over the world and to lead everyone to Hell. Don't trust him I tell you!"

With that, the once sane and professional Lt. Derecks began to scream as he struggled against his straightjacket, while foaming at the mouth. He finally slipped into a restless sleep as the sedative they had given him took effect.

Director Aires turned the video off, sat back down in front of the President's Desk, and said, "Well what do you think, sir?"

Tom looked the director in the eyes and said, "I think he's finally cracked! He's out of his mind with delirium! He's suffering from shock, the poor man. It's hard telling what those creatures did to him up there. I'm also quite sure that they would rather distract us into thinking that they are some sort of evil creature, like Satan, rather than have us concentrate on our defense against the real problem; a race of super intelligent beings, whose motives we haven't a clue"

Richard Aires sat on the edge of his chair and said, "That's what I thought as well until I realized that the enemy might want us to believe that Derecks has cracked. What if there is an outside chance Lt. Derecks is correct?"

The President thought for a moment, as he swiveled his chair away from Aires, then made his decision.

Swiveling back to look at Richard, he said, "No! Richard, these are real creatures from outer space. We've determined that much. Now all we have to do is find out if their friend or foe."

"I believe I can answer that for you."

Both men jumped up and found a stranger standing in the Oval Office of the White House.

Director Aires pulled his gun and yelled, "Freeze! How did you get past security?"

The man laughed and said, "Your security means nothing to me!"

With that the 9mm in the Director's hand flew across the room seemingly of it's own accord. Director

Richard Aires was at a loss as to what to do. He had sworn to protect the President but he didn't even know what he was up against.

As if reading his mind, the stranger smiled pleasantly and said, "Look! I didn't come here to fight with you. On the contrary I've come with information that will ease some of your fears. Then again, where are my manners? Let me introduce myself, I'm Alfred Canards, the reincarnated soul of the man you know as Jesus Christ."

COVENANT POLICE STATION:
September 1st, 2---: 1700 HOURS:

Special Agent Bob Swaggert had mixed feelings about this new Jarrett White. It was understandable that Jarrett would want revenge against Dr. Kamerman for having his brother killed, but the intensity of his hatred worried Bob. He watched Jarrett as he put on his bulletproof vest and took the grenades and shotgun out of Bob's trunk. Jarrett was 6'5" very muscular with short cut brown hair, which Bob still couldn't get used to. Jarrett had always worn his hair long and in a ponytail. The beard he used to wear was gone as well. The face, because of plastic surgery, was of course totally different. When Starvas Creen's assassin's bullet hit Joshua White in the back of the neck, it had passed all the way through Joshua and into Jarrett's face causing enough damage that Jarrett had to have major reconstructive surgery done to his jaw and face bones.

Jarrett started walking toward the police station, and it was all Bob could do to keep up.

Bob said, "Look Jarrett, slow down and think a little bit. You're too intense, you're liable to make a mistake and get yourself killed."

Jarrett stopped so suddenly that Bob ran into his back hurting his nose in the process. When Jarrett turned, it was with such intensity and anger that Bob feared for his safety.

Jarrett whispered through gritted teeth, "I'll tell you this just one time. I've been reactivated! You've done your job! Now stay out of my way and let me do mine!"

With that he resumed his walk toward the station, and Bob followed without saying another word. They entered the station at shift change and many of the officers were leaving to go home. The officers stared at Jarrett not quite sure whether they should draw down on him or not. If it hadn't been for the plastic coated card with the large letters "CIA" written across it they would have at least stopped him for questioning. It's best for them that they didn't have to do that.

Men like Jarrett scared Bob. Oh, they got the job done and that's why they were kept around, but they could be such loose cannons at times and this was becoming one of those times.

*   *   *

Boliczar, demon of Satan, was still attached to Jarrett's spine and was working overtime to keep Jarrett's hatred and anger flowing. His own life depended on the success of this mission, which would once and for all damn the soul of Jarrett White to Hell.

*   *   *

Jarrett walked into Police Chief Grady O'Leary's office without knocking and stood before his desk.

Grady stood up smiled and said, "Hey Jarrett, how are you?"

"Where is he, Grady?"

That's when Grady noticed the great change that had come over Jarrett. He said, "Calm down Jarrett. You look like you want to kill somebody. Remember he's one of your own agents, not the enemy."

Jarrett said, "Look Grady, I don't have time for small talk. President Place put me in charge of this case and wants me to apprehend Dr. Kamerman and his gang, dead or alive. I've been re-activated and that's what I do! I don't do it with pleasantries, however, but with action. So show me where Scorpion is so I can get the information I need to accomplish my mission."

Grady just stared for a minute and then he asked, "You two haven't heard have you? About President Place I mean?"

Jarrett snapped, "Heard what? We've been busy this afternoon and didn't have any TV or radio on. Is it about her speech? How'd it go?"

Grady whispered, hoarsely from the emotion he still couldn't quite control, "She was assassinated during her speech this afternoon along with almost every major leader in the world. It was a gas and bacteria filled missile, launched by a madman and it killed everyone at the U.N. and every person within three blocks. It took some of those poor people over an hour to die." Grady shuddered.

Bob and Jarrett stood shocked. They sat down. Jarrett stood back up and paced. Then he sat back down, his face turning the color of snow, and his voice was as cold when he asked, "Exactly, how did this happen. Tell me everything you know."

Grady shuddered again, took a deep breath, wiped a tear from his eye which was threatening to run down his cheek, and then said, "It started at 2:30 this afternoon with the first attempt on her life..."

THE PENTAGON AUDITORIUM:
September 1st, 2---: 1800 HOURS:

"So you see gentleman, I have come back to earth to set things right again. This has happened several times throughout history; but, of course, this will be the most noticeable time. I've also decided that with almost every major leader being killed, I'll have to stick around for awhile, and make sure things get set up right."

Satan, in the form of Alfred Canards, had laid out his story of lies very logically and had played on every fear and hope that his listening audience held dear. His audience had now grown to include not only the President and Director Aires, but also every major head of the armed forces, as well as, every financial leader in the Government of the United States of America. They were now in a large auditorium conference room at the Pentagon.

Mr. Canards looked out over his audience with satisfaction. Not a practicing Christian in the entire crowd, and these men were buying every word that he had to sell them.

He continued, "I'll arrive tonight in Europe and take over my position as head of the ten country alliance which will be in charge of all financial decisions for the world. We are about to join together, gentlemen, to bring world peace, prosperity, and the fulfillment of basic human needs to all the people of the world. And with your cooperation, everyone else will fall in line. What do you say? Do you want to save the world?"

It was President Holstrum who first stood and began applauding, then others joined, him and soon the entire room was filled with praise for this new savior of the world, Alfred Canards, leader of an alien race and now ruler over all the earth.

COVENANT POLICE DEPARTMENT:
September 1st, 2---: 1830 HOURS:

If Jarrett were angry before, he was furious now. He rambled, "How dare they! President Place was my friend as well as my boss. She was always fair, and she had so much power for good in this world! Kamerman! I know that he and his Committee had something to do with this. This gives me even more reason to bring him in!

"Grady please take me to Scorpion!"

Grady led the way to the computer center of the Police Station. When they arrived they found a small man, whose balding head shown brightly in the overhead light. What hair he did have was gray and sticking out along the sides in an absentminded display of negligence. He was sitting in a desk chair pounding, rapid fire, on the keys of his computer terminal. There were computer printouts covering the floor of the room as deep as the base of his chair, and the printer was heedlessly spitting out more.

Jarrett thought that it was odd that a printer would be printing at the same time as the man was working, but then he noticed that Scorpion was actually working on two separate computers and two separate printers, which would explain the large amount of paper on the floor.

Grady said. "Hi Fred, how's it go'n?"

Fred didn't look up as he snapped, "Get out and leave me alone!"

Grady smiled, Bob turned red and Jarrett got angrier. Jarrett went over, swiveled the chair around and pulled a terrified Fred out of the chair by the front of his ragged, tattered shirt.

Jarrett pulled him close and their noses almost touched which was when Jarrett noticed the stench coming from Fred. Jarrett yelled into Fred's face, "Look you little weasel, don't you ever take a bath?"

Fred sheepishly shrugged his shoulders, which wasn't easy while being held up off of the floor, and said, "It's part of my cover. Now please put me down before I lose the very information that you are apparently looking for. I'll bet you're the famous Eagle that I keep hearing about? Well I'm glad to meet you at last!" He extended his hand in friendship.

Jarrett started shaking Scorpion as if he were nothing but a rag doll and yelled, "Dr. Kamerman killed my brother! He almost killed me! Now he's killed not only my friend President Place, but he has killed most of the leaders from every kingdom on earth! I want him, and I want him now!"

Fred had stopped struggling and just hung there limply in Jarrett's large hands. He had gotten over his initial shock at Eagle's violence and asked calmly, "Could you please put me down? I think I have found him! I must run a couple of more codes and break into another file, if they haven't already discovered my illegal entry and cut me off. Timing is very important in my business and you're wasting the only opportunity we may have to find him." He spoke as if Jarrett were a child, "Now if you'll be so kind as to put me down, I'll get back to my work."

After Jarrett reluctantly put Scorpion down, the little man sat down and with speed and confidence he finished breaking deep into Dr. Kamerman's most secret computer records. Jarrett looked over his shoulder and watched as the screen blinked the word "Searching" on the screen. Then suddenly a list of names filled the screen and everyone in the room gasped at its implications:

THE COMMITTEE AS OF AUGUST 1ST, 2---	
Dr. Kamerman	King Harold the First
Gordi Vochi	High Priest Tzvil Cohen
Holistra Gaduchi	CardinalVincent Vermuchi
Frans Holter	Oscar Welsh
Geraldine Whitehead	Jeremy Lincolnstine
Frank Sorinson	XXXXSECURITY BREECH
OVERRIDE IN EFFECT: ACCESS DENIED.....	

Jarrett screamed, "Get it back!"

Fred screamed back, "Get out of my way!" He rolled his chair over to the next computer and typed furiously. He explained as he typed, "I have this one already set to override their override. There! We're back in!"

> ...Senator Thomas Hol...SECURITY BREECH
> CONNECTION TERMINATED-----------------

Agent Bob Swaggert exclaimed, "It can't be! Not Vice President Thomas Holstrum! He can't be part of this!"

Fred slid back to the other computer, cleared the screen then punched in a code. The printer started its work again and he explained, "When you came in, I had just retrieved this piece of information!"

He rolled over to the printer and tore off the last entry and handed it to Jarrett and Bob.

It read:

> MEMO:
> TO: HOLSTRUM
> FROM: KAMERMAN
> SUBJECT: TERMINAL CLEANSE
> September 1st, have made arrangements to be at UN. Make sure you are not there! I repeat! Make sure you are not there! All is arranged!

Another Memo followed the first:

> MEMO:
> TO: KAMERMAN
> FROM: HOLSTRUM
> All arranged on this end! Happy hunting!

The men just stood there with their mouths open. It was Holstrum!

Jarrett yelled at no one in particular, "What's with these vice-presidents, first Huggens and now Holstrum! Oh no! It's probably President Holstrum by now!"

Jarrett now turned back to Fred and said a bit calmer this time, "Do you know the location of Kamerman's hideout?"

Fred smiled and started digging through the mountains of printouts and came up with one crumpled piece of paper. He handed it to Jarrett.

Jarrett took the paper, looked at it and then said as he ran for the door, "I apologize Scorpion! You are as good as they say." With that he was gone.

Bob said, "We have to follow him. What did the paper say Fred?"

"Covenant Municipal Bank."

Police Chief Grady O'Leary said, "Oh no! I've got my account there!"

CHAPTER NINE
HOW GREAT THE FALL

COVENANT MUNICIPAL BANK:
September 1st, 2---: 1930 HOURS:

Dr. Wilbur Kamerman held the phone receiver with a shaky hand as President Holstrum continued to speak, "Look Dr. Kamerman, this man has power, I've seen it! He's got the answers and technology to solve a lot of our world's problems. He has already established a power base in the European Market and has a wonderful idea for a worldwide computer system. He's willing to work with our committee and keep us in positions of power, but we must acknowledge him as the boss and follow his orders.

"Doc! He's the power behind all of these space ships and is willing to share that power with us. Think of it! A Space Ship! The merchandising gimmicks are endless! We'll make millions!"

Dr. Kamerman was silent for a moment. He stood to his full 5' 5", weighting about 105 lb. with a long beak nose, a sharp protruding chin and a very high forehead with sparse brown hair over deep brown eyes. His, ever present, gray suit had become his trademark along with the long sleeved white shirt with cuff linked sleeves and red bow tie. He didn't look like the powerful man that he was.

Dr. Kamerman finally spoke, "I don't know this guy! I don't know if we can trust him! This is our world not his!"

"I understand all that, Doc, but he is going to take control of this world whether we help him or not, so..." Holstrum shrugged his shoulders, but even though Kamerman couldn't possibly see him, the gesture was implied in his voice.

"So you think we might as well get in on the ground floor. Perhaps we'll get some high positions handed to us while he's in a giving mood?" Kamerman finished for him.

"That's about it, Dr. Kamerman! Believe me! When you meet him, you'll agree! He's the greatest!"

There was a loud explosion, which shook the building and knocked Dr. Kamerman from his feet. He hit his head on the floor and yelled, "AAAH!"

He had dropped the phone and could hear Holstrum yelling, "What was that, Dr. Kamerman? Hello? Anybody there?"

Dr. Kamerman picked up the phone and yelled, "I don't know what that was, you idiot, but it was in this building, and it didn't sound at all good! I have to go! I'll call you when I can."

He hung up on Holstrum without waiting for a reply and rushed to his desk drawer. He slid the drawer open and took out the .357 magnum, as his office door burst open and a very large man came falling in. Dr. Kamerman fired his weapon and hit the doorframe next to the man. The man in turn fired twice at Dr. Kamerman, hitting him in the chest with both shots.

The pain was intense, and as Dr. Kamerman fell he wondered who the man was that had just killed him. He asked in a blood gurgling whisper, "Who are you?"

The stranger walked over to him, smiled and said, "I'm Jarrett White! Remember me now?"

Doctor Kamerman's eyes got big and his face grew pale as he recognized Jarrett's cold eyes. The doctor thought, *" Of course he looks different after being shot in the face!"*

*   *   *

Worl and his guards arrived just in time to see Andy grab his human charge, Jarrett White by the shoulders and yell, "Vengeance is mine saith the Lord! Don't do this Jarrett! Think man, before it's too late! You must let this hatred go just like you did for Brother Keller."

*   *   *

Jarrett White wasn't listening! He was hungry for revenge and violence!

Dr. Kamerman watched in helpless terror as Jarrett aimed his 9mm at his forehead and slowly pulled the trigger. The last thing that Dr. Kamerman heard on this earth was, "This is for Joshua!"

*   *   *

For a second all was blackness. Then Dr. Kamerman heard voices. They seemed like kind voices, whispers really. A hand brushed his hair and a voice said, "Wake up sleeping beauty. It's time to get up and get to work."

When Dr. Kamerman opened his eyes, the scene he took in made him so terrified that all he could do was stare at it and drool. There were two large demons sitting on either side of him and each was holding a very sharp looking knife. He found that he was strapped down to a stone table. He was just becoming aware of how very hot it was. The room was filled with acrid, yellowish smoke, and there were shadows in the far corner that moved of their own accord.

He saw other damned souls sitting or standing in different parts of the chamber moaning over their fate. They were empty eyed, scarecrow people with dried skin stretched tightly across their skeletons and many scars to speak of the torture they had already endured.

Dr. Kamerman whispered to the nearest creature, "What is this place?"

The red eyes of the creature moved closer and intensified until they blinded Kamerman. The creature's voice boomed in the chamber causing damned souls to scurry for cover, "This is Satan's torture chamber, of course, and your home for the next few centuries!" His foul breath made Kamerman nauseous and then fear over took him as the creature lowered the knife to his chest.

As the blade dug deeply into his chest and pain exploded throughout his body, the creature spoke over Kamerman's screams of fear, "Our master Satan asked me to amuse myself until he gets here. That will be in, ooooooh," he looked at his arm as if to look at a watch, "In about seven years!"

Kamerman yelled, "But there is no such thing as Satan. He's a myth and all of his demons with him!"

The demon laughed and said, "You keep telling yourself that while this myth has fun cutting you open for eternity! Maybe this is just a dream!" The gathering demons rolled on the floor with laughter. They never ceased being entertained by the human tendency for denial. No Satan indeed!

The full impact of his fate hit Kamerman when the other souls began to arrive; souls that he himself had tortured for so many years in his hospital. He began to recall all the evil things that he had done to these people over the years. He couldn't take it any more. He struggled and screamed and then struggled some more, until he was engulfed in pain, darkness and loneliness, which would be the only eternal reward he would collect.

Andy wept and turned to Worl, saying, "I'm sorry General Worl, I have failed you and my Lord. I was supposed to stop Jarrett from committing any serious sins, but now he's damned." Andy's head sagged, sadly to his chest.

A tear ran down Worl's cheek as he laid a supportive hand on Andy's shoulder.

He whispered, "The human has a free will, therefore, there was nothing you could have done. There was nothing any of us could've done. As to his damnation, only Jesus can judge the condition of Jarrett's soul. That's not our place."

The angels turned their attention back to Jarrett and tended to his shattered soul, the best they could, as he stood over Dr. Kamerman and alternately laughed and cried.

*   *   *

THE VATICAN:
September 1st, 2---: 2300 HOURS:

His Holiness, Ferdinand Danbury, knelt in his private chapel and prayed, "Oh, Almighty Jesus; the world as we know it is passing away. The terrorists have killed so many of my children today. Please keep the soul of my dear child, President Roberta Place safe for me, Lord. Hug her for me and tell her that I love her, and also embrace John from England and Sam from Germany, and all the others. I'm just too tired and grieved tonight to mention them all. After all I'm...I'm... Oh yes, I'm 86 years old today and I'm entitled to be tired.

"Jesus, on another note. These strange sightings, can they really be space ships from another world? Something just doesn't ring true about them. There have been so many sightings today all across the world. And those pilots that were released in Russia, England and Germany, and I believe one in Japan and one in America. The strange stories they have told about the ships being made of demons. Could they all be suffering the same hysteria? So much to keep track of, so much to pray for."

*   *   *

Unseen by Papa Danbury, as he was affectionately called, was Capt. Mattes, Angel in charge of protecting

His Holiness the Pope. Capt. Mattes stood now at Papa Danbury's side with one hand on the man's shoulder and the other pointing his sword toward Heaven, thus sending his prayers straight to heaven on a beam of spiritual light. When this man prayed, his prayers were answered. He had always been so strong and powerful, but the years and the spiritual warfare had taken their toll.

Mattes didn't notice the sudden chill in the air, so intent was he on sending this man's prayers to the Lord. The shadows moved, first one and then another. The red glow from the demon's sword at first startled Mattes but then allowed him to bring his own sword to bear and block the unexpected onslaught in time. Then there were suddenly two demons fighting Mattes and then a third. Mattes put a call out for back up. He swung his sword at the first demon who ducked allowing Mattes' sword to pass through the unsuspecting second demon who then popped out of existence in a cloud of sulfuric smoke. The eerie lights from their swords danced on the walls of the Pope's private sanctuary. Another flare-up and the third demon disappeared. Now it was just Mattes and the first demon. Block! Parry! Duck! When the demon came in hard and low, Mattes' sword severed the demon's head from his body, and there were two final puffs of smoke.

Just as Mattes turned to check on the Pope, he heard laughter, softly at first, but a little louder now. He looked about the room and saw a dark form streak toward him. He brought his sword to bear, but too late! Satan's claws plowed Mattes' face causing his eyes to fill with his own blood.

137

Satan whispered into Mattes ear, as he held him close to his own face, "You can come back in a few minutes to collect this puny soul. A few minutes are all your precious Pope has left on this earth!" There was a loud "snap" as Satan broke Mattes' spine causing him to puff out of existence and land at the feet of Jesus.

Capt. Mattes looked up from the floor and said to Jesus, "Satan himself killed me! He's after the Holy Father! Can't you help him?"

Jesus whispered as a tear ran down his cheek, "I know he's after Ferdinand and believe Me when I say We can't help. That post must be turned over to the enemy while My church is gone from the earth. It also doesn't matter any longer. Whether you bring him now or he comes up in a few hours with the rest of My body makes very little difference.

"While you were away on assignment, I met with Satan and told him that I was about to remove all Christians from the earth. I tried to tell him that the Christian's removal would harm his Kingdom but as I figured he wouldn't listen. He believes that it will give him free reign upon the earth, but it won't.

"Enough of that for now, let's get you cleaned up and then you can go back and collect My friend. He has earned many rewards, the first of which will be to ride on My cloud as My army joins Me to collect My Body, the Church!"

*   *   *

Cardinal Vincent Vermuchi couldn't see the demons that he served so well. If only he could have, he might have thought twice about what he was about to do.

138

One of the short fat demons was attached to Vermuchi's chest and was swollen like a pregnant tic on a dog's ear. The other was attached to his back and spine. They had controlled him so completely for so many years and their grip had become deeper and tighter, until now it was indestructible.

The Cardinal slipped into the Pope's private chapel, not a hard job for the Secretary of State of the Secretariat. He listened to the fool's bleeding heart requests. It made him sick!

Cardinal Vermuchi, at only fifty years old, had been around long enough and his intense charisma has commanded the respect of enough of the other Cardinals and staff here at the Vatican, that if a vote were taken today, the Cardinal would be selected as the next Pope. Therefore, since it was imperative to Alfred Canards' plans, this old man must die and make room for the new.

Normally he was a patient man, but he was now being driven to action. An action that would just as surely damn his soul as it would herald the end of the earth, as he knew it.

Papa Danbury now felt the chill that permeated the air around him, and he turned to see Cardinal Vermuchi approaching. The Holy Spirit warned him that this man was evil, but Ferdinand had been around his share of evil men, and he feared none of them.

In the gloom of the Pope's private chapel, this man looked even more sinister than usual and Papa Danbury asked, "What can we do for you, Your Eminence?" Papa Danbury had finally gotten used to talking in the plural, but it had bothered him a lot in the beginning. The Pope was speaking for himself and God and therefore spoke as "We".

Cardinal Vermuchi smiled and said, "I thought you might want to take some night air before retiring Your Holiness. This has, after all, been a rather busy day for you."

Ferdinand hated it when Cardinal Vermuchi talked to him as if he were a child, but he supposed that it was a friendly gesture coming from him and the thought of the fresh evening air did sound refreshing after such a hard and emotional day.

The Pope stood slowly. His poor knees cracked and they felt the strain of the kneeling position.

As he slowly straightened one knee, then the other he said, "Yes, Eminence, that would be a nice way to end the day. Shall we step out on my balcony?"

Vincent Vermuchi was overjoyed, inwardly, at the suggestion, and said pleasantly enough, "Yes, the evening is cool, but pleasant. Here allow me to open the door. There, there, watch your step, Your Holiness."

Papa Ferdinand Danbury stepped into the night air, took a deep breath, and then felt the sudden push from behind. He stumbled forward, and when his knees hit the stone railing he almost fell over the edge.

He heard Cardinal Vermuchi's sarcastic voice from behind him, all pretense gone, "Oh, watch out Your Holiness! We wouldn't want you to fall!" Next Papa Ferdinand felt hands on his knees and he was suddenly racing toward the stone pavement some four stories down. Below him was...Light. Lots of Light.

*   *   *

Then this most beautiful being stood in front of Ferdinand and spoke in a most soothing voice, "My name is Mattes. I've been your guardian angel, now your escort." Mattes stepped aside to reveal a long white tunnel and said, "If you would accompany me, Your Holiness?"

Ferdinand felt young again, vital, pain free, and very happy. He walked into the tunnel without even thinking to ask why or where it led. He just knew that it was a good thing. Mattes put his arm around Ferdinand's shoulder and led him through the veils that separate earth from heaven and the two beings passed into the presence of the Lord Jesus.

As the light dimmed somewhat, fields of flowers began to sparkle through with their myriad of explosive colors. Birds began to sing in the trees above, the soft, peaceful rhythm of a distant waterfall soothed Ferdinand's nerves. Ferdinand then saw lions walking toward them in the plush grass. He enjoyed the songbirds and the waterfall, but the lions made him very nervous. Mattes didn't pay them any attention though, and they didn't seem hungry or threatening. Then one of the lions stopped, bit off a tender shoot of grass and began chewing.

Ferdinand asked Mattes, "A lion eating grass?"

Mattes just laughed and pointed up ahead where Ferdinand saw a man standing. As they walked closer, he began to recognize the man. It occurred to Ferdinand that his vision was much better than it had been only moments ago. He realized that he wasn't wearing his glasses. The man was smiling and was surrounded by an intense glow.

At the realization of who this man was, Ferdinand stopped and lay down in the grass face down in front of his Lord and Savior Jesus Christ.

He worshipped, "My Lord and my God! I have tried to serve you on earth and I'm sorry if I have offended you in any way!"

He continued to worship and apologize alternately as Jesus came over and laughed vigorously as he helped Ferdinand to his feet. The Lord said, "You've done a wonderful job for me, Ferdinand, so don't worry. I have so many rewards for you that I had to prepare an especially large mansion for you, right in Mother Theresa's neighborhood."

Jesus gave Ferdinand an embrace and continued, "You've been martyred for the faith, given your life for the cause of right! Now enter into your eternal reward. I wish I could show you around, but I have many preparations to make for tonight. Mattes can explain things until your mother arrives."

With that Jesus disappeared and Mattes said, "What would you like to see first, Ferdinand?"

There was no answer, so Mattes just smiled and let Ferdinand take in the beautiful sights of Heaven. As far as they could see, there were various shades of green grass blended evenly with every sort of blooming flower imaginable. There were, of course, no seasons in heaven only all around beauty. In the distance there was a glorious body of blue water bordered by a pure white sandy beach. Just when Ferdinand thought he had seen the most beautiful landscape possible, he turned to see

New Jerusalem for the first time. His eyes got big and his mouth dropped open.

Mattes said, "Awe! I think that expression answers my question. New Jerusalem it is." With that the pair started up the hill.

*   *   *

COVENANT NEWS ROOM:
September 1st, 2---: 2358 HOURS:

Marla Brinkle O'Leary was dead on her feet. She had been covering stories for almost 24 hours now, emotional, gut-rending stories that had left her drained and spent. First the police had found Starvas Creen, and then President Place and almost every leader of the civilized world had been cruelly murdered, along with 3,000 innocent civilians and now this. This might well be the straw that broke her heart.

She looked at her copy again hoping for a misprint, but no, *"Pope Ferdinand Danbury found dead after accidental fall from balcony. On his 86th birthday (cut to footage of Cardinal Vincent Vermuchi)*

A cameraman ran up and said, "Two minutes Mrs. O'Leary".

Marla took one last look in her portable mirror and said, "Well girl, it's just going to have to do."

"Lights, camera, action," they pointed and Marla said, "Good Morning! This is Marla Brinkle O'Leary reporting to you this midnight from our very own studios right here in Covenant. Our top story tonight, Pope Ferdinand Danbury is dead at age 86. As a matter of fact, he died on his birthday, September 1st. Let's join

Jean Larson in Rome with a live report. Jean?" The screen switched to another beautiful young woman, Jean Larson, who was staring at the camera lens and straightening her hair. When she realized that she was on the air, her face turned a little red as she said, "This is Jean Larson reporting to you live from Rome. I'm standing here with His Eminence, Lord Cardinal Vincent Vermuchi." She turned to the Cardinal and asks, "Can you tell us what happened Cardinal Vermuchi? You were the last to see the Pope alive, were you not?" Vermuchi had plastered a fake mournful look on his face and had turned up the charm as he said, "Yes, it was just horrible. After such a day of tragedy my friend, His Holiness Pope Danbury, had been praying in his private chapel. I went in at about 11:00 and he was just about finished. I was concerned that he might be over taxing himself, especially after all the tragedy at the UN earlier today. The Holy Father wanted some fresh air before retiring and suggested that we step out onto his balcony. As he passed through the door, he caught his toe on the sill and stumbled forward. I tried to catch him, but alas, he fell over the railing before I could reach him." Tears rolled down the Cardinal's cheeks as Jean Larson turned back to the camera, "The world will grieve the loss of this great man..."

There was a loud rumble and the earth, as well as, the camera began to shake. Watching it made Marla a little dizzy and nauseated as fires erupted in the background and a large building collapsed just a block away.

Jean's terror was real but she still managed to say, "It appears we're having an earthquake! We'll try to cover as much as we can before..."

Marla said, "Jean, are you there?" Then she realized that she was back on the air, so she cleared her throat, held down the growing dread of this newscast from hell, and said, "It appears that we have lost our connection with Rome. They may be experiencing an earthquake there, but we'll have to wait until later for more details."

Sam handed her more copy and Marla read it as the color drained from her face. She looked at the camera and forced herself to speak, "Dr. Kamerman was shot and killed earlier this evening by Special Agent Jarrett White. The gun battle ensued shortly after the police and Government CIA agents entered the Covenant Municipal Bank, which was being used as a secret hideout, and attempted to arrest Kamerman. As you know, Kamerman was responsible for both the kidnapping of President Place and the shooting death of police officer Joshua White, this past year. Agent Jarrett White was himself severely wounded in that heartless attack on his brother.

"Kamerman has also been positively identified as the Chairman of that mysterious group of people who call themselves the Committee, and are reported to be responsible for the deaths of hundreds, even thousands of innocent people, from around the world.

"The names of other Committee members are being withheld pending investigation..."

As she spoke, Marla began to glow, as did two other people in the room. Millions of shocked viewers, watched as Marla began rising from her seat. Slowly at first and then suddenly, she zoomed straight up and out of the studio, right along with millions of other Christians around the world. . .

Michael Pro, Marla's faithful cameraman, walked stiffly over to were Marla had just been sitting and looked up at the blank ceiling which gave no clue as to what had just happened. His foot kicked something, and when he looked down he saw the worn Bible that Marla carried everywhere she went. It had fallen from the desk onto the floor and had opened to I Corinthians 15:51-52. Michael picked it up and whispered the words that Marla had highlighted in a soft pink color causing the words to jump out at Michael,

> **"Behold, I shew you a mystery; We shall not all sleep,**
> **but we shall all be changed,**
> **In a moment, in the twinkling of an eye, at the last**
> **trump: for the trumpet shall sound, and the dead shall**
> **be raised incorruptible, and we shall be changed."**

Michael fainted dead away as he realized, to his ultimate terror, that everything Marla had told him had come to pass. Michael and millions like him had been left behind to face the bitter fate of Satan given free reign of the world.

CHAPTER TEN
THE RAPTURE

"And let us not be weary in well doing:
for in due season we shall reap,
if we faint not."

GALATIANS 6:9

JESUS PARK:
September 2nd, 2---: 2400 HOURS:

Rev. Jonathon Smith had stayed after the night's meeting and he, Ellen, and Jarrett White had watched all of the bad news reports. Their heads were spinning! Rev. Smith had a feeling that something big was about to happen.

Jarrett had explained how he raided Dr. Kamerman's office, how he had shot him at first in self-defense and then in cold blood and how he had thought that revenge would make him feel better, but it had not.

Rev. Smith was about to explain the futility of revenge when he noticed that Ellen was beginning to glow a pure white. He looked at his own hands and found that he too was glowing brightly. Jarrett was backing away from them wide-eyed.

He stammered, "W-What's happening?"

Rev. Smith smiled, saying, "If I'm not mistaken, this is the Rapture, Jarrett! Please read Matthew Chapter 24! Believe before the seven years are up and do not worship the beasssst!"

With that he and Ellen soared through the roof of the chapel. Jarrett ran outside and what he saw made him weak in the knees. Thousands of shining, glorified bodies were flying into the sky. The graves of Covenant Park were empty and Jarrett saw...Joshua walking out of his tomb. Joshua walked over to Jarrett and hugged him. He felt real! Jarrett touched his shoulders then hugged him back saying, "Joshua you're alive!"

Joshua laughed and said, "More than you know brother! This is the rapture of Christ's church! I wish you could have believed so that you could join us, but it's not too late. You can still believe and you can still be saved. The Holy Ghost is staying behind to guide people to the way of salvation.

"Now listen to this warning Jarrett! Do not worship the false Christ! Do not take his mark and above all do not lose hope! One more thing Jarrett, you must give up this hatred and violence. Put yourself in God's hands and embrace love, gentleness and kindness. Look to Jesus for Salvation! Well, I hope to see you soon! I love youuuu!"

He was gone just like that! The ground shook, thunder rolled, lightening flashed and the beautiful beings of light were replaced by an oppressive darkness that covered the world like a funeral pall. Jarrett fell to his knees and vomited! Rain beat down upon him in torrents!

Jarrett soon looked up into the heart of the storm and screamed, "What have I done! I've been left behind! Oh my God, I've been left behind!"

He collapsed into the mud and wept bitterly.

COVENANT POLICE STATION:
September 2nd, 2---: 2400 HOURS:

Chief Grady O'Leary sat down and watched his wife give one report after another. She looked older, much more burdened than usual, which of course was understandable. Grady had been dealing with problems of his own. His city hadn't had the violent reactions that other cities had reported, but that could change rapidly. Still his officers were out there right now handling one panic call after another. People were afraid and jumping at every little noise as an excuse to call the police to see if anything new was happening.

He was stunned, right along with the entire World's population. It all seemed so unreal, so unbearable. It was at this moment that the World changed forever. The light had come for Grady as it had for Marla.

NEWS ROOM:
September 2nd, 2---: 0005 HOURS:

Sue Jenkins had tried to stop crying but could not and had finally gone on the air, tears and all. She wasn't alone, however, newscasters all over the world had tears in their eyes and fear in their hearts as they tried to report the terrifying news of the day. She had watched Marla Brinkle and others disappear before her very eyes just as many other people had witnessed their friends and loved one's disappearance. Then on top of that shocking mystery, there was added the tidal wave of disasters, which had suddenly broken out all over the world at the same time.

Sue continued her report; "There was a 9.8 earthquake in Japan, a 9.6 in Russia, and an 8.8 in Alaska but no word yet as to damage. There may be many more disasters to report but communications are down and we can't get access to information in certain areas of the world."

She sniffled, wiped her eyes and then apologized again, "I'm sorry. I-I just can't help it. President Roberta Place is dead, killed by a missile filled with poisonous gas and biological germs. People who weren't killed instantly are beginning to show the first signs of many different rapid spreading diseases. Fear and panic have gripped the people of New York, and the world for that matter. This incident alone has sent the diplomats scurrying for cover as they plan ways to prevent a Third World War. Then there are the mysterious disappearances of the millions of people from around the World!"

Sue stopped as her producer handed her a note. She read it and then continued, "This just in. Russia is arming their nuclear defense system for the first time since their breakup and reunification. The Chinese, Japanese, Iraqis, and the United States are following suit. They are aiming some of the missiles at the sky in the hope of stopping any more ships from entering their airspace while the rest are being aimed at their neighbors to prevent the temptation to cross borders. This is in response to the missing aircraft that disappeared early yesterday morning from various places around the world."

Sue signed to the cameraman to go to commercial. "We'll be back with more news after this!"

Sue screamed! She ran around the studio and knocked things off the desk, kicked wastebaskets and just generally lost it!

She shouted, "Where did Marla go? Where did all the others go? How about these reports that are coming in by the minute of millions upon millions of people disappearing in the last five minutes?"

The producer yelled, "Marla, I mean Sue, we're back in five, four, three, two." "Welcome back to a Special News Report, I'm Sue Jenkins sitting in for Marla Brinkle O'Leary, reporting from our new Covenant studio. We have a lot of news for you today. First of all the President of the United States, Roberta Place, has been murdered. She was giving her speech at the UN yesterday afternoon when a terrorist exploded a missile containing poisonous gas and biological germs. So far the death count is at 3,000 and rising rapidly. Specialists are trying to contain the spread of disease and the armed forces have been called in to control the mobs of panicking people that surrounded the United Nations building. We haven't received any further reports for the last two hours from our reporters trapped in that zone. We have to assume that they are dead or dying.

"Reports of more U.F.O. sightings came in during our break. It appears that more ships of unknown origin or UFOs were sighted over Paris, France, and Berlin, Germany. Several fighter jets were scrambled to intercept but they disappeared from radar just like the ones early yesterday morning."

Once again the producer came forward with a grave look on his face and a note in his hand.

Sue took the note, read it, and her tears began to fall again. All she could do was sit there staring at the camera with tears and makeup running down her cheeks. No one hurried her, they were all numb due to the shear, overwhelming amount of bad news that was pouring into the newsroom from around the World.

Sue finally spoke, though her voice cracked through the shaking sobs that racked her body, "As we reported earlier, Pope Danbury was killed when he accidentally fell from his balcony. In Rome, just minutes ago there was a 10.0 earthquake. This came on the heals of a happier announcement from the Cardinals in Conclave, who announced, 'Annuntio Vobis gaudium magnum!...I announce to you a great joy! We have a Pope! The Most Eminent Lord Vincent Vermuchi!'

"As you know Cardinal Vermuchi was with Papa Danbury when he died. Now in an unprecedented vote by the Cardinals, who were already in Rome, unanimously elected Cardinal Vincent Vermuchi as the new Holy Father of the Catholic Church. The Cardinals explain that with the current state of affairs the church must have a leader on the throne and Vermuchi was the favorite for that position. Then just moments after his acceptance speech to the thousands of pilgrims who filled St. Peter's Square the, earthquake wiped out Vatican City. Thousands are dead, but no word, as yet, if the new Pope survived this newest disaster. It has been verified now, however, that Jean Larson and her crew in Rome have been killed in one of the aftershocks of the earlier earthquake. Please join me in a moment of silence for our fallen comrades."

Everything was quiet for a moment except for the sobs that could not be controlled from around the newsroom. Everyone had liked Jean and she had been so excited about finally getting to go to Rome. It had been a lifetime dream of hers and now the dream had killed her.

Sue continued bravely after getting herself under control once again, "In other news, riots have broken out in several cities here in the States as well as many other countries. People are panicking, they're angry and they're frustrated. The poor economic conditions of our Nation and that of the world have been building tension for years. Today's events seem to be the catalyst that was needed to ignite the fires of rebellion within the souls of these many cities. Stores are being looted and people are shooting each other with increasing frequency..."

Sue put her finger to her earpiece and smiled for the first time in what seemed to be years. She looked into the camera, with more cheer than she thought possible and announced, "Papa Vermuchi survived the earthquake! He's all right!"

Sue basked in this kernel of good news. The cameramen, producers and secretaries all cheered joining Sue in grabbing onto the only ray of sunshine that they had received all day. It was at that very moment that the World around Sue Jenkins and her fellow workers exploded in a kaleidoscope of color and light...Thousands of their viewers watched as the explosion and fire engulfed the entire newsroom. They watched as Sue, still smiling, literally melted before their eyes. The cause of the explosion was a gas main rupture that destroyed the TV broadcast station and all the people in it. Stunned viewers all over the city were left staring at blank TV screens.

THE NEW CHAPEL: JESUS PARK:
September 2nd, 2---: 0015 HOURS:

Jarrett White was a big man and not given over easily to emotion. When Jarrett raised his face toward heaven, his eyes were watery and swollen. Under the caked-on mud, his face was red speaking of the emotional strain that he was under.

It was a strangled whisper that escaped his lips, "The President is dead. Many more are also dead. The Pope is dead..."

Jarrett had been looking right at Rev. Smith and Ellen when they had disappeared. One second they were there, the next they were gone. Jarrett's grief overwhelmed him for a moment and he sobbed.

"Oh Joshua, don't leave me alone on this earth. Not now, when there's no more love left. I want to feel the love you have shown me. I don't want to fear or hate anymore. Oh, Jesus please help me! I'm nothing! I'm dirty and vile! Cleanse me Lord!"

Another fit of weeping overtook Jarrett as he surrendered completely to the Holy Spirit!

$$*\qquad*\qquad*$$

Boliczar screamed, "Nooo! Don't give in to this mushy feeling of weakness!" He was yelling at Jarrett and trying to regain his hold on this human's soul. The moment Jarrett said the name, Jesus, fire had shot from the tip of Andy's sword and Boliczar was knocked free of Jarrett's spine. As Andy advanced on Boliczar, with his sword drawn and a determined look in his eye, the demon decided to make a run for his life. Andy let him go knowing that he would not get far.

*   *   *

Jarrett felt the Earth begin to shake. He vomited from the sudden and overpowering nausea, which struck him. With difficulty, he climbed to his feet in time to watch the entire newly built chapel collapse in upon itself.

Jarrett looked again into the storm as he tucked the already soaked Bible under his shirt for protection. Rev. Smith had handed it to Jarrett just before soaring into the air and disappearing. In the lightening, Jarrett could see the once solid ground moving toward him in a huge wave. It was an unreal, but fearful, sight to see ground move. Then the ground beneath him rose up about five feet and then dropped him into a newly formed valley as the wave moved on destroying everything in its path. Suddenly the darkness of the storm was shot clear through by the light streaming out of the apparition of a man standing in the midst of the storm. The man's hair was white as snow; a blue and white cloak was wrapped around his shoulders, and the pure white robe shown with a supernatural radiance. His eyes flared with the brightness of a million suns going nova and he spoke with the thunder of a thousand jets screaming overhead, "I have returned to claim my own! This is now a dark and lonely world, but don't lose hope! I'll not abandon those who do finally turn to Me! In the end, you'll be allowed to join forces with Me to defeat the Evil One! Stand firm Jarrett White and believe you are running out of time! I will return in seven years to cleanse the Earth of this evil! Join Me or perish in the second death! You've been born a new man this night, Jarrett White! Born of water and of spirit. I baptized you in this rain and immersed you in a puddle. I now baptize you in the Holy Spirit. Be filled with life, joy and wisdom. You will have many struggles ahead of you, Jarrett White, but cling to the peace and wisdom the Spirit offers and you will do fine. Now, go among my homeless people. Comfort them, teach them, heal them and above all bring hope to them. Share what you've seen tonight and make people believe!"

The ground continued to shake even though it had settled once again into its more solid foundation. The voice had died out and was gone. As the apparition disappeared into the clearing night sky, Jarrett saw millions of twinkling lights; the resurrected bodies of the saints, following close behind Jesus. A glitter of light caught the corner of Jarrett's eye, *"A tardy soul no doubt!"*

Jarrett White watched in horror, as a large airliner glided down toward Covenant. It was so close that Jarrett could see the terrified passenger's faces flattened against the interior-lit windows. Screaming for the mercy, which no longer existed in this world. Time had slowed down while the jet dipped its left wing toward the ground and began a slow spiral down. The impact of the jet was lost in the already shaking ground but Jarrett could see the expected fire blossoming up toward the sky just seconds before he heard the distant roar of the explosion. He pictured the hundreds of bodies that were probably already strewn throughout the city of Covenant.

In a daze he walked back toward his apartment, taking no notice of the rain that still poured from Heaven. His apartment was miraculously still standing, for now anyway. The ground seemed to be settling somewhat, but there were still periodic explosions on the horizon. The glow of fires could be seen for miles. When Jarrett entered his ground floor apartment, he switched on the lights, out of habit and was shocked when they came on. He stepped over the plants, the broken glass of statues and other decorations, which had fallen off of the shelves during the earthquake.

Jarrett sat in his favorite recliner and picked up the remote, activating his TV screen.

As Jarrett ignored the wind and the rain that was blowing into his apartment through the broken windows, he watched a visibly shaken news announcer who was trying to keep the news coming at all costs, "We don't know what just hit us. Some speculate that a new form of selective nuclear device was just exploded over several cities throughout the world. Selective because some people were destroyed by the blast of light, while others were left standing just a few meters away.

"We can't keep up with the reports of car accidents, train wrecks, buses going off of the road as the drivers just suddenly disappeared..."

The man stopped as he was handed a sheet of paper, "This just in! An airliner carrying 298 passengers just crashed into the city square of Covenant destroying the large Tablets of the Ten Commandments along with most of the park. All on board are considered dead along with fifty or so on the ground. The cause of the crash is still unknown.

"The earthquake that we've just experienced was very mild compared to most today, but it seems to have broken many of the cities water and gas pipes causing flood damage, and ironically, fire damage at the same time. As a matter of fact our new TV facility in Covenant was, just moments ago, destroyed by a gas line rupture.

"In Egypt, it is reported that the Pyramids have begun to emit a strange bluish/green light. When some scientists got near one of them to study the phenomenon they were destroyed by a static charge. Shortly after that incident, several UFOs were sighted in the area, as if attracted by the energy discharge."

The man stopped. He looked into the camera and said, "I can't take this anymore!" With that, he pulled out a gun, turned it on himself, saying, "I'm signing off", then he fired. They had of course tried to switch to a commercial but his blood sprayed the camera lens before they got it switched off.

Jarrett White sat there staring at a commercial for a local psychic hot line. They said, "Call your friendly Psychic and get a free reading and see what blessings your future holds for you!"

Jarrett started to laugh! At first it was a quiet little laugh, but it soon grew into the full, strangled, choking, laugh of a new born but tortured soul.

CHAPTER ELEVEN
(FIRST YEAR OF CANARDS' REIGN)
THE FOUR HORSEMEN

NEW JERUSALEM: THE THRONE OF JUDGMENT

The twenty-four elders, consisting of the twelve great Prophets of the Old Covenant, and the twelve Apostles of the New Covenant, stood around the Great White Throne of Judgment. Jesus was sitting there looking out over his Kingdom.

Lightening flashed from His entire being and lit heaven with beautiful bright flashes of multi-colored light. This light then reflected off of the walls of New Jerusalem. The gold, diamonds, rubies and other precious gems that made up its walls, exploded in a kaleidoscope of color and glory!

The great crystal sea also reflected the light onto the pure white robes of the millions of souls who lined its borders. They, along with the elders, were worshipping Jesus the Christ. The singing was glorious and filled heaven with joy, as angels flew overhead or stood amidst the crowd of the redeemed. The raptured church, people from every nation of the earth, basked in the warmth and peace of their salvation.

One of the great Archangels flew up to the Lord and handed him a sealed scroll. Jesus stood and the crowd became silent. As the light shot out from his eyes, he broke the first seal and heaven trembled with the release of its power.

A white horse appeared, and its rider was given a bow and a crown of power was placed on his head.

Jesus said to the Anti-Christ, Alfred Canards, "You've obtained what you've always wanted. Go and rule the earth! But remember that you have only seven years before I return to reclaim my world."

Canards rode off to rule mankind with his iron fist.

After he had gone, Jesus unrolled the scroll to the second seal. When he broke that seal, explosive violence swept throughout heaven and then raced back toward the Lord. Jesus held up his hand and the violence slowed and finally stopped. A great red horse appeared before the Lord Jesus Christ. Angels and redeemed alike trembled in fear and fell to their faces and worshipped their God!

Jesus said to the horseman on the red horse, "Follow my enemy to the earth. For the next seven years, I empower you to take away the peace from the earth and bring war from one side of the earth to the other."

As the horseman rode off to strike fear into the hearts of humans with the great sword in his hand, Jesus opened the scroll a bit further, uncovering a third seal.

When he broke the third seal, a darkness churned and rolled toward the Lord. The Angels and redeemed moaned in empathy for the unsaved world below. They dared to peek from their prone position, only for a moment. Then from the dark, churning cloud emerged a black horse that stood obediently before the Lord Jesus!

He said to it's rider, "Bring famine to the earth, but do not affect the rich!"

As the black horse disappeared from sight, Jesus opened the fourth seal, and a yellowish green mist rose out of the Crystal Lake, which lay at the foot of His throne. Within the mist could be seen the terrible pale horse, upon which rode Death. Everyone among the redeemed was glad that his hold had been broken. They wept for the poor souls left on earth, which would experience the cold touch of death, and in the cruelest way possible!

Jesus said, "Spread sickness throughout My world and bring death to a fourth of the earth's population."

The pale horse rode off to the earth to spread disease while those in heaven continued their adoration of the Lamb. Jesus laid the scroll aside for a time and watched with joy as His church worshipped God the Father, Son and Holy Ghost.

After this experience had passed, Joshua White found himself walking the streets of Gold once more. There was no time here to separate one experience from another. He simply did one thing and then another and enjoyed each and every experience immensely. Joshua still wasn't used to his new body, but truthfully it wasn't much different than what his soul had experienced up to now. He never got hungry, tired, anxious or angry, at least not with any of the inhabitants of heaven. He still felt anger against Satan for all the evil and pain he had caused, and now he felt confusion, as did many other people. Several people asked if he would go and talk to the Lord and find out what these horsemen meant. How could their Lord send these evil things upon the earth? Joshua trusted his Lord of course, but ever since Jesus had taken this glorified form He seemed a bit more terrifying than he used to and just a little less approachable.

161

Just as Joshua White decided to try and speak with the Lord, Jesus smiled, stood and addressed the assembly of Saints and Angels. "I am!" He shouted causing thunder to roll across the heavens, lightening to flash, the ground to shake and every being in the assembly whether Angel or Saint fell face down on the ground. They worshipped Jesus, the Son of God!

Jesus continued, "Please rise My children and listen to Me."

Everyone rose, their hearts swelled with love and awe for the Lord.

Jesus smiled that radiant smile and everything was peace and harmony again, "I have sensed your concerns My brethren. Believe Me you have no cause for concern. You've passed the test; you've fought the good fight. You listened to My prophets and My Holy Word, the Scriptures. Now you're basking in your reward; eternal, resurrected life with Us in heaven!"

"Those left on the earth are not without hope, but they didn't listen. They now must come to Me the hard way. For the next seven years, it pleases God, My Father, to release Satan upon the earth. Satan feels that he can turn everyone to him; but he'll find that with him in control, people will run all that much faster to find Me, and I'll be there to collect them. The Holy Ghost has not left the earth, but neither is He going to restrain evil any longer. Satan will have his way and that was the first horseman, Alfred Canards, the Satan possessed Anti-Christ. I send the other three horsemen without Canards' knowledge. They will bring My judgment upon the cold, heartless men and women of the world. In the trouble that will follow, many will repent of their evil ways and will once again turn to the Lord for Salvation."

"Satan will, after about three and a half years, get very desperate and he'll show his true self to a terrified world and even more will flock to be saved. Add to this the fact that I will send the two witnesses, Moses and Elijah, to preach and they will bring many souls to them and will convert the 144,000 evangelists out of the Jewish faith. Twelve thousand from each of the following tribes: Judah, Reuben, Gad, Asher, Naphtali, Manasseh, Simeon, Levi, Issachar, Zebulun, Joseph, and Benjamin. These are the tribes that stayed faithful to Me throughout the hard times. They kept themselves pure and undefiled by the evils of the world. They will be blessed again when these sealed representatives walk the land and preach the good news of the coming of the Lord. This time they will know the exact moment of My return and will prepare the people for this glorious event."

"After the harvest will come great persecution as Satan takes his revenge on the Holy Saints of God! They will be purified by their sacrifice as they give up their lives for the faith. Yet, Satan will not be able to stop the constant flow of repentant sinners who will flock to Me. He'll go mad in his quest to stamp out all reference to God. For the last three and one half years of the great tribulation, he will attack not only the Saints, but he will begin to murder and rape the entire earth. And finally, he will turn on My chosen people, the Jewish Nation, whom he will have seduced with magic. He will show his true nature, causing many of the Jewish faith to surrender to Me as their Savior. Their eyes will be opened in time for them to flee the wrath of Satan and to come to the peace and love that is God. No longer will they be burdened by the law which has strangled My people for over three thousand years."

"All of this you have been spared, because of your faithfulness to Me during the hard times. When you did not see, you still believed, and suffered greatly for your belief. Enjoy the pleasures that await you."

With that Jesus pointed toward the great-jeweled walls of the New Jerusalem, which suddenly glowed a bright blue. As the gates swung open, reds, oranges, purples and greens escaped from the interior. The sound of Angels singing filled the Heavens! They burst forth in a rainbow of colors, flying this way and that. It was purity in motion. Then God the Father soared through the gates! This magnificent being of Light began to fill the outer courts completely!

Joshua's breath caught in his lungs! Gone was the fear of Judgment! Gone was the anticipation of what was to come! Gone were the questions of the unknown! Joshua looked over at Daniel Derecks, who having just been freed from his cell on earth via the Rapture was totally overwhelmed.

In front of them stood a line of Angels, Capt. Worl among them. He stood there, tall, strong and filled with power. On either side of Capt. Worl were his ever present guards, Left and Right. Joshua and Daniel watched them in total awe. The angels' wings were half extended and slowly flapping back and forth. It was as if the angels were absentmindedly preparing for instant flight, anxious to get back to the battle at hand. Joshua had heard that Capt. Worl was to lead all of his favorite soldiers into battle one more time. They were to protect Daniel's brother Natan and his lovely wife Chava.

Joshua watched as Daniel put his arm around the fully-grown shoulders of Moshe, who after meeting Moses face to face didn't mind the name so much. Sara, Tzvi, and Esther were there also, and their hair began to blow in the gentle breeze of God's presence.

God began to move at the outer edges of the vast crowd. As he touched them, they were lost from sight, fully immersed in the presence of their Almighty God. Joshua felt the cool breeze of God's approach. Joshua hugged Ellen and then Patricia as they too disappeared into the awesome, overwhelmingly, presence of God's love. The power of the encounter, which would have totally destroyed their old bodies, now only filled their new ones with power. In the end all that was left was Light and Love in all of its pureness and perfection. Heaven sighed! Phase One was complete!

CHAPTER TWELVE
(FIRST YEAR OF CANARDS' REIGN)
FALSE MESSIAH

EUROPEAN WORLD HEADQUARTERS OF W.E.L.:
September 2nd, 2---: 0730 HOURS:

The Newly elected President of the "World Equality League" or W.E.L. for short, stood on the platform overlooking the crowd of thousands of enthusiastic followers. President Alfred Canards, using his demon ships and his own Satanic powers, had preyed on the fear and confusion of world affairs to get every leader to hand over to him the reins of their governments. This would never have happened if it were not for the circumstances in which these new and inexperienced leaders found themselves. All of their experienced leaders, with the exception of Committee members, had been killed at the U.N. attack! Strange diseases were spreading quickly throughout the United States and even becoming a threat to other countries, because no one stopped the delegates from boarding jets and flying home. The world was falling apart at the seams. New and numerous natural disasters occurred almost weekly. Human wars that were the result of fear were breaking out all over the globe, and finally there was the instant and simultaneous disappearance of millions of citizens. Into this scene of disaster and chaos stepped Alfred Canards, Satan's empowered, charismatic leader, with the power of thousands of space ships behind

167

him and a knowledge that left the leaders speechless.

They saw instantly that they could throw off the overwhelming burden of leadership from their own shoulders and put it squarely onto Canards' capable shoulders, and they did so happily. They had gathered here in Germany for that very purpose, and the incredible spur of the moment gathering was made possible by transportation on Canard's Demon Ships, which had worked throughout the night to accomplish the task. The Center of World Finance instantly became the new headquarters of W.E.L. with Canards, not surprisingly, its President.

Alfred Canards had surprised his new following by announcing a plan that would bring all Jewish people home to Jerusalem. Loud protests arose from the crowd but Canards spoke patiently and with confidence, "Listen my people and learn."

The room got quiet and everyone listened intently, if suspiciously, as Canards smiled and said, "Have you not noticed that there is no representative here from Israel. Why is that? I wanted a chance to gain your help and support before approaching them. Publicly, I want our stance to be one of support and respect toward our Jewish brothers, but secretly you and I will know that we are setting them up for their final demise." He had everyone's attention now.

He continued, "I am going to give them what they've always wanted, all of Jerusalem and their precious Temple. I will seduce them with their own religion. Then after they are completely under my spell, I will crush them. You may help as well!"

He ground his right fist into the palm of his left hand for emphasis with the cheers that arose from the crowd lasting a good five minutes. It only took a thirty-minute meeting with the Islamic leaders to convince them of his sincerity compelling them to embrace his entire plan and agreeing to play their part.

Now it was time for his news conference and his public plan. He wasn't afraid of leaks because he had shown them the horrible death that awaited traitors. He smiled at the memory of the shock of the unsuspecting security guard whom he had used as the example.

The man next to the camera held up his hand and counted down, five, four, three, two...

NEW YORK COMMUNITY HOSPITAL:
September 2nd, 2---: 0800 HOURS:

Natan Cohen sat next to his wife's bed holding her hand. He still couldn't believe that he'd survived that fall with only a slight concussion, but even more wondrous was his wife's miraculous recovery. He had thought her dead for sure. Steel pipes had been sticking up out of her chest and stomach area. When he had felt for a pulse there was none to be found on Chava or his children. He had collapsed and awakened when the rescue people lifted him into the ambulance. Next to him lay his wife and the paramedics were working on her injuries. Before he passed out again he heard, "Her life signs are weak, step on it, Steve!"

Natan had thought, *"Life signs weak! She's dead, how can her life signs be weak?"*

He had awakened a couple of hours later in a room with his wife. Chava was hooked up to wires, tubes and all manner of scary equipment. Natan had stood up and except for a moment of dizziness, he felt fine. For the rest of that day, right up until this moment, he had sat by her side, holding her hand, watching the bad news roll across the TV screen.

They had announced that a man was about to speak, a man who had the answers for these trying times. He watched as the man ascended the stairs to the raised platform. As he walked up the stairs, men in the background were raising a banner with large letters W.E.L. and smaller letters saying, "FOR A SAFE AND HEALTHY TOMORROW!"

By the time he reached the top of the platform, the banner was stretched tight and tied off. Natan looked this man over and noticed his slender, muscular body. He stood about six feet tall. He had neat brown hair that was streaked with gray and as he stood staring into the camera those emerald green eyes pierced Natan's soul. The man wore a green, unadorned uniform and his smile was contagious, making Natan feel better. He sat forward as the man began to speak.

EUROPEAN WORLD HEADQUARTERS OF W.E.L.: September 2nd, 2---: 0805 HOURS:

The continuous applause lasted for five minutes. From the moment he had ascended the stairs throughout the time he had stared at the audience and the cameras, they had applauded. Canards wasn't in any hurry, he basked in the glory of their adulation. This was the way he had always pictured it. He thought, *"Today they herald me as their Savior, tomorrow they'll worship me as their God."* He waved to his adoring audience and smiled that captivating smile.

Finally, he held his hands high and asked for silence. The obedient crowd fell silent by degrees until finally all that could be heard were scattered, hoarse coughs.

Canards emanated feelings of good will and happiness toward the crowd. His green eyes glowed with hypnotic power as he spoke, "Good morning, citizens of this New World Order. I am your new President, Alfred Canards. I am no stranger to your planet, as I have been here many times. I am the leader of the people who you've seen in the skies over the years. We, in fact, transplanted you here millions of years ago. I was here at the beginning and now I'm here at the end.

"How is this possible you might ask? We're a race that has evolved to the fullest. When our current body dies, we are reincarnated into that of a child, just as you are. The difference between you, and us however, is that we don't lose the memories of our past lives as you do. The memories and experiences just build one upon the other, so we have evolved into a highly intelligent race of beings which no longer needs war and which has the means to take care of everyone.

"We've decided that it's time to help you once and for all. I came here over two thousand years ago in the form of a preacher, named Jesus of Nazareth. I tried to teach you humans how to care for one another. The people of the earth thanked me for my efforts by killing my body. After a three day meeting, it was decided to reincarnate me back into that body and teach my followers about life after death.

"This may have been the biggest mistake I ever made! After I left in one of my ships, I came back years later to find that my followers had interpreted it all wrong. They had gone away from my Jewish faith and started their own. They'd decided to worship the events of my life instead of me. They had even turned their back on their Jewish heritage. The series of bodies that I have used over the years can be traced back to the House of David. I am the rightful heir to the throne of Jerusalem and all of Israel and I am here to claim the right of king!"

The applause could not be stopped as the crowd cheered for another five minutes.

As the celebration died down, Canards continued, "I knew, however, that in order for me to take my rightful place, I would have to do something to prove myself. Last night, at about midnight New York time, I had my ships remove all the Christians from the face of the earth. They'll be transported to another world where they will no longer be able to twist the truth into an unrecognizable fable of stories. We found that people who believe in their Jesus and their God have a defective gene, which prevents them from developing and evolving properly. I know that we've removed all the Christians off planet, but I'm afraid that we couldn't get all the infected people off the planet. So citizens of the world, be on the look out for symptoms of this disease called Christianity. If it creeps into your neighborhood you'll be ruined. I'll be giving you some phone numbers that you can call, anonymously, in order to report any neighbors who are beginning to show symptoms of this disease. These are people who preach that believing in this dead Christ is the only way to heaven; that one must be born again of spirit and water and one must give his all to the Savior. What ridiculous hogwash! I gave them their faith! I know the truth! And the truth shall set them free!

"The truth is that when you die your life essence is released back into the cosmic force, making you one with the universe from whence you came. Then after a time of purification and rest, you are returned to the body of a new born infant, which isn't human until your soul enters it at birth. That's why I'm making abortion legal again; it's only tissue until it's born. In my kingdom, sex is a gift to be used anyway that two consenting people wish, no matter of race, gender, age or any of those limits that those sick Christians put on it's fulfillment and the joy it brings. I'm here to release you from all inhibitions and fears." Again, the applause was explosive and people felt good about this man.

"But I digress!" he continued, "There'll be time to straighten out all those misconceptions over the next few years. Anyway, removing the Christians was the first step to healing Mother Earth." Canards chuckled before he continued, "You know I was just thinking of how twisted the Christians had become over the years. Take for example this quote from Luke17: 34-36, 'I tell you, in that night there shall be two men in one bed; the one shall be taken, and the other shall be left. Two women shall be grinding together; the one shall be taken, and the other left. Two men shall be in the field; the one shall be taken, and the other left.'

"You may ask me what this all means. The poor Christians got it all twisted up. They thought that I was saying that I would come back and take the good people into heaven and save them from some great tribulation. On the contrary! I meant that I would remove those who didn't follow my ways so that they couldn't cause The Great Tribulation! The ones left, which include all of you here watching me, will get to stay and participate in the greatest worldly kingdom ever created. However, you must all follow my instructions exactly as I give them to you. You'll all have to attend some classes so that you will understand all the secrets of life. I'll hide nothing from you! You'll be co-inheritors of Mother Earth's treasures with me! Thunderous applause filled the room.

When the crowd fell silent again, Canards continued, "You may have noticed the horrible, terrifying, reaction of Mother Earth last night. She's alive and she's angry! You people have mistreated her and she's taking her revenge. I've appeased her for a time by removing those most responsible for the Earth's corruption and by promising that we'll undo the harm that the Christians have done. We are guests on this planet and must bow to the greater need of Mother Earth. Therefore, we must have an educated population on this earth, one that can take care of her instead of destroying her. With this in mind, every citizen will be asked to attend a training seminar in your area. At this seminar you'll be taught the basics of our New World Order. Shortly, there will be laws enacted that will protect the environment from any further abuse and our religion will reflect our honor and worship of Mother Earth. I'm calling for all police forces, reserves and military to put themselves at the disposal of the green army for reassignment. There will no longer be any crime or wars to fight; my ships will take care of peacekeeping. The green army will enforce, with deadly force if necessary, all the laws that are forthcoming, which has been agreed upon by the world leaders. In the mean time, I'm afraid that Mother Earth will continue to strike back for the years of abuse you've heaped upon her head. She'll be causing droughts, storms, earthquakes and all manner of plagues."

"But remember my friends that no women gives birth without some bloodshed and Mother Earth is no different! We're simply witnessing the birth pains of a new civilization. Be at peace, my friends and follow my lead and you'll be fine. I've already put some plans in motion that will do away with poverty and want. I'll see to it that everyone has a home, food and fun!"

"After last night's removal of the Christians from the earth, millions even billions of jobs need filling. There are fewer people breathing our air, drinking our water and eating our food. This will give us the time we need to more equally distribute the world's goods. This will of course mean a few sacrifices from the affluent people of the world. We will all soon be equal."

The thunderous applause that followed caused him to smile.

He thought, *"What idiots these people are!"*

He signaled for silence and then continued, "My friends, I have another piece of good news. I know that there has been animosity between many of you and the Jewish nation of Israel. Since, as I have told you, I am the new leader of Israel, I hope to end all this conflict. I've convinced the leaders of Islam that I must have

Israel back. The Muslims have agreed to allow me to move their great monument to my brother Mohammed, the great "Dome of the Rock". I'll be moving the great Dome and their many other monuments, as well as the entire populace to the lands of Iraq and Saudi Arabia."

"I am giving all of Israel back to my people! I believe this should show that God has given me the power to rule!"

Again the applause was thunderous from this crowd, who had been well rehearsed for effect. Canards let it go uninterrupted for quite some time before signaling that he wished to speak again.

He smiled and pointed to a large screen on the far wall and said, "Watch what I do and see that I Am!"

OUTSIDE THE WESTERN WALL, JERUSALEM:
September 2nd, 2---: 0845 HOURS:

"What am I doing here," thought the great High Priest Tzvi Cohen. He had received word from President Holstrum, via the still secret Committee communications network, that the newly elected President Canards, was taking over not only the World Government but also Israel. He had requested that the great High Priest be here at 8:30 this morning to witness a great miracle. He hadn't been told what this great miracle was, so he just stood here feeling foolish. The miracle was fifteen minutes late getting here and there were no signs that one would be here any time soon. The High Priest was very nervous! Ever since the murder of Dr. Kamerman, none of the Committee members could stop looking over their shoulders, fearing at any moment to be arrested or

killed. The disappearance of the Christians had eased that fear, but it had not been totally eliminated. Many of his Jewish brothers and sisters stood behind him. They had come to see what was of interest to their High Priest. It was a beautiful day. The sun was up but not yet too hot. Birds sang a melody to God's creation. The air was sweet and the breeze slight. A caravan of cars could be seen pulling up to the mound on which sat the Dome of the Rock. Tzvi recognized the Israeli president, Soden Colenhoff, as he and his guards left the cars. Tzvi's nervousness grew worse. He walked straight over to Tzvi and said, "What's this all about? I've been informed that an Alfred Canards has claimed the right of ascension to the throne as king of Israel. He claims to be the long awaited Messiah! What do you know of this Tzvi?"

"Only that I've been told the same thing and that there's supposed to be a miracle here today that'll prove his claims, but it seems to be late. Personally I have my doubts that anything can prove this claim. I for one..."

Before he could finish his statement four large space ships simply appeared over the great Dome. There was no sound, no wind, and no terrifying announcements. They simply appeared. The light which shown from them was immense and the men had to shield their eyes from their searing radiance.

Tzvi thought he saw, "No", he whispered, "This can't be!"

As they watched through the brightness, they saw the Dome shimmer like a mirage. Then it simply disappeared along with every Muslim in the city.

Tzvi spoke to the President; "First he took the Christians out of our City and now the Muslims. He has, according to the message, given us back all of Israel. The Arabs no longer occupy the East, we're free to move in immediately."

Tzvi praised God. The President was closer to deciding to turn the power over to this man, for the good of the Nation of Israel, **as** the world watched the miracle in awe.

One of the many TV reporters, who were stationed around the Dome, came over to Tzvi and the President and asked, "Can you tell the world what your thoughts are?"

President Colenhoff spoke first, "This man, Canards, is truly a man of power. Whether he be the Messiah, you need to ask the High Priest Cohen."

Tzvi was about to answer when again the ships interrupted him. This time beams of light shot out of the ships and the ground exploded! Dirt, rock and sand showered the crowd, most of who had already been knocked to the ground, from to the explosion. The earth shook and moaned. A pillar of fire rose high into the air and surrounded the entire mound area. It was hot. Men began to sweat even more profusely than they were already, due to both the heat and the fear that this new phenomenon produced.

The streaks of light stopped suddenly leaving only the billowing clouds of dust that still blocked their view. The people rose to their feet straining to see through the clouds of dirt and debris as Tzvi's stomach began to churn with excitement. As the dirt cloud dissipated, he dropped to his knees, tears running down his cheeks. He then stood and in a very non-priestly gesture he began to jump up and down with joy, shouting, "All Hail our God! All hail our new Messiah and King."

He turned toward the camera laughing and jumping and said, "I, as High Priest, give my allegiance to Alfred Canards. I declare him The Messiah! He'll lead our people to new glory."

The world listened to his proclamation, but their eyes were not fixed on him but on the object that stood behind him. On the mound for the first time in thousands of years stood the original, newly restored Holy Temple of God. Israel was once again the powerful stronghold of God's own religion, the Jewish faith.

NEW YORK COMMUNITY HOSPITAL:
September 2nd, 2---: 0845 HOURS:

Nurses ran into the room to see why Natan was suddenly yelling! A man who was both crying and laughing met them. He yelled, "It's a miracle! Look Chava, my wife! She's awake and sitting up!"

They looked into the bed and sure enough the woman who, just a few minutes ago, was in critical condition, was now asking for a drink and some food. They agreed with Natan. It was a miracle, and they shared his joy. Unnoticed, behind them on Chava's TV monitor, was the great miracle of the Temple that had appeared on the TV at the same moment her cure was granted by God.

EUROPEAN WORLD HEADQUARTERS OF W.E.L.:
September 2nd, 2---: 0845 HOURS:

This was going to be easier than Canards thought and much more fun. He watched the awed expressions on the faces of the audience who hadn't believed his claims even though they had agreed to follow him. Now, however, they believed in him completely. This would be very helpful in the completion of his many other goals. Not only did he want to completely destroy the Jewish nation, as a whole for all the trouble they had given him over the years, but he also wanted to destroy all humans. Damn them all to his kingdom for all eternity, and except for the few million Christians that had escaped, he was well on the road to achieving his goals.

He spoke with new power and benevolence; "My faithful followers prepare yourselves for a new era of peace and prosperity! To my Jewish subjects, I say, rejoice. The day of the Lord has arrived! I ask that all Jewish people arise and come back home. Worship in the Temple of your fathers. Bring the glory back to our nation!"

The huge screen exploded with activity, showing every detail of the newly resurrected Temple. In front was High Priest Tzvi Cohen jumping and shouting his loyalty to Canards before the entire world. After a moment of stunned silence, explosive applause filled the meeting room. Canards smiled at the camera and thought, *"The simple idiots are so easy to manipulate! Why didn't God takeover while he had the chance? Well, who cares? I'm in charge now! This is my world, now and forever!"*

CHAPTER THIRTEEN
(FIRST YEAR OF CANARDS' REIGN)
ENDANGERED EAGLE

JARRETT'S APARTMENT:
September 2nd, 2---: 0900 HOURS:

Jarrett slammed the phone down! *"Who could have taken it? Who indeed! You only gave your Swiss bank account code to one man, Winter!"* Jarrett flopped into his chair, devastated.

When he had been under cover on his last job, he had played the part of the leader of the Demon Slayer gang; Winter was his second in command. Jarrett had entrusted to him the codes of his Swiss bank account, which held over a million dollars. The Demon Slayers were made up of fifty of the most wanted men in America and their families. They had been paid to come to Covenant, mess things up, and kill people at the whim of the Committee. Jarrett had set a trap for them, and they were all captured or killed.

"Obviously Winter got away somehow and had accessed the Swiss bank account and was now on his way here to settle the score!" Jarrett thought.

He had hoped to use that money to lay low! He knew that President Holstrum was already looking for him; he had found Agent Bob Swaggert dead in his room just a few minutes ago. He had been killed execution style as a message, that anyone who had seen the list of

Committee members had to die and Jarrett was no exception.

"I wonder if Winter is still mad about me turning him in? Yeah right! The only reason you're not already dead, White, is because Winter would've given orders not to do anything until he gets here! He wants to kill me in person!"

Jarrett put on the old clothing he had dug out of rummage and stood before the mirror. He hadn't **shaved** for a couple of days and he actually did look like a street person. Jarrett would go into the streets and find Scorpion, who had disappeared shortly after breaking the code on Dr. Kamerman's computer records. Jarrett would seek him out and see if he could help him. Jarrett could lay low and still do something constructive while seeking the faith he had thrown away.

He was pleased with his own makeup work and while he admired himself in the mirror, Jarrett saw in the reflection, a man silently climbing through his bedroom window. Jarrett reached into his shirt, pulled out his 9mm, turned and fired, hitting the man in the forehead. He, of course, went down, but was followed by two more black clad men, and they were already shooting. A spray of automatic gunfire potted the walls all around Jarrett, as he tried desperately to take cover in the hall and then the kitchen. He was pinned down behind the serving bar and the firefight was on.

*　　　　*　　　　*

Lt. Andy, Jarrett's guardian angel, drew his sword filling the chamber with the pure white light of his sword. Boliczar, a demon who was hungry for Jarrett's soul, had his own sword out and at the ready. It's reddish glow caused eerie shadows to dance on the walls of the chamber. As Andy made his move on Boliczar, he was struck from behind by two demonic shadows that he had failed to sense. He fell forward, rolled onto his right shoulder and then bounced to his feet! He pivoted left, lifting his sword as he did so, just blocking the reddish sword before it could come down on his head. The clanging of steel on steel echoed throughout the chamber, followed quickly by a scream from the second of the sneaky attackers. The source of his pain, which had invited the scream, was the snapping of his kneecap, which Andy had just broken with a well-placed kick. While this demon was distracted, Andy concentrated on the first. He slid his blade across the demon's blade. As the demon applied more pressure to Andy's blade, he inched closer to the tip of the demon's blade. Then suddenly Andy stepped back causing the demon's blade to slip off of his blade, just missing his nose. As it swished past his face, Andy swung around in a long sideways arch and succeeded in removing the shocked demon's head. Through the sulfuric smoke Boliczar emerged with his sword held high over his head. He struck downward and connected with Andy's sword knocking him to the ground. Andy did a quick back roll and was again on his feet before Boliczar could finish him.

This time Andy did sense the approach of the second sneaky demon, the one with the broken kneecap. Andy took out his dagger, flung it backward over his left shoulder, and hit the demon in the throat. Before the demon had disappeared from sight, Boliczar was on Andy again. He came in low this time, forcing Andy to jump over his blade and then Andy struck out with his own. He connected with Boliczar's shoulder, who then emitted a very undignified groan and hastily shielded the wound.

*   *   *

Jarrett White ducked down just in time to be showered with splinters from his counter top. He really wished that he had the wings of an eagle right about now. After the emotional strain of seeing his friends, amid their smiles and good wishes, all taken from this earth and realizing the mistake he had made in not following Jesus, his fuse was very short. He raised, aimed and quickly shot his 9mm. One of the intruders went down, but the other opened up again, removing more counter top. Jarrett had gained his bearings, however, and this next shot would bring this to an end. He moved over slightly, raised and fired, but only received a loud "click" as the firing pin fell upon an empty chamber.

"*Ooh Ooh!*" thought Jarrett as he dove for cover once again.

*   *   *

Boliczar screamed in rage, but held his ground. Blood oozed from his shoulder and he stood there panting, every muscle tense with fury! He screamed again! As he flew from the room he yelled, "I'll be back,

Angel!" With that the attack was over. Andy turned toward Jarrett and his eyes went wide with horror!

*　　　*　　　*

Jarrett had dove down just in time for another splinter shower as the rapid fire from the automatic weapon ripped the rest of his counter top to pieces. This was getting old fast. He looked down into the barrel of his own empty gun, wishing that he could end it all right now. He knew, however, that he could no longer do that. Joshua had once told him that there was always hope and that he only had one chance, Jesus!

"That might be," thought Jarrett, *"But I have also been trained to take care of myself!"* With that he pulled out a hand grenade, pulled the pin and then lobbed it in the direction of the intruder. The result was deafening. What was left of the counter top blew in on Jarrett cutting a large gash into his back. The sound of splintering wood was mixed with the surprised scream from the unsuspecting intruder.

It was then that the cell-phone in Jarrett's pocket rang. Out of habit Jarrett took it out and answered, "Hello, White here."

"Oh, I see you have the same phone Spike. Whoops! You're not going by Spike these days are you?"

"Winter, I was expecting you. Glad you could make it to the party." He said this with mixed feelings. On the one hand he was glad that he could still guess the enemy's movements, but discouraged that the enemy had the upper hand in this case. Winter had always called him Spike in such a way that reflected respect. Now, however, his intention was anything but respectful.

"Spike! I knew you'd get out of my little trap alive. In fact, I was counting on it! I've got some good news for you. I'm not going to move in and kill you, just yet anyway. With the new government that was put in place last night, you've nowhere to go. Your accounts have all been drained, your bankcards are canceled and you have no car. You're a sitting duck! I'll be watching you all the time. You'll never know when or by whom, but one day soon you'll meet death in person! When you do I'll be there to watch!"

After a fit of laughter, Winter hung up the phone and Jarrett began to dig himself out of the rubble that had once been his very comfortable apartment.

CHAPTER FOURTEEN
(BETWEEN THIRD AND FOURTH YEAR OF CANARDS' REIGN)
STATE OF THE WORLD ADDRESS

EUROPEAN WORLD HEADQUARTERS OF W.E.L.: November 16th, 2---: 0800 HOURS:

"Good Morning, you're listening to the World News Center, and I'm Hans Rupple reporting live from W.E.L. Headquarters' here in Germany. Our Master, President Canards, will be here to speak momentarily, but first he has authorized me to tell you the good news.

"As you know, for the past three and a half years President Canards has tried his best to stop the disease of Christianity from spreading, but his efforts have been hampered by the Two Witnesses. They keep preaching their poison throughout the streets of Jerusalem and the world via television. They've even disrupted our Jewish brothers to the point that there is a hundred and forty-four thousand of their number who have joined the Prophets in preaching their poison throughout the world.

"Last night, however, President Canards personally went up against these two false prophets at great risk to his own safety. To date, these two prophets have killed over eight hundred people with their satanic weapon; that fire from their mouths. Our leader, President Canards, approached them and...well, we have a tape of last night's battle, so watch and see for yourself..."

The lights dimmed, and not only did the picture appear on the large screen behind the announcer, but also on every TV set throughout the world.

As the camera zoomed in on the Temple Mound in Jerusalem, the world saw for the first time the feared, "Two Witnesses".

The News Anchorman spoke in the background as the picture on the screen zoomed in on the two Prophets, "Some believe that these two men are the reincarnation of Moses and Elijah, but our leader knows that they are just two crazed men wanting to spread their poison throughout the World. Many have tried to stop them and have died for their efforts. These two men have done so much damage to the Jewish faith that President Canards is determined to stop them himself! Let's watch, as he approaches their location."

A military car pulled up and Canards climbed out of the back seat. He had on his blue field uniform complete with his blue beret. He carried no weapons with him and wouldn't allow any of his soldiers to accompany him. He walked straight up to the Two Witnesses and stood in front of them, glaring at each in turn. The Witnesses calmly and patiently waited for Canards to begin the battle.

Instead of fighting, Canards spoke, "I demand that you surrender to me immediately!"

The Two Witnesses were sitting in front of the Temple and the crowd that had been around them had fled upon Canards' approach. The Witnesses stood and faced Canards, saying in unison, in a very loud voice, "We are here upon the authority of God and will preach his coming until the day we face the Evil One himself! For the last three and one half years, we have shut the sky from giving any rain. We've turned many of your rivers and oceans to blood, and you, of course, know how many people have already died from our plagues. Yes, we are responsible for all of your troubles, under the authority of Jesus Christ. Now begone!"

Canards smiled and said, "Prepare to die!" At this, the Two Witnesses opened their mouths and fire shot out and engulfed Canards. The watching audience gasped in horror at their leader's demise. Moses struck Canards with his staff, splitting his skull wide open. Blood sprayed from the wound, but was lost in the flames. Hair and skin around the wound shrank away, singed, and discolored. Canards dropped first to his knees and then fell onto his face. He lay there dead and the world mourned its loss. His soldiers stood stunned and didn't know what to do. They feared these two men of God and none knew if they could be killed.

Just as the Captain of the Guard was about to give the reluctant order to attack, Canard's dead body shuddered. Light began to shine out from him and he pushed himself up to his knees. People around the world watched in awe, as he climbed to his feet. The right side of his head was dented, discolored and hairless, but it was nonetheless healed. It would forever remain the mark of a fatal head wound, from which Canards recovered. It would become the proof that Canards was a god.

The two Prophets didn't look surprised. They said, again in unison, "Then you've arrived! Do with us what is written, but know that we will return!"

Canards backed up a step or two and screamed at the top of his lungs, while at the same time he held both hands out toward the witnesses. Bolts of lightening shot out from the palms of his hands and struck the Two Witnesses in the chest. The look of surprise and pain brought shouts of joy from the TV audience as well as the live audience on the scene, about fifty thousand or so, now. They cheered their leader on and as the Two Witnesses fell dead at his feet, his guards ran up to take away the bodies to bury them and good riddance as far as they were concerned.

"No!" Canards said, "Hang them on a pole in a jeep and drive them around town as a warning to others who may insist on opposing me!"

With that, Canards walked away.

The screen went dead and the announcer, after drying tears from his eyes, continued, "That was wonderful! You see how powerful our leader is and how he cares for our welfare? He will..."

The announcer paused and held his earpiece tighter so as to catch all the words. Then he looked at the camera and smiled, "I was just informed that one of our Master's great ships has just deposited him on the roof. He's just getting back from Jerusalem and his victory. So with no further delays, here's our President and ruler, President Alfred Canards!"

The studio audience rose to its feet and applauded. Even people at home found themselves rising to their feet and applauding. Canards marched onto the stage amid the celebration of victory and he grinned from ear to ear. He wore the fresh head wound like a medal of honor, as the floodlights reflected off of the bare spot on his head. After about five minutes of congratulatory welcome, Canards signaled for silence. He stepped up to the microphone and said, "Citizens of the World! Rejoice! It's over! Did you see it? They're dead!"

More applause!

"I'm declaring a world-wide Holiday! Later this afternoon I'll lift all rationing tickets for one day. You can get yourselves a mighty meal. Prepare it and celebrate. No work for the next three days for anyone! At the end of those three days, we'll once again visit our mysterious pair of troublemakers and you'll see for yourselves that they are frauds! We will then bury them and have done with it!" The applause was even more riotous than before.

After taking a drink of water and waving his arms above his head, Canards continued, "Now to the business at hand! The State of the World, what can I say? There are still many unbelievers among you. This is what causes all the curses that you are bringing upon yourselves. If you had enough faith, you would be well! At last count, there were over thirty million people dead from Virus X; these people didn't have faith!

"Mother Earth still continues to take her revenge upon those of you who do not worship her as she deserves. At last count, sixty-five million people have been lost to natural disasters, like tornadoes, floods, earthquakes and disease.

"Finally Mother Earth will not release her rain and she bleeds into the oceans and rivers. This is not due to the false prophets as they claim, but can be traced back to the abuses to Mother Earth.

"I picked this particular day to speak because it marks the anniversary of my first three and one half years in office. As you've just seen, I'm keeping my end of the bargain. I destroyed the pests for you! Across the world I have established camps for the Christians. This was, of course, for your protection and for theirs, to prevent them from defiling you with their lies. These camps are very necessary, but very costly. I'll be raising your taxes in a month or two bringing them up to about 50% across the board. This is unfortunate but necessary for our survival!

"The other problem to be discussed is the fact that you people can't get along. I wanted to bring you peace, and yet you insist on fighting your petty little wars. This is what causes all of your diseases, droughts and cash flow problems. But today and for the next three days, let's not fight! Let's just go out and have a good time. Drink! Eat! Make love! Enjoy the pleasures of life!

"It's not as bad as it seems, my faithful followers, and things are looking up a bit. I just finished speaking with Pope Vermuchi and he reported to me that all earthly faiths have agreed to unite under one World Faith. As a matter of fact, that's what we're going to call it, The True World Faith. Pope Vermuchi has also been selected to serve as its leader, second only to me. Starting tomorrow, everyone must report to a church in his or her area and receive the Sacred Mark that will enable him or her to buy, sell and function in our new paperless society. The Mark will be a red dot on the forehead or on the back of the hand and will be scanable.

It will hold all of your health records, as well as your personal file and financial records. Once you've fallen on your face and worshipped my image, and received your mark, you'll be shown how to find your Spirit Guide. Then you'll be a powerful disciple of Mother Earth, just like I am!" Canards turned to leave, but hesitated for a moment to think.

Hans Rupple shook himself free from his trance and spoke pleasantly into the microphone, "Stay tuned for more updates and may you all be in Canards Book of Life!"

There was very little enthusiastic applause this time. Instead people filed out silently. They were heading for the food lines, which were already miles long around the world. For the first time in months, they could take advantage of rare unrationed food, clothing, toiletries and pet supplies. Beef, however had been declared unclean and so very few would buy steak anymore.

Canards watched the crowd and could barely contain his laughter, *"These idiots really do believe everything I tell them! I've been able to explain away every single disaster as being their fault! Ha! Haaah! I love this work! Just two more days, and I can launch my plan against Israel! I'll finally make the Jews crawl to me! Worship me! Then I'll crush them!"*

Canards marched from the room followed by his usual circle of vultures vying for his attention, as the new Anchorman summed up.

"There you have it fellow citizens of the World! President Canards has blessed us with the removal of rations for a day and he's finally arranged for our faith to

193

be formalized under the capable guidance of Pope Vermuchi.

"Our next broadcast will be in six hours, we are trying to save energy as well. Until then, this is Hans Rupple, reporting to you live from the European World Headquarters of W.E.L. Good day!"

Hans disconnected his mike and ran for the door. He had a steak to buy!

CHAPTER FIFTEEN
(BETWEEN THIRD AND FOURTH YEAR OF CANARDS' REIGN)

GOD'S HOLY TEMPLE

JEWISH TEMPLE IN JERUSALEM:
November 19th, 2---: 0600 HOURS:

Natan Cohen walked up the long flight of stairs, which led to the Temple of their Holy God. He had arrived here two and one half years ago, just about one year late. His wife, Chava, had received such extensive injuries from her fall that he just couldn't leave her. As a result, he had lost his position as apprentice to High Priest Tzvi Cohen. Oh, they had welcomed him when he finally arrived and had given him a job as a servant of the Temple. He had the honor of preparing the altar for the sacrifices and the Temple for the services and various other support tasks, but it just wasn't the same as serving the High Priest himself.

As Natan entered the courtyard of the sanctuary his supervisor, Rabbi Shilistein, hurried toward him.

Natan thought, *"Oh God spare me another day of this man's nagging and abuse!"*

Rabbi Shilistein whispered loudly, "Natan you're late again! Come, come, there is much work to be done this morning!"

He hustled Natan along toward the Altar of Burnt Offering located in the courtyard.

He said, "Natan, you've got the great honor of lighting and tending the fire in the altar. We'll have many sacrifices today. Remember today is the day that His Honor, King Canards, buries the Two Witnesses, after he comes here to offer a Sacrifice to our God, right here on this altar. Your job is to clean it, shine it and make sure it stays lit. First, however, you need to go into the Holy Place and trim the lamps. Come now Natan look alive!" Shilistein hurried off to harass someone else much to Natan's relief.

Natan walked across the courtyard and walked through the curtains that separated it from the Holy Place. This was the large room just before "The Most Holy Place". Once it had held the Ark of the Covenant but now a replica of it was housed here. Although it was a beautiful replica, or so Natan had been told, it had none of the power of the original. No one was allowed into the holy place except the High Priest and then only once a year. He had described it to Natan once in one of the rare moments when Natan got to talk to the High Priest by himself.

A chill of excitement ran down Natan's spine as he entered the Sanctuary. There against the South wall stood the Candlestick that held seven lamps. His job was to fill all of the lamps with oil and light them. During the night only one was left lit; but during the day, all seven burned.

Natan took a moment to take in his surroundings. He never tired of this holy place. On the West wall was the large heavy veil that separated the Sanctuary from The Most Holy Place. It was a beautiful curtain with embroidered angels standing guard over the holy place.

Just in front of the veil stood the altar of incense into which Natan would soon place some coals from the altar of burnt offering. Onto the hot coals, he would then place incense thus filling the Sanctuary with sweet smelling smoke, which would rise to the heavens taking along their prayers and offerings. He touched the altar of incense and prayed, "Oh Lord my God, please help me through this day. My heart is breaking for my poor wife who, I'm afraid, has the Christian disease. That's all she wants to talk about anymore. Jesus this and Jesus that. Heal her Lord, please..."

"Natan Cohen, stop stalling and get to work!" yelled Shilistein as he passed the Sanctuary on his way to harass yet another poor priest.

Natan continued, "Help me, Oh Lord, my God!"

Just then another young priest entered. His name was Jericho Worthing. Natan liked him. He was always joyful and had a good sense of humor. Jericho was carrying a tray of shewbread or "bread of the presence" because it sat in the presence of God all week. Jericho took the old tray off of the Table of Shewbread that was over against the North wall and placed the new tray in its place.

He then yelled across the Sanctuary, "Hey Natan, you hungry?" with that he threw Natan one of the old loaves of bread. It was the responsibility of the young Priests to eat the old loaves, which had sat in the presence of God all week and was always a bit hard and stale, but it was an honor nonetheless. Each of the young Priests would eat one of the small loaves, thus sharing the honor and lessening the amount they each had to eat.

Natan caught the loaf and yelled back, with an exaggerated lack of enthusiasm, "Thanks!"

Jericho laughed and turned to leave, so he could distribute the rest of the tray of bread. As he left, he yelled over his shoulder, "Hey Natan, I'll be back as soon as I can to give you a hand."

"Thanks Jericho, I could use it."

Natan thanked God for that relief. Jericho's presence always cheered him up. Jericho was a kind and gentle soul and Natan always felt lighter of heart as he walked back out into the courtyard to tend to the coal fire of the great altar of sacrifice.

GENERAL RUMPUS' CHAMBER:

Satan was sitting on Rumpus' throne and Rumpus was bowing low before him.

Satan spoke, his voice echoing off of the chamber walls, "Well, General, report!"

General Rumpus began to rise, but Satan yelled, "Did I tell you to get up? Report from your knees! Slave!" This last he spat out with such contempt that it made Rumpus shudder.

General Rumpus said, "Yes, my Lord. Angels still guard Jarrett White. Ever since we attacked him three and one half years ago in his apartment, they have increased his guard. Lt. Andy has several more angels helping him now. We've tried to turn him but he fell in with those Christian street people and got saved for real this time. He has fought off every group that we ever sent to crush those Christians. He's learning more about self control and he even feels bad about violence now, even though he is still very effective in its use. He is out of our reach..."

Lightening flew from Satan's fingertips. The streaks of fire struck Rumpus in the chest and then lifted him into the air. As he dangled there shaking like a rag doll, in the hands of an angry master, Satan yelled, "Don't you ever say that in my presence again! No one is out of my reach! No one! Do you understand me?"

Rumpus nodded profusely and Satan released him, dropping him to the floor with a painful thud. Rumpus said through his agony, "Sorry Your Honor. As I was saying, we are working on getting Jarrett White back to our side. I have a plan that might make him fall. He has an attraction to Genulata, one of our greatest sorceresses, and I believe that she might be ready to seduce him. She has a score to settle with him anyway, we can use her to get to him."

Satan smiled, "That's more like it. See to the details. Now, how is my plan going with the United States Government?"

Rumpus smiled broadly, "Your Honor, I'm happy to report that we now have enough votes to do away with it's Constitution and they will, this very day, officially join the One World Government.

"Also, my Lord," all churches have now given allegiance to Pope Vermuchi. Your trick worked in having Canards pass the law that no churches will be funded or be allowed to stay open unless they are affiliated with The One True Church!"

Satan smiled, "Yes, purse strings have always been my best weapon against worldly churches and their blind followers. Enough of these reports! Get your soldiers ready; today Canards will make his public proclamation of Godhood! It's about time we finally, once and for all, separate all believers from my people. I will not rest until all humans either bow down to me or die. Then will I own the world and my kingdom will be safe."

JEWISH TEMPLE IN JERUSALEM:
November 19th, 2---: 0900 HOURS:

Natan was very excited! The King and Messiah was coming here! He would be using the very things that Natan and his friend, Jericho, had spent the last three hours preparing. No early morning sacrifices were allowed! King Canards had ordered that everything be prepared and ready but undefiled by any other offerings.

It was an unusual request, but then again since he was the Messiah, he could do pretty well anything he wanted. Natan and Jericho were at the altar of incense causing a fresh supply of sweet smelling smoke to rise up and fill the Sanctuary. They had been ordered to stay by the Altar and make sure that it, the lamps, the incense and the bread remained ready until the High Priest and the Messiah arrived.

The Temple was alive with activity as the older, more powerful Priests vied for positions of honor. They wanted to be the first ones to be seen by the Messiah, Alfred Canards, when he came in.

Suddenly, a thought occurred to Natan, "Hey Jericho!"

Jericho looked up from scooping incense from the censor that Natan was holding and said, "Yes, what is it Natan?"

"It just hit me that the Messiah Canards hasn't stepped foot in this Temple for the entire three and a half years that he's been our king. Doesn't that seem odd to you?"

Jericho looked around before answering to make sure no one could hear and whispered, "It doesn't seem strange to me. I don't believe that Canards is the real Messiah."

Natan almost dropped the censor as he gasped, "What! Are you nuts! You can get kicked out of the Temple for a statement like that!"

Jericho nodded, but kept his serious expression as he continued, "Yes, I know, and I can go to hell for worshipping the wrong Messiah too. No, let me finish Natan. I listened to Rabbi Jenson the other day and he..."

Natan's face was red with anger, "Jenson's an outlaw, banned from teaching or preaching. As a matter of fact, he's wanted by the Government as well. His outlaw radio program is spreading the disease of Christianity all over the world." Natan stopped and then stared at his friend with shock, as he whispered, "Jericho, No, You haven't caught the disease as well have you? Why? First my brother, then my wife gets it and now my best friend?" Tears formed in Natan's eyes.

Jericho said, "Jenson is just one of 144,000 Jewish evangelists who have been preaching about the true Messiah, Jesus Christ. This whole thing with the Temple here and Canards is just a lie, a fake. He has more of Satan about him than he does God."

Neither of the young priests had noticed Rabbi Shilistein listening just out of sight in the courtyard.

Natan whispered back, "Don't tell anyone about this or you'll be banished or worse, killed!"

Jericho smiled and said, "The Lord will watch over me, of that I'm sure!"

Shilistein slunk away as the two young men walked out into the courtyard. From the commotion outside, it would appear that the Messiah Canards had arrived.

Natan went over and checked the water level in the Laver. The High Priest would wash his hands there before he offered the Sacrifice for the Messiah, this morning. Luckily, it was full of fresh water. Jericho no doubt had remembered to take care of it.

Natan looked over at Jericho who smiled back nervously and Natan thought, *"Jericho my friend, what have you done to yourself? You have committed a grave sin against God and the faith. I can't stay around you or you'll pull me into your sin. I must..."*

His thought was interrupted when a wall of people entered the Temple through the East gate. Suddenly Natan was faced with the great Messiah Canards himself! As the man walked toward him at a fast pace, Natan could feel the man's mighty presence. A chill dripped down Natan's spine and he fell to his knees and bowed his head down to the ground in worship. Natan peeked to the side and found that Jericho hadn't even knelt down.

Canards walked straight up to Jericho and said, "You must be the Priest, Jericho Worthing, that I've heard so much about. Your supervisor, Rabbi Shilistein, was kind enough to verify for me that you have the sickness. One of my own Priests! Is this true?"

He paused as the pale Jericho gathered his thoughts and his courage. Natan had scrapped up enough of his own courage to make himself stand up, as he watched his unusually brave friend face down this giant of a man.

Jericho spoke loudly and clearly, "I have no disease, unless you call the truth a disease. Jesus Christ is the true Messiah, not you! Jesus Christ is the true King of Israel and the entire World for that matter. Only He can save us. You, sir, are an impostor! A pretender to the throne!"

One of the guards with Canards pulled a revolver and was going to shoot Jericho, but Canards raised a hand and stopped him. He smiled and said, "Just as I thought, you are too far gone for help. But you can help me."

Canards turned and addressed the assembled Priests and said, "I am!"

The crowd gasped at the blasphemy!

Canards continued, "It's not blasphemy to tell the truth, and I am God! I have come down to earth to show you the truth, to rule over you, hard-hearted people, with a rod of steel. I have come here today to crush this lie once and for all! Today, I declare my rightful place as God of this world and of this Temple!"

With that Canards turned back to Jericho, and with one hand raised but still about five feet away, he lifted Jericho off of the floor and threw him onto the sacrificial altar. Instantly his clothing caught fire and the shocked crowd heard the sizzling of roasting human skin. Jericho screamed, "I worship Jesus Christ alone and Him alone do I fear!"

Canards walked up to Jericho who was being held down by some unseen force. As Canards watched Jericho struggle to free himself, he pulled a ceremonial dagger out of his pocket, took it out of its sheath and raised it above Jericho, poised to strike.

Jericho yelled one last time, "Don't you fools see what he is. He's an abomination to God. A stench in his nostrils. He's Satan incarnate! Would God sacrifice a human on his own altar?"

With that Canards buried the knife deep into Jericho's chest.

Natan stood there! Tears of sorrow and anger mixing with the sweat of doubt. His friend had been right all along!

Canards pushed on the knife cutting deeper until Jericho finally lay still. Then he turned to Natan and yelled, "And you! Where do you stand? Will you bow to worship me?"

Before the terrified Natan could answer, people standing by the East door began to scream in fear. Canards turned in that direction, forgetting all about Natan. The crowd began to part and suddenly standing in their midst were...The Two Witnesses, Moses and Elijah!

Canards just stared in disbelief as the two old prophets approached him.

He stammered, "But I...I...killed you myself!"

Moses answered him, "Yes, you did! And as He did Jesus Christ before us, God, Himself, breathed life back into us."

Without taking his eyes off of Canards, who was froze in rage; Moses spoke to the crowd of terrified Jewish leaders.

"The Holy Scriptures were written to Prophecy about Jesus Christ, the true Messiah, whom your ancestors killed and whom you still deny to this day. From Genesis through Revelation, the Word of God speaks about Jesus. Every Prophecy in Scripture has been fulfilled by Jesus Christ or will be in the very near future."

Moses pulled a sealed scroll from his sleeve and held it high as he shouted, "As I once brought you the Ten Commandments, I now bring you proof of Jesus Christ's true identity. This was written by the Apostle Peter himself and given to a local Rabbi, who quickly hid it, for fear of the Jews. It is time for the facts to be known. I will give this to you, if you follow our commands."

Moses looked over at Elijah who had been waiting patiently. Elijah now continued, "You've allowed the Evil One to enter this Holy Temple of God and defile it with a Pagan Human Sacrifice. For this you should be killed where you stand!"

As if on cue the room was suddenly filled with Angels, swords drawn and fire in their eyes!

Elijah continued, "You are a stubborn people, Oh Israel! You've turned your back on God's plan from the moment you disagreed with him. In that you're no better than this puppet of Satan who defiles the Temple with his presence. He killed us in hopes of silencing the truth, but God will not be silent! Just as the writer of Revelation warned, God has raised from among you

144,000 Evangelists, to open your eyes to the truth. Some of these you have already killed, and the others you are hunting down like animals. They hold the truth! Seek them out, they have the knowledge you seek, and only one of them can translate this scroll. Peter hid the truth in a secret code which has been given only to Rabbi Jenson, a mighty warrior for God..."

Canards screamed, "Silence them! Turn off the cameras! Stop..."

General Worl, pointed his sword at Canards, and his throat was closed off to speech and he was forced to stand there choking, as he heard all of his secrets being exposed one by one.

Elijah continued, "Thank you Capt. Worl. Now as I was saying, Rabbi Jenson is a very adept Scripture Scholar, unrivaled in this generation, and you all know it. Run to him and beg his forgiveness, while he'll still give it. He's the direct descendant of King David's Line. You must make him your King if you are to survive this final three and one half years of Canards' rule."

While Elijah was speaking, Natan had walked over to the Altar of Sacrifice on which lay what was left of his friend, Jericho Worthing. Tears ran down Natan's face as he realized that his friend and, of course, Chava had been right all along. Canards was a false Messiah. Natan reached down and slid his hands and arms under his scorched friend, searing his own arms in the process. He ignored the pain and lifted his friend from the fire and laid him gently on the ground. Natan then sat there with Jericho in his lap. Natan was holding Jericho's head to his chest and rocking back and forth. Jericho's blood that had caked onto his chest was now oozing out onto Natan. Natan sat there oblivious to the mess and filth that used to be his friend and listened to the Prophet Elijah as he continued.

"During this final time, the World will turn against you at the prompting of this impostor, Alfred Canards; Satan possessed puppet! Look at this Holy Place!"

The audience obeyed and what they saw turned their blood to ice. Horrifyingly powerful Angels stood all around the outer walls and the number was growing by the minute.

Elijah smiled at their reaction and then pointed to the Sanctuary and said in a whisper, "Watch!"

The T.V. crews stepped aside as mighty angels took over running the cameras. People around the world were watching these miracles unfold. An angel reached up and tore the Eastern curtain down exposing the entire Sanctuary area. All seven lamps were lit and they suddenly flared and brightened. The altar of incense puffed forth-beautiful clouds of colored smoke. Then to their horror, a second angel tore the curtain to the Holy Place and exposed their replica of the Ark of the Covenant. When the angel struck it with his sword, it burst into flame and was quickly consumed by heavenly fire.

Elijah continued, "Thus we have purified this Holy Place! We are about to entrust to you the most Holy Symbol of all time, the Ark of the Covenant. People have been looking for it everywhere, but it hasn't been on earth for years. If you had just read Rev. 11:12 which says in part, "And the temple of God was opened in heaven, and there was seen in his temple the ark of his testament:" I tell you brothers that same ark will destroy you if you do not obey and soon. Watch!"

Thunder rumbled and echoed throughout the Temple. Lightening flashed and the very foundations of the Temple shook causing the men to scream in fear. But they could not move, the angels prevented their escape. Suddenly, over the very spot on which they had placed their fake ark, a beam of light pierced the roof of the Temple and dug into its floor. Out of the floor grew a stone table. Angels descended carrying the bottom half of the Ark of the Covenant. Bright pulsating light shone out of the center of it and beamed straight into Heaven.

Moses pointed to the light and said, "Behold the very presence of our God! The Old Testament was fulfilled in the person of Jesus Christ who was the Holy Sacrifice, and became the New Covenant between God and his people! Just as I led your ancestors out of Egypt, Jesus will lead you out of your bondage to Satan! Turn from your unbelief, turn from your sacrilege to God and his Holy Messenger, His Messiah, Jesus Christ!"

As Moses said Jesus Christ, the light flared to such brilliance that the men present had to cover their eyes. They heard a loud booming voice come from the fire and it said, "Come Up!"

Elijah said as the pair walked toward the light, "This is a Holy Place! No one is allowed to tend to this room but Natan Cohen. It is given to him to care for this Temple. He will come here daily to speak to Jesus Christ. He will then report to Rabbi Jenson whom you will make King! The King will only be allowed to come here in person once a year on the last day of the year, the Day of Atonement. He'll come in and offer prayers to

Jesus and receive the Lord's blessings, which he will then return and share with you. Anyone else who dares enter this room will die!"

Moses spoke as the pair began to rise into the light and disappear from sight, "Angels of the Lord, please remove Alfred Canards and his people from among the Chosen people. Canards return no more to this Holy Land. The day you do will be your last!"

The word "last" echoed loudly and the two mighty prophets were gone.

The two mighty angels at the entrance to the Holy Place waved their swords and a fire red, thick velvet curtain, with golden angels embroidered onto it, appeared across the entrance to the Holy Place.

The angels said in unison, "Though you will not see us, we will strike down any who tries to enter this place except as laid out by the Prophets." With that the two angels took up positions on either side of the curtain and disappeared.

Several angels attacked Canards and his guards forcing them into their demon ships and then escorting them out of Israeli air space.

Capt Worl, who had stayed behind in the Holy Temple of God, bent down and lifted Jericho off of Natan. He picked Natan up and hugged him, filling him with the Holy Spirit of God! Natan wept as this new knowledge and strength filled his empty soul. He hugged Worl and wept the words, "Can he ever forgive me for not believing? I'm so ashamed of my doubt and fear. I was fooled by Canards and I almost turned my friend in. How could I?"

As he wept on Worl's shoulder, Worl stroked his hair and whispered, "It's all right! Jesus forgives you. Forget the past and concentrate on the future of your country. You must now worry about the spiritual welfare of this mighty nation as well as their physical well-being."

Worl nodded, and two separate angels went to the entrance of the Sanctuary and erected a heavy White curtain signifying the purity of this place. The Holy Spirit swept through the entire Temple and the Priests, learned Scribes, and men of Israel were all touched and given the wisdom of Salvation through Jesus the Christ. They fell on their face in shame before their God. The crowd at the Temple alone, all of who were saved numbered five thousand. The number of people watching on television, who were saved reached about ten million, about two million of them were Jews. The largest revival in history had just begun.

Worl, still holding Natan, nodded again and several angels left the Temple. Seconds later a huge earthquake shook the city of Jerusalem. The valleys rose high into the air forming new mountains. The hills sank quickly causing valleys and all was destruction. It lasted for all of three minutes, but when it was over, seven thousand non-repentant sinners lay dead under the rubble of their own greedy establishments. The over two million Jews who survived in this Holy City of God, were all now true believers in Jesus Christ as the Messiah.

Natan jumped suddenly and said, "Capt. Worl! What about the scroll that they promised us, the proof?"

Capt. Worl laughed out loud and pointed to Natan and said, "It's in your pocket!" Natan looked down and then stepped back in shock. He was dressed in a long red robe bordered in gold. It was of the same material as the curtains to the Holy Place. Next to Natan was another robe of the same color and a crown.

Capt. Worl spoke, "You are now wearing the robe of the High Priest, which is the post you hold! This robe and crown are for Rabbi Jenson when he arrives. You will present them and give him God's blessing. You will then go into the Holy Place and receive a message from Christ himself for the new King of Israel. Do you understand all this?"

Natan nodded but asked, "What about High Priest Tzvi Cohen?"

He lies dead on the floor over there. Killed by his own greed and ignorance, for he worshipped the beast in his heart. As Natan looked over at the dead High Priest the body burst into flame and was gone instantly.

When Natan looked back, Worl and his army were gone from sight. Everyone stood there for a few more seconds, dumbfounded by the events of this morning.

Natan turned to the camera and looking into it said, "I hope you are watching all of this Chava. I believe!"

*　　　　　*　　　　　*

Chava had been watching it all, lying on her bed, as tears of joy ran down her cheeks. She had spent the last three and one half years in great pain and agony, bed ridden from her wounds at the bombing. She longed to die and get relief, but it had all been worth it. She picked up a note pad and spoke out loud as she wrote, "Be happy in your new position and stay faithful. In just another three and one half years we'll be back together, when Jesus returns to reclaim the Earth. I love you! Chava."

She laid the note on the table and lay back exhausted from the effort. Liberty, Chava's guardian angel bent down and helped her out of her dead body and happily wrapped his wings around this brave soul. Chava felt wonderful, as they passed through the veils that separated this life from the next.

CHAPTER SIXTEEN
(BETWEEN THIRD AND FOURTH YEAR OF CANARDS' REIGN)

THE MARK OF THE BEAST

**"Having a form of godliness,
but denying the power thereof:
from such turn away.**

II Timothy 3:5

**EUROPEAN WORLD HEADQUARTERS OF W.E.L.:
November 19th, 2---: Noon**

"This is the Noon news with your reporter, Hans Rupple."

As the announcer introduced Hans, pictures of President Canards killing the Two Messengers flashed onto the screen.

Hans smiling face appeared on the screen and he said, "As you can see, President Canards did kill the two mad men three days ago and just a short two hours ago. . ."

Pictures flashed on the screen as two coffins were lowered into the ground. Hans said over the pictures "As you can see, President Canards was present at their burial this morning. Unfortunately, what you saw on the live broadcast this morning was a trick by a radical Christian. His expertise in the C.I.A. was to fool people with the type of special effects that you saw this morning. He has played many parts in the past three and a half years. This morning, with the help of a renegade T.V. crew, he pulled off quite a hoax. This man, whose name is Jarrett White, has stolen two million dollars from the Government and used it to buy the special effects that you saw this morning. I know it looked real, but it was just a very good special effects trick. Daniel's Magics have taken the blame as one of their employees; another Christian took it upon himself to create the fake scene that you enjoyed this morning. The company was fined; but since they didn't authorize it, the President pardoned them. President Canards is dedicated to the truth and will fight to bring the truth to you at any cost!"

While Hans had been speaking, the scene behind him changed and the audience witnessed the brutal beating of the "suspect" employee as he was dragged from his office, beaten and then shot in the head right in front of his place of employment.

Hans continued, "While President Canards likes fun as much as the next guy, he cannot put up with hoaxes that threaten the peace and security of the entire world. Jarrett White is being brought here to Germany so that President Canards can speak with him and give him one last chance to repent.

"Well on a happier note, President Canards is here to unveil his new economic program that is sure to stop robbery, theft, loss of money, stolen checks, etc. President Canards, would you join me please?"

Hans stood and shook the President's hand as he came out from the wings. Both men were smiling and the president leaned very close and whispered, "Well done, Hans. I almost believed your story myself!"

Hans swelled up with pride, that was quite a compliment from the King of Lies, himself. He applauded as the President walked up to the podium.

Canards smiled and said, "My fellow World citizens!" Applause filled the room as Canards continued, "I have wonderful news! After two days of delays and set backs, we finally have our mighty MNO (Money Neutralizing Operation) computer up and running! With it we've effectively stopped thefts of any kind, because from this moment on the World will exchange credits for services rendered instead of paper currency. When you get paid at your jobs your account will receive so many credits and when you buy something the price of the items will be deducted from your account. You won't even need credit cards anymore, because all of your credit transactions will also be tracked through your account."

"How does this work you might ask? Well starting tomorrow, local offices of the MNO will open up to take your money and add the appropriate credits in your account. Rates of exchange will be posted on the walls. In order to sign up for this service, you'll have to go to a local church; bow low before my likeness and worship me as your God, which I am! You'll then be stamped with an invisible mark on the forehead or the back of the right hand. We had first intended it to be a red mark and then we changed it to the symbol of W.E.L., the green globe with World Equality League written around the edges and in the middle the MNO mark. My advisors told me, however, that people had called in and complained about any mark that would be visible. To prove that I listen to my people's complaints, I've agreed to an invisible mark.

In a quick, painless procedure, a small computer chip will be injected under the skin of the right hand or the forehead. When the chip is scanned it will tell us your medical history, financial account balance, family information, your employment file, and many other things that are essential for your safety and convenience.

"Getting back to the MNO symbol for a moment I want to explain how it works. If you look on your telephone, MNO is on the number six, so in the middle of the green globe I placed a six for each letter, therefore the number 666 appears in the middle. That prefix (666), which by the way is the numerical computer equivalent of my name, will precede your personal I.D. number. When the prefix is entered into your personal computer at home, it will get you into the "Beast", which is what I have affectionately nicknamed my computer. When you enter your own personal I.D. number, you can access many important items, through a globalnet connection, which will be of great assistance."

"When you bow to my statue, all you have to say is, 'I give all praise and honor to President Canards, My Lord God', sign the pledge card and then you will be free to go about your business. If you will not bow down to my image, one of my faithful employees will escort you to the nearest police department. From there you'll be taken to one of my many Christian Work Camps, which are already beginning to exceed capacity. Any Jews caught outside Jerusalem will be tortured and then shot. They will not be allowed to receive the 'Mark of my Beast'. I will soon destroy them all and wipe them, once and for all, from the face of the earth!" President Canards had to stop for a moment and calm himself down. Hans cut to a commercial.

When they came back, Canards was once again in control of himself and he said, "In order for us to start off smoothly, I've arranged for Jarrett White to be brought here. As you know, for the last couple of years he's been stirring up trouble among the homeless people. He's been spreading vicious rumors and spreading his Christian poison everywhere he goes. Well, just yesterday, we caught him, and now I'm going to offer him the mark, in full sight of the entire world. If he doesn't take it, you'll witness his immediate execution."

"Now remember, if you don't get the mark", Canards pointed at the television audience for emphasis, "you will not be able to buy or sell anything. You'd simply be declaring yourself a renegade Christian just like Jarrett White. Well, good-bye for now and have peace!"

Hans stood, shook the President's hand and said, "Thank you Mr. President for those words of hope and encouragement! Also thank you for clearing up the mystery about this morning's hoax. Congratulations on a speedy capture of the responsible parties."

JERUSALEM: NATAN'S APARTMENT:
November 19th, 2---: 1230 HOURS:

Natan just stared at the screen. He had picked up a New Testament Bible on the way home, intending to read it with his wife Chava. When he had arrived home, however, Chava was already dead. He wept over her kind note and his own loss for at least an hour. He then called some friends, who in turn had called other friends and now his apartment was full of people preparing Chava for burial and giving him support. He had hurriedly read Revelation and his heart was racing in his chest. The answer had been there all along but he had not even read it before. Then when the President mentioned the mark, "666", and his new computer, "The Beast", Natan's blood ran cold. Everyone in the room was quiet for a moment trying to take in all the changes that had hit them this day. Their people had spent centuries denying all the things that they now knew to be true. It was as if God had removed the scales from their eyes.

Natan said, "Oh, God! Your ways are above our ways! You have the mysteries of life and death! Thank you for calling us to believe in Your Son, Jesus Christ. Help..."

There was a knock at the door and the closest person opened it and gasped! Everyone turned and there in the doorway was their new king, Rabbi Jenson, himself.

He was a rather tall man, about six feet two inches tall. He was heavily muscled and wore a full beard, which was brown in color except for the streaks of gray that shot through his beard and his short haircut. He was in his middle fifties. He wore a suit and tie commanding respect by his very presence.

He walked into the room through the parting people who just stood with their mouths open and walked right up to Natan.

Jenson said in his deep booming voice, "Natan Cohen, I share your sorrow at the loss of your wife and of your friend and mine Rabbi Jericho Worthing. I saw the respectful way that you treated him and the way the angel healed your arms and hands afterward. As King, I bow to you as the Great High Priest of Israel; God has so ordained. I also saw your heart today and I agree with his choice. After we bury our friends and loved ones, we must prepare to defend our country. I'm sure hard times are ahead for us."

Natan had just sat there during the King's speech with his mouth open. Now that he had finished, Natan got up, bowed low and said, "I give to you my obedience and loyalty, my mighty King. May God fill you with the Spirit of the Christ, and may He lead you to victory."

King Jenson then said, "Duty calls us to perform the anointing of the king this evening, then you must go into the Holy Place and receive a message for me. Will you be up to it?"

Natan smiled, "Yes, of course, your...what should we call you?"

It was Jenson's turn to smile, "Just call me Rabbi Jenson, I'm used to that, everyone will know that I'm king, we don't have to rub it in. When a title is appropriate, let's stick to Prime Minister."

"Very well, Rabbi Jenson, I'll be ready at 6:00 p.m. This should be done at sunset at the end of one day and the beginning of another."

As Rabbi Jenson bowed and turned to leave, he said, "Until then, may Jesus Christ keep you safe!"

*   *   *

Unseen by the humans, Capt. Worl and his personal guards Left and Right, smiled at that statement. These two men had been assigned ten angels each. They would be very safe. As the Prime Minister left with his Angelic guard surrounding him, Worl gave last minute instructions to Lt. Aaron and then departed. He had to attend to Jarrett White who was in the gravest danger and Andy would need backup forces.

*   *   *

On Natan's television set, Hans Rupple came back on with a live report from Rome, where President Canards was meeting with Pope Vincent Vermuchi.

Hans Rupple said, "We join them, now, live from Rome."

The picture on the screen changed to President Canards and Papa Vermuchi sitting in one of the Pope's dens at the Vatican.

The Pope said, "Welcome Mr. President! I'm glad to announce to you that I've completed all the documents needed for us to start our new World Church. This is now the official religion of our world and you, of course, will be the center of that worship. The Pope stood, then knelt before the President bowing to the ground and said, "All hail to our God! The Almighty above all things! The..."

Natan switched off the set and said, "I've had quite enough of their lies for one lifetime, how about you!"

Everyone agreed and Natan said, "Shall we get prepared for tonight and then bury our dead? We have preparations to make for the war that will surely come!"

CHAPTER SEVENTEEN
(IN THE FOURTH YEAR OF CANARDS' REIGN)
GATHERING STORMS

SATAN'S REALM:

Satan sat upon his throne! Canards lay in the corner in a fetal position, waiting like a lifeless puppet for his master's touch.

Satan stood and smiled down at General Rumpus as he said, "Well done, General! The world folded just as planned. Jesus struck down many souls, which we got to harvest. Our pits are the fullest they've ever been and we've millions yet to harvest. I, especially, like the camps you've set up for our Christian and Jewish friends. Keeping them alive was a stroke of genius. We can't touch their souls, not yet anyway, but we can break them down and possibly win a few of them over. Well, anyway, I just wanted to thank you personally.

"Now the only bad thing that I've heard is that Jarrett White has escaped our grasp, again?"

General Rumpus who had been puffed up by all the praise, now looked slightly afraid of the consequences to his next report, "Yes, Your Honor, he has escaped, with the help of his angelic friends, but we'll find him and kill him."

Satan sat back down and smiled saying, "Thank you for your reassurance, General Rumpus. Now sit and enjoy the entertainment."

Satan nodded and his guards brought out the human souls of Rabbi Shilistein, and High Priest Tzvi Cohen. In their arrogance, they had tried to enter the Holy Place and had, as promised, been immediately struck down by the Angelic Guards posted there.

They screamed, "But we're children of Abraham! You can't do this!"

Their screams echoed off of the chamber walls, as their nerves were slowly cut, one by one.

Satan sat back, comfortably in his throne chair, crossed his legs and whispered, "Aaah! Now that's sweet music to my ears!"

EUROPEAN WORLD HEADQUARTERS OF W.E.L.: November 20th, 2---: 0900 HOURS:

After four years of hiding among the homeless people in America and saving untold numbers of people for the glory of Jesus, Jarrett had been captured. He had then been brought to Germany to stand before the President himself. He was told that he would have to worship him or die. Jarrett had then promptly escaped again. However, through one bad break after another he had been recaptured by three-o-clock this morning. Now he awaited the televised worship service. He, of course, had no intention of worshipping the man.

His guard came in and pulled him to his feet and it was all Jarrett could do to restrain himself from fighting back. He knew that he would have to wait for the right moment. As they left the room Jarrett felt his shirt where he had hidden the plastic gun. He had made it through the metal detectors, as expected. Rev. Smith had shown him the gun, once, back at Jesus Park. He had told Jarrett about Sam Crawford and how he had been intimidated into killing Rev. Smith by Dr. Kamerman of the Committee. He had explained how Sam had a change of heart and turned the gun in, instead. Jarrett had taken the gun when he left Jesus Park over four years ago. Now he would allow the gun to serve its purpose finally and against the proper person.

Jarrett had been a warrior all of his life and these habits were hard for him to break. The way he looked at it, they were at war and this was going to be self-defense. President Canards had to go, for the safety of the World!

The guards pushed Jarrett onto the stage and nudged him forward to where President Canards and News Anchorman Hans Rupple were holding hands. They smiled to themselves when the couple quickly parted. They had heard the rumors that Canards and Rupple were lovers, but this proved it. *"So What!"* they thought, *"To each his own."* That was one of the first things that Canards had set straight in the world.

If he had said it once, he had said it a million times, "What you do with your sexuality is totally up to you."

Free expression of sexual desire was one of the things that the World Government Religion would teach.

When they arrived in front of Canards, each of Jarrett's guards kicked the back of one of Jarrett's knees forcing him down to the floor. Canards motioned for Hans.

Hans turned to the camera, his heart racing with anticipation. The world was about to watch Jarrett White cave and Hans was a part of it! The man next to the camera counted down three, two, one..." they were live!

Hans said, "Good morning! We're here today as promised, with President Canards and the accused and broken prisoner, Jarrett White. White will worship our Lord, or he will die! President Canards?"

President Canards walked up to Jarrett with a very smug expression. Jarrett kept his own expression neutral.

The president got right down in Jarrett's face and said, "Well, Jarrett White, you have been a royal pain, but now you must choose! Will you choose life or death?"

Jarrett smiled up at the President and thought, *"You fool! Didn't any of your guards teach you anything about security?"*

Then he prayed, "Oh, Lord, guide me in my path. I know you have told me to stop the violence, but this man must be stopped! Please forgive me if I'm doing the wrong thing!" he said to Canards, "I will choose......death!"

Jarrett had paused for a moment, as if he were having second thoughts. Then moving with all the speed his training and conditioning would allow, he pulled the gun, brought it up and fired. Lightening flashed from Canards' hands and Jarrett's gun hand was knocked to the side just as the gun discharged. The bullet raced past Canards' ear and straight into the right lung of the very surprised Hans Rupple. He stood there with a shocked look of pain. When he tried to speak, he coughed up blood instead. A weak plea of, "Alfred help me", bubbled out with the blood and then he fell to the floor dead. Canards' expression was a mixture of pain and surprise! Hatred and respect!

As the guards moved in, Jarrett jumped up and kicked the first guard breaking his left kneecap! He then turned and kicked the second guard in the face. Within seconds, a shot rang out and Jarrett went down, hit in the right leg. Guards swarmed him and tied him up.

President Canards put his smoking side arm back in its shoulder holster, his face ashen gray as he looked down at his mortally wounded lover.

Canards knelt down and held Hans to his chest and wept. Satan saw an opportunity in all of this, so he allowed his power to leave Canards and enter the lifeless body of Hans. Hans coughed, wheezed, and then coughed again. Canards jumped and lifted Hans' face toward him and he saw life!

Hans whispered, "It's gone! The pain is gone!" Canards stood up and then bent over to help Hans to his feet. Hans, however, pulled away and knelt before President Canards and began to worship him.

Hans lay on his face on the floor in front of Canards and yelled, "All hail to our Lord and Savior, The Almighty Canards!"

The television audience of millions gasped and some lost their faith in Jesus and found it in Canards instead.

Canards walked over to Jarrett, who was being held down by four guards, and he kicked him in the face, several times, screaming at the top of his lungs in a very ungodly way.

When Canards stopped and calmed down for a moment, he squatted down and whispered to Jarrett, "I should kill you right here and now, but you've done me a great favor, so I'll return it in kind!"

The malice in Canards voice was unmistakable and wasn't softened at all by the smile that appeared on his face, as he continued, standing and talking to the cameras, "To show that I'm a forgiving god, I'm going to let Mr. White live! I'm ordering him sent to Christian detention camp number twelve, just outside of town here. I'll try to visit him whenever I can to see if he's ready to repent."

Jarrett tried to spit out a retort but lost a couple of teeth, which Canards had loosened, and he spit blood instead. His face was already swelling up into an ugly mass of black and blue welts.

Worl placed a hand on Jarrett's shoulder and whispered into his very soul, "Jarrett it's not your will but God's will that must prevail. It's not by your might but by the Holy Spirit that God's plan will be carried out. Give yourself over to God!"

Tears formed in Jarrett's eyes as his soul was convicted. He pledged to endure whatever Canards had prepared for him and without any violent reaction. He would try to respond with love. He thought, *Lord this is going to be the hardest thing I have ever tried to do, please help me!"*

As Jarrett was dragged from the room, President Canards continued speaking to the people, "As you can see, I have power over life and death." He paused for a few seconds and let the overwhelmed crowd think about that for a moment. He said, "So don't waste your life trying to kill me or my people. Now I have another wonderful announcement. Well, first, I should review the problem. The Nation of Israel has officially anointed Rabbi Jenson as their new Prime Minister and Rabbi Natan Cohen as their High Priest."

"They then announced to the world earlier this morning, that they would no longer honor any existing treaties. They'll not trade with the world on any level and will not allow anyone into Israel unless they can prove their Jewish heritage. In my case, they won't let me in at all. They've rejected me as their God and have fallen to the madness of Christianity and after all I've done for them.

"I tried to reason with them, but it isn't possible. I've warned them that I can't restrain the neighboring nations for long, and I'll not be held responsible for them when they are attacked, which is exactly what happened at seven o'clock this morning on the Northern border of Israel." The large screen behind President Canards lit up and showed a massive movement of tanks and soldiers stirring up a wall of dust as they raced toward the Israeli border. In front was a jeep carrying a large flag, which waved in the wind. The flag's large black cloth carried the figure of a huge fierce red bear with teeth bared and claws ready.

Canards pointed at the close up of the flag and smiling he said, "The Russians will make short work of the Israeli's."

"Once we rid this world of the Christians, both Gentile and Jew, we'll finally be at peace and can begin to build again what they've torn down.

"Now, for my good news! I proclaim this day, that Christians are no longer to be considered human beings and can be treated as such. There will be no penalty against anyone who kills or tortures one. They can hold no property; therefore, all such must be immediately given back to the State. This includes real estate, cars, jewelry, cash and any other type of property.

"Children under the age of five will be taken from Christian parents and raised by sane couples of any gender, who want to adopt them. Children over five will stay with their parents and share their fate. This, I decree as your god, and it will be obeyed by all or the violator shall share the Christian's fate as well. At last count, we had about six of the ten million known Christians in our camps and we're rounding up more every day!"

"Each day, we will execute a few from each camp for the amusement of the guards and the people from the surrounding towns with many of these being televised for your entertainment. We'll call the show, THE ULTIMATE REALITY EXPERIENCE! Also, some scientists have put in their bid for a few hundred of the Christians, with whom to conduct stem cell research. This will once and for all allow them to cure such diseases as cancer, aids, and yes, even Christianity itself."

"So my friends, eat, drink, make love, and use drugs; there is nothing at all to worry about! I'll protect your interests while you indulge your passions, lusts, and desires. I'll try to keep you informed of our progress, but in the mean time watch your local listings for the time of the execution near you. Remember, many will be televised!"

Hans came running up and whispered into Canards' ear. The President's face lost all color and he staggered backward toward a nearby chair and collapsed.

Hans stood in front of him so as to hide the President from the camera and to the shocked audience, both in the studio and in the millions of homes around the world, he reported, "At eight thirty-five this morning, the Israeli Government shot two missiles into the Russian army and detonated..." Hans' voice cracked, he stopped, picked up a glass of water with a very shaky hand, took a drink, and then continued, "...They detonated two nuclear warheads. Early reports indicate that five sixths of the Russian army has been destroyed. We will, of course, keep you up to date on all this fast breaking news."

Behind Hans, President Canards got up and silently walked out of the studio.

His thoughts were about how to take Israel back, *"The first thing I need to do is get Wong's army prepared. At last count he had 1.5 million soldiers prepared to move out. Yes, I'll call Wong and tell him that he has my permission to sweep down on Israel from the East that ought to do it. If not? There's always my own nuclear stock pile!"* Canards laughed out loud as he walked toward his car. His guards didn't react to his laughter; they had learned the hard way not to ask questions or to make comments. But they knew that Canards had just solidified a new plan in his head, and they figured it had to be more vicious than anything thus far. Beads of sweat broke out on their foreheads as they tried to imagine what Canards was plotting.

CHAPTER EIGHTEEN
(IN THE FIFTH YEAR OF CANARDS' REIGN)
FOR THE FAITH

CHRISTIAN DETENTION CAMP # 12:
November 20th, 2---: 1800 HOURS:

Henry Ganal stood at his post at the gate to #12. He had been very glad when he first got this job. It paid 300 credits per week, which wasn't bad under the new rules. It had fed his family, paid for his new car and would put his kids through school. Even after the 10% that the new Government Church took out of his pay automatically, he considered himself very lucky. Yesterday, Henry had celebrated his 25th birthday. He had slept in this morning and had a nice afternoon watching a football game that he had recorded on Sunday. He now stood at his post watching a very depressing scene that threatened to stress him out all over again.

The Christians had been moved in here about two weeks ago. It had taken President Canards over two years to organize and build these camps. Some of them were old army bases, but not #12...this camp was new. It had towers all around the perimeter of the double barbed wire, electrified fence. As darkness slowly descended over the camp like a pall of death, the wind began to pick up. The night was going to be very dark and chilly. Henry pulled the collar of his uniform coat up around his neck a little further and settled in for a long shift. He would stand duty from 1800 hours to 0200 hours.

It was depressing for Henry to watch the Christians, as they milled about each other trying to stay warm. In the courtyard in front of him, there were about three thousand Christian men, not counting the women and children. Henry didn't believe in God, but he wasn't sure about this business of Christians not being human. President Canards had announced just one year ago today that these Christians were not human and so they were not, but Henry knew it was all political. After all, how can anyone just suddenly dehumanize another person and make it legal to kill them or worse. Henry was really shocked and disappointed when Canards had declared himself god. Henry didn't believe in any gods. Therefore, he was suspicious of any religion, even this Government one. He knew, however, that in this New World Order there was no room for disagreement. You either believed Canards' way or you were marked a Christian and brought here.

Henry had also gotten a little nervous about these people since they arrived. They had been denied every human dignity. They had no buildings in which to sleep. Buildings housed only the guards and administration. The "guests" as they were called had to sleep out in the open, on the ground, regardless of weather or temperature. There were no restroom facilities, which forced them to relieve themselves in a ditch on the far side of the compound, away from Henry's gate, "thank goodness!" So far they had been allowed to keep their clothes, but some of the guards were already picking out certain girls and dragging them to their beds for the night. The next day, they were allowed to keep what was left of their clothing, which at times wasn't much.

Every day for the past two weeks these people had endured beatings and starvation. They were only fed bread and water once a day. That was another strange thing; the guards purposely didn't give them enough bread. They wanted to see a fight ensue among the guests but that just never happened. These people would take the bread, break it into pieces, pray over it and then in an orderly fashion they would share it. Nobody got much, but they all got some.

Henry looked over at the new addition that had been brought in earlier this afternoon. The man's hands were tied to the top of a pole and his entire 6'5" frame was stretched with his toes just barely touching the ground. His clothes were covered in blood, some of it his and some of it belonged to guards who got too close to him. Henry shuddered at the thought of the President's lover being shot by this man. Then according to what Henry saw on television, Canards brought his lover back to life and beat this man, Jarrett White, senseless. With power like that, Henry knew that these people didn't stand a chance.

Henry had heard of the White brothers even here in Germany. Joshua White had been quite famous with all of his healings. It was rumored that Jarrett also had that power. Henry smiled, and thought, *"If he does, he better use it on himself. He looks pretty bad."* He could only imagine what the last year had been like for this tortured soul. Jarrett White had started out here; the very night of the Canard's televised broadcast, but then it had been decided that he would be passed from one prison to another and then from one camp to another until he had finally ended up back here.

Henry looked at his watch and realized that it was already 1830 hours and time for supper. Right on cue the door to the mess hall opened, the smells of delicious food for the guards, of course, wafted out to further torture these poor souls. There were three guards who walked out with large tubs of freshly baked loaves of bread. They went to the center of the compound, dumped the bread on the ground and walked away. A single water faucet stood in the center also and that was their only source of water. They had no cups in which to put the water so they had to use their hands to drink. Those that were too sick were carried to the faucet and helped to get what little water they could manage.

Henry shook his head, as the people got in line in an orderly fashion while other men passed out portions of the bread as if it were some delicacy. Then they did something that Henry hadn't really noticed before, they all held the bread until everyone had a piece. From the oldest to the youngest, they just waited. Henry couldn't understand such self-discipline. These people had to be starving! They should be killing each other for bigger portions!

Now what where they doing? Henry strained to hear and when he did his jaw dropped open! They were praying, "Sweet Jesus, we thank you for our daily bread. You have met all of our needs. We have bread and water for our bodies, and we have the Holy Ghost for our souls. Lord, we pray for these guards and their families. They are starving spiritually, and we pray that they will see the light and be saved before it's too late. We ask you to bless them and keep them safe from the Evil one."

A shiver ran down Henry's spine. This was weird! To pray for someone who was treating you badly and keeping you a prisoner, he just couldn't understand these people.

Henry watched as a little girl of about seven asked her mom, "Mom, what about him?" As she said that she pointed to the new arrival hanging from the pole. The mother said, "You're quite right, honey."

The mother walked over to Jarrett White, breaking her already small piece of bread in half as she did so. When she arrived, she reached up and held the bread to his mouth. He tried to eat it but his mouth was just too swollen and too dry. The woman walked back to the water faucet and tearing a strip of her skirt off, she ran water over it until it was soaked through. She then walked back to Jarrett White and squeezed the cloth forcing the water into his mouth. He greedily slurped the water into his swollen mouth and allowed it to trickle down his parched throat. Water had never tasted as good as it did this very moment! Then the woman used the wet cloth to gently wipe his face. She then broke the bread even smaller and a crumb at a time fed it to this stranger.

Henry watched and began to feel a little jealous at the gentleness and love that this woman was showing a perfect stranger. Henry had been straining to see this scene through the dwindling light and was, therefore, almost blinded when the automatic floodlights suddenly came on without warning.

The woman gave White exactly half of her bread, and she then ate the other half. She went back to the water, cleaned the rag the best she could and filled it with water again. She repeated her earlier act of kindness and squeezed water through his abused and swollen lips again.

Henry was touched by this act of kindness and had been so intent on watching this gentle woman that he hadn't noticed Sgt. Boris Chillier approach. He walked up to the woman and kicked her in the groin. She doubled over in pain. He grabbed her hair and roughly dragged her back toward the other Christians, screaming the whole time, "Never, ever, feed the animals! He's an animal and is not to be fed at all! Do you understand?" He stopped, let the woman drop and then he backhanded the woman's little girl as well, knocking her to the ground. "Animals!" he shouted with disgust, and then walked over toward Henry.

Henry thought, *"I've had it now!"*

When Sgt. Chillier got to Henry's position, he was laughing!

He said good naturedly as he lit his cigarette, "Did you see that Ganal? This is fun! Ever since the Master declared them non-human, we've been able to treat them anyway we wish. I have enjoyed inflicting lots of pain. I take my pick of the women and...well you get the picture? You should have seen what I did at my last assignment." He winked, slapped Henry on the back and laughed as he walked away.

Henry thought, *"Talk about animals!"*

The Sergeant stopped, turned around and said, "Oh yeah! I almost forgot, at 1900 hours we're going to carry out our new orders. We're to separate the children under five years and ship them off to the new Government Home for Children. I'm sure there'll be trouble. So be ready."

The sergeant walked away whistling a happy tune.

Henry was sick to his stomach. His own little girl, Judy; and his little son, Franky, were both under five. He couldn't stand the thought of his own children being taken away and sent to those cold schools. There were rumors that Canards was planning on taking everyone's children eventually and raising them in the homes. It had been in his original plans when he took over five years ago, but he had second thoughts about actually doing it because of all the opposition. It was just too foreign an idea for people to grasp.

The Christians were finished eating their sparse supper and they all, as one body, knelt on the ground. Again, they prayed in a loud voice, "Oh Lord Jesus help us and our children, most of all though, help our guards..."

SATAN'S DOMAIN:

Unseen by the Christians, the demon world was turning upside down. The pain and agony was caused not only by these humans but also by all Christians around the world who were praying at the same moment, under the prompting of the Holy Ghost, for the salvation of their enemies' souls.

Satan writhed in pain and fury as the prayers continued to heap coals of fire upon his head and those of his soldiers. Erie screams and howls could be heard echoing all through the Nether World as the prayers intensified with the desperation of the Christians.

Satan moaned! He should never have agreed to this deal with God! He had been tricked! God had asked Satan to agree that if people would pray for their enemies that he, Satan, and all of his demons would live in torment as long as the prayers lasted and that God's Angels could help souls during this time. Satan had agreed, because from his narrow point of view, he couldn't believe that anyone would actually do it. That was a mistake that he and his warriors have been paying for profusely ever since.

*   *   *

Henry Ganal watched the Christians pray. He listened to the words of their prayers and he finally felt something stirring in his heart. He was, suddenly, filled with the Holy Ghost and just about fell to his own knees. However just at that moment, the mess doors opened and the men started filing out. The camp commander came out last and spoke to the crowd of Christians who had now stopped praying and were getting up off of their knees. Satan sighed with relief!

"Listen honored guests, President Canards, has decreed that all children under age five must be taken to the Government houses where they will be raised as good citizens of the world. We are going to take your children tonight."

Without another word, the guards rushed the shocked people, but except for a couple of desperate souls, who actually tried to stop them and were immediately shot down, most of them just knelt down and prayed for deliverance.

Henry could make out some of the words, "Lord, Jesus, I know you will not allow our children to be taken. Please send your angels to protect the children!"

The guards loaded the screaming, wiggling, crying children into a waiting truck. As the truck started off, it died. When they tried to start it, they found that the battery was dead. They got the children out of that truck and loaded them into the next one. This truck started and drove toward the gate where Henry stood. The truck cab was occupied by the driver and one guard with two more guards in the back of the truck along with the children. The Christians continued to pray.

Henry felt the Angels more than saw them. He did see a streak of unexplained light pass through the truck. The driver slumped over the wheel, and Henry had to jump out of the way as the truck crashed into his guard shack. As Henry climbed back to his feet, he looked again and found that the two guards, who had been on the back of the truck, now lay on the ground dead. The children jumped out of the truck and ran back to their parents' loving and thankful arms.

The camp commander was so angry that he ordered his men to open fire.

*　　　*　　　*

Worl, who had been flying overhead, watched sadly as the commander gave the order to fire. He landed next to Andy, who was standing guard over Jarrett, still painfully hanging from the post.

Worl whispered, "So it continues just as the Lord predicted! The blood of millions of innocent people has already been shed and before this great Tribulation is over, many millions more will lose their lives."

Worl and his guards watched sadly as the Christians were mowed down by automatic weapon fire. As they died, their souls were tenderly collected by their waiting Angels and lovingly transported to Jesus to gain their Heavenly reward. No longer would they have anything to fear.

*   *   *

Henry Ganal stood frozen at his post. He was appalled by this senseless slaughter. He was sick to his stomach as he watched innocent children and their parents being shot down in cold blood. He hadn't signed on for this! He couldn't do this!

Sgt. Boris Chiller came over to Henry's post.

Sgt. Chiller, with madness in his eyes, laughed, and said, "That's what I call fun, man! Did you see the shocked look on their faces when we shot them?" He stopped for a moment when he heard a moan over to his right. There was a Christian boy about fifteen years old lying on his side. He was holding his stomach and moaning.

Chiller smiled at Henry as he pointed to the boy and said, "That one's yours, boy. Go put him out of his misery!"

Henry's face got hot. He felt dizzy and nauseated. He finally whispered, "I-I can't, sir."

Sgt. Chiller got right in his face and yelled, "Go put him out of his misery now! There are plenty more where these came from! Now get to it!"

Henry started crying and yelled, "No, I can't!"

Sgt. Chiller walked over to the boy, pulled his 9mm Beretta and fired at the boy's head at point-blank range. The boy died instantly.

Sgt. Chiller walked back over to Henry and spoke in soft, comforting tones, "Look, I'm sorry I yelled at you. I forgot that you haven't received the Mark of the Beast yet. During dinner, we all took the pledge and were blessed by the Priest. I'll relieve you here. I want you to walk over to the mess hall and get your own mark now, along with the other sentries."

Henry was numb, his mind reeling! *"I don't want The Mark of Canards' Beast! I don't want to kill innocent people! The world has gone mad and left me behind!"*

Henry's thoughts were disturbed as he passed Jarrett White and heard him praying, "Lord Jesus, please forgive me my sins and don't allow this to happen to these good people. That woman was so kind to me; please don't let her die like this. Lord, if you will use me to heal this woman and her child, I will never be violent again. I've been trying not to fight back, Lord, and I know that I have failed miserably. If you will only give me another chance Lord, Work your miracles through me again Lord..."

Henry had stopped to listen but Sgt. Chiller yelled, "Hey Ganal get going! I don't want to be out here all night!"

Without thinking, Henry took out his knife and cut Jarrett down from the post and freed his hands. Jarrett looked up at him and said, "May Jesus the Christ bless you!" Jarrett placed his hand on Henry's shoulder and smiled at him.

Then a strange thing happened! Henry felt the weight of his own sins lifted from his soul. The scales were removed from his eyes, and he saw this atrocity even more clearly. His own safety wasn't the issue any longer. He helped Jarrett walk over to the dead and dying people.

Jarrett looked down at the woman and her daughter. They had been so kind to him and he wept at their deaths. As he reached down and touched their heads, first the mother and then the daughter, he whispered, "God is the God of the living not of the dead! Arise for the glory of Jesus' Name!"

A powerful wind swept over the camp and the woman and her daughter were healed of their wounds instantly, stood up, and smiled at Jarrett and Henry. Not only them, but also about four hundred of the other dead and dying stood up, healed.

Henry gasped and asked the woman, "Weren't you dead?"

The woman nodded and said, "Yes, I was dead and I saw the most glorious of places. The Lord Jesus himself greeted us when we arrived. Heaven is such a wonderful place..."

As the woman explained about her experiences, many of the guards, who had been on their way to get their mark, stopped to listen to the woman. The camp Commander, who had gone back inside to prepare for the next group of guards, came out now to see what was taking them so long. He stopped in his tracks and stared at the scene before him. There were twenty of his guards standing around talking to the prisoners. Then the commander went pale. Not only were they talking to the prisoners, but to the prisoners who had been shot down, who only moments ago were dead!

Fear gripped his heart and he yelled to the other guards, the ones with the mark, "This disease is spreading throughout our guards! We must save ourselves!"

Henry ignored the Commander, the Sergeant and the commotion around him as the guards surrounded them. Henry asked the woman, "Could this Jesus possibly love me?"

The woman hugged him, and said, "Yes, of course! Just ask him into your heart."

It felt so good to be hugged in this loving way by another human being. She was so gentle and kind. He whispered, "But I don't know how."

The woman whispered into his ear, "Just say, Jesus I believe that you are the Savior who comes to take away my sin. Please come into my heart and live. Forgive me my sins and send me the Holy Ghost!"

Henry had repeated her words and he really meant them. So did most of the guards around him and so did Jarrett White. For the first time, he really understood gentleness and kindness through this woman. He renewed his vow to Jesus, to be non-violent for the rest of his life, no matter what they did to him.

Jarrett walked over to Henry and the woman and said, "Mam, would you give me a hug too?"

The woman patted Henry on the shoulder and could tell by the joy in his eyes that he had received the

Holy Ghost. She then turned to Jarrett White and said, "My name is Mary. Please call me Mary." She took him in her arms and hugged him tightly to her. He hugged her back and wept heavily. Her touch was so loving and tender. He felt something at his leg and looked down to see the woman's daughter hugging his leg. He patted her head.

Mary then whispered into Jarrett's ear, "The Lord sent a message back for you Jarrett. He said to tell you that he is with you, that you're not alone. He wants you to stop the violence and start using your opportunities to spread his word while you can. The only thing that your acts of violence have done so far is to make you the object of Canard's attention. Speak out as the Holy Ghost directs you. And don't be afraid, we'll all be with you in spirit and peace."

With that she squeezed him, kissed his cheek tenderly and then backed away, taking her daughter with her. She said, "Don't be sad for us, Jarrett White, today we'll be with the Lord in Heaven."

Mary turned to Henry and said, "Don't be afraid Henry. It doesn't hurt for long and then you'll be free of all cares and worries. This world is no longer fit for saved souls, but a time is coming soon when the heavens and the earth will be renewed and we will dwell here in peace, under the rule of Jesus Christ."

A couple of guards, with the mark, came and dragged Jarrett away and held him, though he didn't try to fight. The commander, who was afraid of these people and angry at his fear, gave the order to fire. The guards opened up with their automatic weapons and had quickly re-killed all the resurrected "guests". They also shot several of their own newly saved guards. The only one left was Jarrett White whom they tied to the pole again.

All over the world these same scenes played out in one camp after another. The more Christians they brought in and killed, the more guards they lost. They would catch on, eventually, that only the guards with the mark were safe and they would make this a condition of employment. For some reason, they were immune to this Christian disease.

*   *   *

Worl and his soldiers had a busy night! He looked around himself and never in all of his experience, not even in early Rome, had he seen so many Christians killed in one day. Neither had he seen so many people saved in one day. This was the greatest harvest of souls in the history of mankind and it brought joy to Heaven. The celebration was in progress and songs of joy filled the heavens. The awed look on the faces of these people was something to see. They praised God for his goodness and kindness, and they all flocked around Jesus, who had been explaining everything to them. Angels posted throughout the crowd talked to the people they used to guard and reminisced about old times. The Lord told stories of the past and the future. All was going as planned.

Worl smiled and said to his faithful guards, Left and Right, "It never ceases to amaze me how Jesus is always right. I was a little put out, when he made that deal with Satan, letting him take over the World and making us back off, but he was right. With Satan in charge, people have been flocking to our side daily. Within a couple of days only people sealed with the mark will be left on earth, along with the Christian Jews. Which reminds me, we have to be leaving for Jerusalem."

The three took flight in perfect formation, which came from their years of practice together. Several angels joined them as they went to prepare for the largest battle that would ever be fought on earth. They only had two years left and the time was passing fast!

CHAPTER NINETEEN
(IN THE SEVENTH YEAR OF CANARDS REIGN)

THE HOLY PLACE

HOLY TEMPLE: JERUSALEM:
December 8th: HANUKKAH'S EVE: 1900 HOURS:

As High Priest, Natan Cohen walked up the massive steps of the mighty Temple. He couldn't help but marvel at the spectacle in the sky. It had been on the news for weeks how the Doran Asteroid was heading for earth. Canards' mighty Demon Ships had tried to stop it, but all they had managed to do was shatter it into smaller pieces. It made for quite a light show as they entered the earth's atmosphere and burned. Of course, Canards was taking the credit for saving the earth. It was also predicted that two more asteroids would impact the earth in about three months. Canards assured the world that he could handle anything that came along and not to worry.

"Makes me feel a whole lot better. Right!" thought Natan as he entered the Temple.

He stood before the great curtains that separated the Sanctuary from the Holy Place. He had stood here every evening since this all had begun three and a half years ago right after his appointment as High Priest. Tonight was different, however. Perhaps it was because the Angels, who had been invisible since that first day when President Canards was chased from of the Temple, were now standing by the entrance fully visible and highly intimidating. Their swords were drawn and

247

flaming brightly. One touch from the tip of either sword would reduce Natan to charred bone. Their wings were fully extended. The right tip of one was touching the left tip of the other forming an arch of sorts, an arch through which Natan would have to pass in order to enter the Holy Place.

Perhaps the difference was the fact that tomorrow was Hanukkah, always an exciting day full of miracles and hope, or it could be knowing that President Canards had raised an army of two hundred million warriors which were, even now, on their way to Israel to, "Wipe out the nest of vipers that infest my Holy Land", as Canards put it.

But Natan knew that for him, the air of tension and anticipation came from the fact that soon he and the Prime Minister would meet with Jesus, their Savior. This was a change from the norm. They had never met with Him at the same time.

Natan, and his fellow Jewish Christians had grown spiritually over these years as well as in wisdom, and God had blessed their efforts. They now grew enough food to support themselves without any help from the outside, which, of course, they hadn't received. Life had improved for all of Israel and they were once again God's chosen people. The daily reports, which had slowed over the last few months, showed staggering numbers of Christians being killed throughout the world. Israel was ironically the largest stronghold of Christians left in the world, consisting of about two million Christian Jewish men along with their families. Natan had watched, via television, the day that President Canards had gone to the city of Covenant and had personally supervised the complete leveling of the city and the famous Jesus Park.

Canards had then built a Christian Detention Camp on the very spot! Natan had studied the efforts of Joshua White and the Christians who had followed him. Joshua, who was Natan's hero, and the Christian were all gone now except for Jarrett White, who was still on public display. Daily world wide on all channels at exactly ten o'clock or 2200 hours, President Canards would publicly ask him if he were ready to worship him. Jarrett White always answered with a sermon on how Jesus was the Messiah not Canards, and several people in the audience would be healed of various afflictions. Each day that Natan watched Jarrett looked even more emaciated and abused. He was suffering for all Christians since Canards' methods had limited the number of Christians available for abuse.

No one in Israel had taken the "Mark" and they all worshipped the Lord Jesus Christ as their Lord and Savior. Natan was very nervous with these odds. If every man in their entire country were to join their rather small army and face Canards, it would still be two million against Canard's two hundred million!

"200 to 1 plus God!" thought Natan, *"Well on second thought, that's not bad odds!"*

Rabbi Jenson walked into the Temple. The air crackled with the hustle and bustle of activity that always followed the man wherever he went. Natan slipped out into the courtyard to greet the Prime Minister.

Rabbi Jenson smiled as he approached Natan and said, "I'm really looking forward to this!" He passed Natan up before he could be warned, ducked through the curtain, walked right into the Sanctuary and straight to the awaiting Angels.

Jenson stopped dead in his tracks. The heat, the sheer power that radiated from these Angelic beings, was immense. The Prime Minister started to kneel but a booming voice from one of the Angels said, "No! We are not to be worshipped! Only God is to be worshipped! Enter the Holy Place, the Lord awaits you!"

When both men stood frozen in fear, the Angel spoke with a softer, kinder, more human voice, "Peace! Don't be afraid of us, we are here to help you. Please go in and meet with the Lord Jesus. No harm will befall you here!"

The two men, still reluctant, took a very tentative step toward the glory of the Angels. Their wings were still extended forming an arch under which the men must pass. Their clothing was as white as new fallen snow and shone like the sun. The hem and sleeves of their garments were lined with gold. Golden threads were woven throughout the cloth sending out little glittering shards of light and their clothing pulsated with varying degrees of brightness. As the men passed under the arch, they ducked even though the top of the arch was at least three feet above their heads. As they walked into the Holy Place, they were stunned by the Glory of the Lord Jesus Christ! Once again they fell on their faces.

Before them a bright shaft of light shot out of the Ark of the Covenant straight up into heaven. To this they were accustomed, but what they weren't expecting was to see the resurrected Jesus Christ, standing in all His Glory dressed for battle!

His hair was white as snow and from his eyes shot fire, which could cut a man to his very soul. His skin was bronze in color and his clothes were the same as the Angels, except that he wore a blue cloak that was attached to his golden breastplate.

As the men laid face down before their Lord and Savior worshipping Him with love and fear, the Lord spoke to them, "Why does it trouble you so that I'm dressed for war? Are we not at war more so now than any time in history? The army is approaching your outer borders and will reach them at daybreak. As it is written in the Scriptures, you must meet them at the valley of Armageddon near the Mountain of Megiddo.

When you leave this place, you must gather up all the people and leave the city at once! President Canards will use the last of his atomic weapons on Jerusalem just before sun up. He will level the city and anyone left here will die! Take your people to the ancient cities of Bazrah and Petra and stay there until I call for you in the morning. Then you must march your men to the Mountain of Megiddo and have them face the enemy, all two hundred million of them. Canards has fierce warriors and they will try to kill you. Trust me, they will not succeed. I had Beriak and Liberty appear to you outside so that you would remember the power of even our low ranking angels. The Angel on your left as you entered was your Guardian Angel, Natan. Liberty on your right as you entered was Chava's, but now he also guards you, Natan. I assure you Rabbi Jenson, that yours are just as impressive.

Tomorrow at about noon, the first of the enemy's army will arrive at Armageddon. Before that time, I'll call you to gather all of Israel at the base of Mt. Megiddo. You, Prime Minister Jenson, will stand with your back to the enemy and will read the scroll that was given to you on the day of your appointment. Do you have it?"

Natan looked up from the floor and said, "Yes Sir.

We do!"

Jesus smiled and said, "Come, get up! We must speak, openly and quickly, I must get back to the plans at hand."

Natan and Jenson got up and noticed that the intensity of Jesus' light had been toned down so as not to blind them. As they watched, another figure came out of the light and walked up behind Jesus. Natan recognized him as Moses, one of the two witnesses.

Moses, carrying a staff, walked up to Natan and handed to him, as he said, "Natan, this is the same staff I used when the Red Sea was parted and your ancestors were freed from the Egyptians. Now you will use it once again to free Israel from the rest of the world. Have faith tomorrow, God is with you!"

With that he turned, went back into the light, and was gone.

Jesus once again addressed the overwhelmed pair of men; "You must follow My instructions exactly as I give them to you. For years you've lacked faith in Me and must prove your new loyalty tonight and tomorrow, beyond a shadow of a doubt. Prime Minister Jenson, you'll be tempted to stop reading and turn around to watch the action, but don't give in to that temptation or your people will perish! Do you trust Me?"

Jenson said, "Yes, my Lord and my God!"

Jesus then turned to Natan, "High Priest Cohen, your arms will get tired and you'll be tempted to lower the staff, which you're to hold high and pointed toward the enemy at all times. You'll need two men to help hold your arms up and up they **must** stay or your people will be destroyed! High Priest Cohen, do you trust Me?"

Natan exclaimed, "Yes, of course, my Lord and my God!"

Jesus then addressed them both, "You will take no weapons but the scroll. Anyone with a weapon will die! Your people must stand unarmed before the great army of the enemy, totally trusting in Me to save them for that has been the way of My people from the beginning. Do you both trust Me?"

Both men were distressed that the Lord kept asking them that question and they answered in unison, "Yes, my Lord and my God!"

"Warn your people that no matter what they see, hear, feel or smell they are to stand firm and strong, praying for help from their Lord and Savior, Jesus Christ. I will deliver them from this army if only they will trust Me! One other thing! All your men must come out to the mountain. If they stay in any of the cities, they will be destroyed along with the cities not one stone will be left upon another. So fierce will this battle be, that the very foundations of the earth will be shaken. The world, as you know it, will cease to exist and a glorious new kingdom will be born, but you'll just have to see it to believe it!

"This is your final test, so you'd do well to rid yourself of everything you've ever learned about fear or doubt. There won't be any room for either. Remember, I Am!"

With that, the light of Jesus intensified and exploded into a Kaleidoscope of color and the voices of thousands of Angels singing rang from Heaven.

Tears streamed down the cheeks of the two men as they fell to their knees overwhelmed by the beauty and majesty of the Angels' song. For two hours, they knelt there and listened as the Angels revealed one secret after another about God's Kingdom. When the Angels were finished, there was a thunderous explosion. The lid to the Ark of the Covenant was lowered into place onto the bottom half of the Ark. When it slid into place, it cut off all light from the interior of the Ark. The Holy Place was now suddenly dark except for the light of one angel's sword.

The Angel said, "Men of Israel, arise! Prepare your people for their journey. Time grows short and the journey is long. You must leave soon if you are to make the dead line. Pick six groups of four men each who will then take turns carrying the Ark. When you are called in the morning to travel to Mt. Megiddo, have them carry the Ark at least a mile closer to the enemy than you will be standing. Have them set it down, turn and walk away. Then at a point at least a mile closer to the mountain than the Ark, I want you, Prime Minister Jenson, to stand with your scroll and your back to the enemy. High Priest Cohen, you stand at the Prime Minister's side facing the enemy and raise your staff until the battle is over.

"Now one last thing! Tomorrow is Hanukkah! This is the Festival of the Lights! Have your Priests carry the lights, incense and shewbread. Set up an altar on your side of the Ark of the Covenant right in the field of battle. Just as every Temple has been dedicated to God, the new one, which will arrive tomorrow, will also be dedicated in like fashion. The miracle you are about to witness is easily greater than any miracle ever performed for this Nation and at the same time a fulfillment of them all.

Satan defiled this Holy Temple. You are about to enter into the new, pure and undefiled New Jerusalem!"

With that the angel disappeared! The dazed, overwhelmed and utterly drained men slowly walked from the Holy Place. The people, who had been waiting anxiously in the Sanctuary, gasped when they saw the men. The hair on both their heads was pure white. Their faces shown with the glory of God, Himself! They literally glowed from within. The people had heard none of the words but they had heard thunder, had seen lightening and the fierce moaning sounds as of an animal in pain. Now, they saw two men who had emerged alive from a meeting with God!

The two men spent the next hour explaining their meeting with the Lord. They implored the people to listen to them and to follow their instructions to the letter. Then all two million men along with their wives and children put on their best clothes and headed for Bozrah and Petra to await their confrontation at Mt. Megiddo on the great plain of Armageddon.

BOZRAH:
DECEMBER 9TH, 2---: 0600 HOURS:

Prime Minister Jenson and High Priest Cohen hadn't slept at all the previous night even though they had been so advised by many people. Who could sleep knowing what was coming! They stood together in the only safe place in the world, Bozrah. It had taken them about two hours to drive the fifty-five miles from Jerusalem to Petra. They left about half of the women and children there with enough supplies for a month. Then the rest had driven the remaining twenty-five miles to Bozrah.

As everyone busily unloaded the trucks, Jenson and Cohen just stood and watched the beautiful light show, which still streaked across the sky every two minutes or so. It had been an unforgettable night.

Natan looked over at Rabbi Jenson and asked, "Would you read it to me again? I just can't believe that it was there all the time!"

Rabbi Jenson smiled and nodded his agreement as he opened his copy of the Holy Scriptures and read aloud,

"Micah 2:12 and 13. I will surely assemble, O Jacob, all of thee; I will surely gather the remnant of Israel; I will put them together as the sheep of Bozrah, as the flock in the midst of their fold: they shall make great noise by reason of the multitude of men.
The breaker is come up before them: they have broken up, and have passed through the gate, and are gone out by it: and their king shall pass before them, and the Lord on the head of them."

256

Natan shook his head as he said, "It's exactly what the Lord told us to do. He knew thousands of years ago what would happen this very day! Glory to God and to his Son, Jesus Christ!"

Except for the light of the streaking fiery masses of asteroid, it was still very dark. The sun wouldn't rise for another hour. The Jews were gathered amidst the mountains and could not see the plains from their vantage point. Suddenly, the night became day as the last five of Canards' atomic bombs went off in and around Jerusalem. In a flash, every ancient building in the city was leveled. Every tree, every animal and every human left in the area were vaporized. The ground rumbled, then rolled and finally cracked from this major attack on its fault lines. Huge fissures opened up under the front half of the Chinese army, instantly swallowing about one hundred million men and women along with all of their equipment. Canards had effectively destroyed Jerusalem but at what price? What was to be a happy moment of triumph turned into a moment of, "Who can I blame for this?"

Canards turned to General Butts and asked, "Which General was at the lead?"

Butts looked at his list and said, "Lee Wo Chung."

"Good, then it was his fault that the troops were too close."

The General made notes and smiled knowingly.

The mountains groaned as the Jews knelt and prayed to their God. The eerie lights in the night sky, the rumbling of the ground, the smoke that filled the air struck terror in the hearts of the enemy while the hearts of God's people were breaking over this violation of their home land. However, even through this immense experience, God's love and protection filled and healed their souls.

They looked up and saw the Angels standing around their stone fortress. The people began to stand one by one with their mouths open in disbelief. Apparently their trek to Bozrah had not gone unnoticed by Canards, he had sent several jets to attack their new location. He must have been livid with anger when he found out that the Jews were not in Jerusalem when it was bombed. The jets intended to fly over the top of the compound to drop their bombs, but once they reached the ridge of the mountains the angels shot lightening at the jets causing them to explode instantly. However, no matter how much debris filled the skies or dropped toward the huddled Jews, not one piece of it fell upon their heads. It just seemed to disappear.

As the Lord had promised, the world was turned inside out and upside down this morning yet not one of their number was harmed in any way.

The Jews had been huddled together in praise and thanksgiving for two hours when an Angel approached them and said, "It's time to drive over to Mt. Meggido. You'll just have time to make it before the attack. I'm General Worl and my warriors will clear your path. I'll leave plenty of protection for your families."

The men said good-bye to their wives and children and left for the last battle this world would ever see.

CHAPTER TWENTY

ARMAGEDDON
(THE MOUNTAIN OF MEGIDDO)

**"And then shall that Wicked be revealed,
whom the Lord shall consume with the
spirit of his mouth, and shall destroy
with the brightness of his coming:"
II Thes. 2:8 KJV**

**HEAVEN:
December 9th, 2---: NOON**

The Throne of God was under siege! God the
Father, God the Son and God the Holy Ghost were not
worried! Indeed, they felt rather sad because Satan had
finally gone over the edge just as they knew he would.
He would be God or die trying. This had to be the
inevitable outcome; Satan was blinded by his own pride
and arrogance.

Without warning, Satan, in a heightened state of
madness, attempted an assault on Heaven. He had led
his host of fallen Angels, too many to count and yet only
numbering a third of the total Angels that existed, in an
attempt to overthrow Jesus and defeat God on his own
ground. Jesus had called most of his Angels back to
heaven for this confrontation. He had foreseen the
attack and was more than prepared with Michael the
Archangel leading his troops against Satan and the fallen
Angels.

Satan, making one last ditch effort to take over the throne of God, screamed, "Charge!" and a wall of powerful, dark demons streaked across heaven toward the Seat of Power. About halfway to their destination, they ran into Michael and his guards. Swords clashed in a mighty effort to kill the enemy. Some of the demons got past the Angelic guard and were instantly devoured by the four Creatures that protect Heaven's Throne.

Michael watched as Satan stayed in the rear. He was pushing his men forward and getting them cut down due to the two to one odds against them. Heavenly Angels swept in literally overwhelming the Satanic army. Heaven began to fill with the reddish yellow, sulfuric smoke of the demon army's demise.

Jesus watched as his brave army swept the enemy from these Holy grounds. Michael was fighting his way closer to Satan himself and would soon be within a sword's reach of him.

Suddenly thunder rolled throughout heaven as the two mighty swords clashed. Satan's eyes grew big and round filled with doubt and fear, as the force of Michael's blow took him by surprise! Michael was relentless in his attack! His sword's blade had no sooner bounced off of Satan's blade than he swung again and again. Satan was backing up under the onslaught of Michael's wrath!

Clash! Ping! Pivot! Block! Parry! As soon as Michael's blade had hit the metal of Satan's blade, Michael kicked out with his right foot breaking Satan's knee.

Satan let out a scream that turned the demon's blood cold. His fury was at its peak! He finally made the mistake of leading a limping charge toward Michael and

ARMAGEDDON

his heavenly hosts. The demons with Satan were quickly snuffed out of existence and thrown down onto the earth. Satan swung one last time at Michael, who blocked it easily, then struck out with the hilt of his own sword striking Satan full in the jaw and knocking him senseless!

Michael, the mighty warrior of God, grabbed Satan by the scruff of the neck and carried him over to where Jesus sat on the Throne of Judgment.

As Satan began to come around, Jesus said, "You've lost this battle and shall now be banned from heaven forever! No longer can you come before me to accuse My followers!"

Jesus now addressed Michael, "I thank you once again for your faithful service. I will allow you the privilege of removing Satan from heaven yet again. We will turn him loose on the world one more time."

Michael bowed low and then threw Satan onto the ground. Satan disappeared from sight and reappeared on the earth. He was angry, and he denied his defeat reasoning that he would still beat God by stealing all of his people and destroying his favorites the Jews. He decided that he would not wait or even hesitate in their destruction. Satan called a meeting of his most trusted commanders and planned the most daring attack of his career.

EUROPEAN WORLD HEADQUARTERS OF W.E.L.: December 9th, 2---: NOON:

"Good afternoon! I'm Hans Rupple with the twelve o'clock world news. Another plot by a male/female

261

marriage was uncovered today. The couple was found to have a new infant, which they had hidden from the authorities. When the green army tried to take the baby, for good of the State, the couple resisted and had to be shot." On the screen behind Hans, the world watched as the couple was executed. They were kneeling down with their hands tied behind their backs and then they were shot in the back of the head. The baby was held up to show its happy, innocent face as the authorities removed the infant to one of their many youth homes, which had gone up around the world over the last few years.

Hans continued, "Here's some brighter news! Movie stars Bobby Taylor and Juan Barbo entered into a year contract of marriage today. The two men were joined together in the Temple of the Moon in London this morning at around ten. The happy couple will honeymoon in Egypt and visit the site of the glowing Pyramids. The screen behind Hans showed the couple kissing as Juan raised the veil on his wedding dress.

"A new type of bug was discovered today. As if it were not bad enough that the ants are in our food, our beds and our wardrobes; we now have a new and much more vicious threat." As Hans said the words "Vicious threat", the screen behind him changed from several consecutive scenes of ants doing what he described to fields full of angry looking locusts seen in black, crawling waves covering the fields and leaving nothing in their wake. A close up of the bug, held by a man dressed in protective gear, revealed an ugly angry looking bug with sharp teeth and a stinger each connected to a poison sack.

Hans continued, "The death count is already over one hundred thousand and rising as this moving ocean of death sweeps across the world.

Hans held his hand to his earpiece and a smile began to creep onto his face, "I have just been informed that President Canards is in place and ready to report live from the plains of Armageddon near the mountain of Megiddo." As Hans said this, the screen behind him projected a satellite map of the region as two crossed lines zeroed in on the spot and then enhanced it till it was big enough for the television audience to see. The screen then changed to live footage of the plain of Armageddon.

A man dressed in a tan camo-uniform stood next to President Canards, who was also dressed in a camo-uniform except his uniform shirt was covered with medals and rank insignia.

The field reporter spoke first, "Thanks Hans. This is Julius Hober III reporting to you live from the site of the largest build up of troops anywhere at anytime in history. Here with me to explain what is happening is the World President, himself, President Canards."

President Canards smiled, looked into the camera, and said, "I welcome the citizens of the world to this final battle. This is the largest, most powerful army ever assembled in one place. It makes even the Roman Empire's army look small. We're the New World Order, the New Roman Empire if you will. After I have totally destroyed the Jews, and thus all of Christianity, I'll have total control of this world. We can then get down to the business of purifying and purging it of all the warped thinking that the Christians left behind. We have already made great strides in that area, but more needs to be done. Before I share with you what will take place in what I expect to be a very short although extremely bloody battle at least for the Jews; I have provided us with a little entertainment. Julius, if you'll follow me?"

President Canards walked about a hundred yards to the east and the bumpy view steadied, as the cameraman reset the camera. The viewers were met with a gruesome sight. There on the back of a jeep was tied the most abused and hauntingly, sad man alive. His eyes were swollen shut, his nose was broken in several places, his lips were cut and swollen and his face was, in general, beyond recognition as human.

Canards continued, "You probably can't recognize this fool, but his name is Jarrett White. I have successfully killed every Christian in the World except the Jews and this man, Jarrett White. I wanted to show you what will happen this afternoon to the Jews, who have gathered not one mile from here, in the largest gathering of Jews in decades."

Canards pulled out his 45 cal. pistol and said, "Jarrett, after three and one half years of torture are you now ready to denounce this false Messiah, Jesus Christ, and bow down and worship me instead?"

Julius held the microphone close to Jarrett's lips so as to catch his last words as the entire world sat on the edges of their seats. What hate would this man shout? What spells of condemnation would he cast? They all knew the mistreatment he had received ever since his capture.

Jarrett was dizzy and his head was throbbing from the combination of dehydration, loss of blood and starvation, but he suddenly felt the power of the Holy Spirit swell up inside him. His mind cleared and he knew, for the first time, what was about to happen.

Jarrett thought, *'Thank you, Lord, for filling me with your Holy Ghost! I have tried over the past few years to control my temper and through your help I have been able to do away with the violence that waged war in my soul. Now you have given me the knowledge that was, until now, hidden from me. I offer myself up to you Lord Jesus. Take me into your Kingdom, as one of your most humble servants. I am not worthy of the gifts I have received.'*

President Canards' smile faded as Jarrett's smile appeared. President Canards had a bad feeling about this. Before he could stop it, Jarrett White spoke his final words into the microphone that Julius held for him, "Jesus Christ is coming back today! Prepare to meet your Creator-God, Jesus Christ, through whom all things were..."

President Canards pulled the trigger and stopped Jarrett, but the damage had been done. People all over the world and even in Canards own army were now full of fear.   The conviction in Jarrett's voice was unmistakable! He seemed to see something just before he was shot and that smile! It remained on his face even in death.

Canards turned to Julius and motioned him closer. He put the microphone in front of Canards, who said, "We are still over one hundred million strong against only two-million Jewish Christians. Even after my General's gross miscalculation this morning, which cost me the lives of over half of my troops, our army is ready.

I don't see any reason to wait another moment. Canards gave the signal! It was passed among the troops and the entire army started their tanks, jeeps, half-tracks and helicopters at precisely the same moment. It was very impressive and got everybody back on Canards' side. The roar was deafening, and President Canards knew that it would strike fear into the very hearts of his enemies.

JEWISH CAMP--ONE MILE AWAY--Hanukkah: December 9th, 2---:1215 HOURS:

Prime Minister Jenson was in position in front of his two million men. He held the scroll still sealed in his hands. He was very anxious to see what it had to say. They had all watched as Canards murdered Jarrett White. They had television sets, which ran off of auxiliary power, scattered throughout their large camp. He wanted everyone to be able to hear and see what was going on. It had taken the better part of four hours for his engineers to prepare the necessary configuration. It had allowed them to watch Canards and now it would allow them to see and hear their leader.

Mt. Megiddo was at their backs. There would be no escaping the onslaught that was about to begin. No way, that is, unless Jesus came through for them as he promised.

Just as Jesus requested, Prime Minister Jenson had moved his army up to the front facing the enemy with no one carrying a weapon. Neither side would be allowed to use aircraft. It took Canards about four hours of jet crashes and hundreds of lives for him to believe Jenson, who had warned him last night following Jesus' orders to call Canards with the warning. The smoke from the crashed jets could still be seen some five miles out in all directions.

Jenson's hands shook slightly as he heard the engines of the enemy equipment start. That was their cue. The Lord had said, "When you hear the thunder from their camp, turn your back on them, break the seal on the scroll and begin reading. At the same time have High Priest Natan Cohen raise his staff into the air and shout what I've instructed." Now the time had arrived to fulfill the orders of their Lord and Savior Jesus Christ.

Prime Minister Jenson, as instructed, turned his back on the one hundred million-man army, not an easy task, and broke the seal on the scroll. Immediately thunder, even louder than the combined noise of the engines of Canards' army, rolled across the Eastern sky. The ground shook, the sun turned in on itself and the dark sky turned even darker, becoming darker than night. Even the warnings they'd received from the Lord, hadn't prepared Jenson or his people for the power that was being unleashed upon this earth.

The High Priest raised his staff and shouted into the microphone in front of him, "But when the fullness of time was come, God sent forth his son, Jesus Christ, the son of David, the son of Abraham! The Lord God shall give unto him the throne of his father David: And he shall reign over the house of Jacob for ever; and of his kingdom there shall be no end."

There was a man on either side of Natan ready to hold his arms up if they should get tired. All was set! They were now in the Lord's hands.

Jenson opened the scroll, which glowed with its own light and began to read what it said as loudly as possible while trying to ignore the world around him, which was quickly falling apart.

He read loudly,

"But he was wounded for our transgressions, he was bruised for our iniquities: the chastisement of our peace was upon him; and with his stripes we are healed.

And I will pour upon the house of David, and upon the inhabitants of Jerusalem, the spirit of grace and of supplications: and they shall look upon me whom they have pierced, and they shall mourn for him, as one mourneth for his only son, and shall be in bitterness for him, as one that is in bitterness for his first-born.

For my love they are adversaries: but I give myself unto prayer.

Thou hast ascended on high, thou hast led captivity captive: thou hast received gifts for men; yea, for the rebellious also, that the Lord God might dwell among them..."

As Jenson read on, his people, one by one, had begun to kneel being convicted by the words and yet comforted by them. They began to understand that reality operated through prayer and nothing else. They began to ignore the chaos around them and got caught up in the Spirit of their God.

HEAVEN: JESUS PREPARES HIS ARMY:

Jesus looked out over the massive army before Him. He had divided his angels into divisions with an Archangel in charge of each and Michael over them all. The Christians, dressed in their best whites, knelt and prayed with their Jewish brothers and sisters on earth. The power of God was everywhere.

Jesus stood and walked down the stairs leading from His throne to the golden street below. Jarrett White, walking next to Andy, strode the golden path toward Jesus. His peaceful smile beamed and gone were the signs of abuse, pain, loneliness and doubt. Gone were the violent rages that had warred within his soul, he had finally understood the message. He had accepted Jesus as his Savior and had suffered greatly for his belated faith.

Jesus hugged Jarrett, when he was close enough and said, "Welcome home, Jarrett White! I'm glad you've finally joined Me. I wish We had time to show you around but as you can see, We're preparing for the biggest battle in human history. You can join us if you like?"

Jarrett laughed, "I wouldn't miss it for the world! Just tell me what to do!"

Jesus said, "Andy show Jarrett to his brother's group and we'll begin."

PRESIDENT CANARDS' CAMP ON THE MOVE:
December 9th, 2---:1215 HOURS:

"I'm finally going to rid the world of this disease once and for all! No more goody-goodies! No more false worship of that false Messiah! Just disciples full of fear and respect for me!" President Canards thought while standing in his jeep and watching the slow advance of his massive forces. Were it not for the immense quantity of lightning and the multitude of vehicle lights, the darkness would have totally robbed the Chinese army of the usual gleaming of their bright red helmets and breastplates as they passed in formation before Canards. It had taken Canards over two years to convince them to join him in his quest. They had made-up over a hundred and fifty million of the original two hundred million troops present here today making them still the single largest group in the remaining troops. The rest were fragmented forces from all over the world, men and women with nothing better to do with their lives now that all individual Governments and armies had failed. Now they all belonged to the World Equality Force, the stinger of the W.E.L. Organization.

President Canards watched the screen as the Prime Minister of Israel broke the seal on the scroll.

Satan was hidden safely within Canards' body but as the earth began to tremble so did Satan. Canards mimicked Satan's thoughts as he whispered, "Where did he get that scroll? That scroll can't be unsealed until the end...Oh no! The end...I didn't think he would ever do it! He can't do this to me!"

JEWISH CAMP:
December 9th, 2---: 1225 HOURS:

As President Canards' troops advanced, fear swelled up in Natan's stomach. He couldn't breathe. The enemy's army was very impressive wearing their red breastplates, which shone despite the lack of sun. Once the Prime Minister broke the seal of the scroll from which he now read, Natan felt dizzy and his mouth and throat were very dry. His arms after just ten minutes were burning pillars of aching muscle, screaming for relief. His guards lifted his arms even higher sending sharp pains into his chest. He heard the shuffling of his people as they knelt and then lay prostrate before their God. Within the same ten minutes, all the people lay convicted before their God and Lord, Jesus Christ. Their prayers of acceptance of Jesus rose to heaven with the dust of the desert. God was pleased and He sent lightening to light up the eerie darkness.

Natan whispered, "I need something to drink." His throat was parched. One of the guards gave him a drink of water and after swallowing several mouthfuls, Natan yelled into the microphone, "Now!"

Instantly from every direction at once arose the sound of the trumpet blasts! Then silence! Then into that eerie silence came the combined shout of all two million Jews, "Jesus Christ is our God, and we await His return!"

Tears ran down Natan's cheeks as he remembered Chava and his children. He knew they were on the way down with Jesus, and he couldn't wait for their arrival.

Natan had been counting to one hundred as instructed by the Lord and he shouted again, "Now!" Again the trumpet blasts and again the shout from the people. As Natan watched, millions of flashlights and lanterns came on in the enemy camp creating a very impressive sight that was more frightening than reflecting armor. Natan sensed a glimmer of fear from his people at this sudden site and offered a silent prayer for his people and himself for the events to come.

He then looked over at the Altar of Incense that they had carried from the Temple, and the Candle Stick, which held the seven empty lamps. The Lord had instructed them to bring the altar but not to put incense into it and the same with the Candlestick. Bring it but do not fill it.

It was beginning to look bleak. The dust cloud, which rose thirty feet above the advancing enemy army reflecting their ghostly shapes against the dust filled sky, striking fear into the Jewish men, who were forced to watch helplessly as the enemy approached.

Natan had been counting, "99, 100...Now!" Again the trumpets and again the obedient shout, "Jesus Christ is our God, and we await His return!"

Then instantly there was...silence and darkness as every piece of equipment and every flash light in the enemy camp died at once! Both sides were stunned and shocked, they just stood one half mile apart and looked into the darkness of the noonday sky!

PRESIDENT CANARDS--ANTI-CHRIST:
December 9th, 2---: 1230 HOURS:
LAST DATE AND TIME OF THE OLD ORDER

President Canards was scared and angry at the same time. He was no doubt feeling Satan's own frustration; he knew what was about to happen. He had denied the possibility for all of these thousands of years. Yet, here it was, unfolding before him as predicted. He thought God had been bluffing all of these years.

"God won't hurt his little pets," Satan had told himself many times. Now in an instant he knew he had been wrong.

"I should be happy that he is going to destroy these people for me, but I want them all!" he pouted greedily.

After listening to the roar of engines for half an hour, the silence was by far more deafening now than the engines had ever been. The darkness was closing in like a pillow being lowered to snuff the life out of his army. Canards couldn't breath! He coughed and then choked on his own fear.

Satan, after quite a struggle, got Canards back under control and was trying to think what to do next. Satan whispered into Canards' soul, Canards shrugged his shoulders and yelled, "Charge!"

JEWISH CAMP:
THE ORIGINAL HANUKKAH MIRACLE REPEATS ITSELF

High Priest Natan Cohen was trembling with fear as he heard the order of charge given and then the collective scream of over one hundred million men and women as they ran forward to kill the Jews with their bare hands if they had to.

Natan thought, *"Oh, Lord have I led my people to their death? I think..."*

His thoughts were interrupted when the Candlestick suddenly flared into life. All seven lamps lit up at the same moment. In the new blinding light, Natan could also see incense rising toward heaven in one pure, sweet smelling cloud of hope.

Every Jew there knew that the lamps and the altar had been empty, and they knew that God was repeating his miracle of the lights. Whether a Jew was schooled in the miracle of the flask of oil, which burned untended for eight days found in the story of Elijah and Elisha, or whether they believe that the Sons of Hasmonean the High Priest who defeated the Greeks, entered the temple and found eight spears there on which they lit eight candles or any of the other stories surrounding the Hanukkah miracle; allowed them here and now to know for certain that Jesus Christ was coming back to reclaim his throne.

Natan's pain was forgotten as he smiled into the flame. Nothing, not even the charge of millions of angry and scared enemy solders, could pull his gaze away from the miraculous flame. Nothing, that is, except what happened next.

ENEMY CHARGE:

President Alfred Canards had gone mad with rage! He was running in front of all of the troops oblivious to the danger, fear, or even the consequences of his actions. He just wanted one thing--to choke the life out of that High Priest!

Then he stopped dead in his tracks, as did all of his troops! Lights had come on in the enemy camp. Canards squinted into the Jewish camp and saw the lamp stand and the Altar of Incense with its billowing cloud of smoke.

The earth began to tremble again, with more force this time. A buzzing noise filled the air. Canards and his men looked around but could see nothing. Then they were struck with such surprise and ferocity that the barbarian army panicked. Millions of the most vicious, ugly, frightening insects ever to walk this earth began to attack Canards' army. They were a form of locust that had sharp teeth and a stinger, both of which injected deadly poison into its victims. A slow, painful death always followed a bite from this type of insect. The army of millions began swinging their heavy swords at the insects, the result of which ended in about a fourth of Canards' army being wiped out within the first five minutes. Then the earthquake hit!

The ground under Canards' army began to shift and roll. Men and women began to vomit, sweat and cry. Large sections of the earth disappeared and were replaced by open pits of fire into which fell another fourth of Canards' army.

Around the world, cities crumbled into ruin, whole islands disappeared into the sea and the world was turned upside down. In Rome, at the Vatican, Pope Vincent Vermuchi was buried in the rubble that was once the home of holy men of the past. Then the entire city of

Rome was swallowed up by the earth as it opened, and then resealed.

Canards had only fifty million men left!

Suddenly with a terrifying roar and a blinding light, the Eastern Sky was torn open, rent beyond time and space, right into the very being of God Himself! Immediately a heavenly glow poured out of the wound in the sky onto the dark and tortured earth below.

Canards stood there helpless with rage. His face turned red, veins popped out on his forehead bursting, shooting blood onto his near-by guards.

Natan, his arms still held high, watched in awe as the army of God descended from heaven!

CHAPTER TWENTY-ONE
THE BOTTOMLESS PIT

THE ARMY OF JESUS:

Jesus spoke from heaven causing thunder to roll across the Eastern sky. Both human armies looked up at the sound. "Father, the time is here! Split the Eastern Sky and reveal the Glory of Your Son!"

The two armies watched in helpless awe as the Eastern sky was split open. The Glory of God filled the skies with the glorious light of heaven itself, which chased away the gloom that had filled the earthly sky all morning. They could see Jesus, riding upon a beautiful, powerful, pure white horse. Jesus was clothed in gold and wore a golden crown embedded with priceless gemstones. His pure white hair shot streaks of light in every direction as he rode closer to the darkness that, of course, fled from his presence.

Canards and his army had forgotten about the Jews and were now running back the way they had come.

Behind Jesus flew Michael the Archangel and his many guards. Angels began to fan out in all directions. Behind the Angels flew the mighty Christians, who with their resurrected bodies could defy all of the old rules of earth. They could no longer be killed, a handy trait when fighting a war; and they never got hungry, thirsty, hot or cold. They felt no pain nor did they have any of the very annoying human weaknesses, which used to accompany them wherever they went. The Christians were dressed in flowing white gowns, which were composed of one piece of seamless cloth. They glowed with the radiance of God, Himself.

Natan, the Prime Minister, who was now allowed to watch, and their fellow Jews all stood by and cheered as this new army came to their rescue. The Christians drew swords of their own, The Word of God, and began to praise God for his wisdom, power and glory. As they sang out, the ground turned to quicksand under the remaining enemy and their foes sank to their waists in the muck and mire. Angels swept in and, with a few swift, well placed thrusts and slices of their mighty swords destroyed Canards' soldiers. Blood poured from the millions of bodies that lay twitching and screaming in the muddy ground. In places, the rivers of blood ran four feet deep all across the plains of Armageddon.

Natan fought the urge to throw up and held his staff high; the battle was not over.

As Canards breathed his last, Satan ripped himself from the disgusting human host and stood to face the Lord. Satan's demons, which had also been hiding in the bodies of their victims, now stood behind Satan! The lost human souls gathered to watch this unbelievable sight! Most of them had not believed in the existence of Satan, much less Jesus, a mistake that they would live with for all of eternity.

Jesus pulled up short, sitting on His beautiful white horse and turning to Michael He said, "Would you like to do the honors?"

Michael smiled, as he brought his right fist to left breast in salute of his Lord, and then shouted, "Forward men!"

Demons flew out of the ground to assist their brothers under attack until all demons were finally present. Swords clashed! As the demons were killed, they didn't flash and disappear in the usual puff of smoke, but instead they were paralyzed on the battlefield and forced to watch the complete demise of their mighty army.

The mighty General Worl and his two guards Left and Right fought their way over to General Rumpus and Captain Crygen.

General Worl smiled at General Rumpus. Rumpus wasn't the proud eager demon of just a few years ago. His robes of office were torn and dirty. Fear literally oozed from his eyes.

Worl said, "Want to surrender now?"

Rumpus' fear turned to hatred and he attacked! He brought his sword down hard toward Worl's head, but Worl simply blocked, stepped back and swung his sword upward cutting through Rumpus' left shoulder and his neck severing both his left arm and head in one swing! Then suddenly, Worl saw a streak out of the corner of his eye. He turned to meet this new danger, but burst out laughing instead. Standing before him was the mighty General Tumult, except that now he was only four feet tall and had no muscles at all.

Tumult yelled in a weak high-pitched voice, "Worl! Prepare to die!"

As the puny Tumult attacked, Worl easily sliced him in half. He felt only pity for what had once been a mighty warrior.

Worl's guards, in the mean time, had killed Crygen with a minimum of effort. As quickly as it had started it was finished!

Satan stood before Jesus Christ alone!

Jesus said, "Satan! You've condemned yourself and your entire army to the punishment of death and eternal fire! Watch!"

As Jesus said this, he pointed toward Satan's defeated army and the damned human souls who trembled together in fear in the middle of the battlefield. They screamed and moaned for mercy, but got neither. The ground beneath their feet became like oil, and they sank slowly into the depths. When they were about chest deep in this liquid blackness, the entire surface of the ground exploded into flame and the damned souls were burned, but not consumed, as they slipped into hell not to be seen again until after the thousand years of Jesus' reign of peace.

JEWISH CAMP:

The sky filled with a black cloud, which seemed to be coming from every direction at once. As each stream of blackness intersected over the pit of fire, they merged into a twisting, turning tornado, which bored a hole into the ground. Screams of rage, hatred, pain and the knowledge of their own damnation filled the sky causing Natan and Jenson to flinch as the mournful sounds coming from hell overwhelmed their being. These were the souls of the damned from all over the world. They were being gathered into this place of torture from which there would be no escape. The last to go in were the souls of Alfred Canards, who had misled many people, and Pope Vincent Vermuchi, who had sold out his faith, his church and his God for the Anti-Christ whom he had worshipped in exchange for power and wealth in a world that had become extinct. As he slipped below the rim of the fissure, his eyes locked with those of Pope Ferdinand Danbury, who was standing in Jesus' army. He looked happy and fulfilled. Vermuchi could see the pity in his eyes. Then all was blackness and pain.

Natan watched as the flames licked across the surface of the ground. He saw Jesus motion to Michael to do something. Michael, who was now holding a large chain gleaming in radiance of the light Jesus' presence, flew toward Satan. Worl and his guards held Satan as Michael chained his hands and feet and then for good measure, wrapped a great length of chain all around his body, which when it reached the end simply melted into the other chain forming one piece.

Satan stood there struggling, but to no avail.

Jesus, still sitting upon his white horse, spoke loud enough for his entire army to hear, "My faithful followers! You have waited long and suffered much to see this! Today all the blood spilled by this being will be vindicated! I hold the keys to heaven and hell, and this creature will not escape My final Judgment!"

A large bottomless, pit appeared beneath Satan's feet and he fell straight down.

He screamed, "I'll get you for thisssssssssssss!!!"

His voice could be heard for a good five minutes before it faded to silence. Jesus opened his mouth sending lightening forth into the pit and the resulting explosion sealed the opening tight. As the pit sealed, so did the fissure sealing hell until the Day of Judgment.

Jesus looked toward heaven and said, "Heavenly Father, we give you all the honor and glory for this victory! Let Your Will be done!"

The world around Nantan disappeared and was instantly replaced by the most beautiful country he had ever seen. He would discover later that he now stood on a world with no oceans. He and his people, as well as Christians from around the world and of course the resurrected, supernatural Christians, all stood in a great field with mountains off in the distance on all sides.

Jesus stood before them and spoke, "Watch as the glory of your God is revealed!"

Out of the sky came a shadow! A shadow that they would soon discover was a cube with all sides being 1500 miles across, down and high! Natan stood with his mouth open as he watched New Jerusalem descend from heaven! The walls were 216 feet thick, and the entire city was made of transparent gold, as of glass. The twelve gates were made of rare, expensive materials as well as gemstones.

The gates were open as it set itself down with such a jolt that it knocked the Christians off of their feet. That's when they noticed that the desert floor had been replaced by plush green grass. They laughed with the joy of God's presence as they rolled in the soft, sweet smelling fields of New Jerusalem. Jesus led them all into the City of Gold. They all just watched in awe as the Angels flew through the sky. As the Angels passed each building it lit up and sparkled, with the Angel's light reflected in such gem stones as diamonds, rubies, and emeralds, to name just a few.

The Christians knew instantly that this New Jerusalem had no Temple; God was to be worshipped everywhere!

Jesus spoke! Each of the millions of Christians present heard him clearly as he said, "You have all fought a good fight! Rest now in the peace and tranquility of my Father's City! We've spared no effort in making sure that each of you have a mansion in which to live and you'll each be fulfilled in God's purpose for you! Welcome, finally to your just reward!"

Surprise and awe slowly gave way to joy and exploration! Natan and Chava met their children who were, like everyone else, full grown adults. They were all safe, happy and felt joy as Natan and Daniel finally had a chance to embrace for the first time since their separation.

Joshua White and his brothers Jarrett and Chad, all ran in together! They were laughing and anxious to meet up with their friends to talk over old times.

The city glowed with the intense presence of God. He poured His Spirit upon its citizens. The veil had been rolled away and would no longer separate the people of earth from their God. The Eastern sky had split revealing the Glory and Wonder of God and at the same time melding Heaven and Earth in eternal piece and harmony.

Jarrett stopped suddenly and began to weep. Joshua and Chad stopped and looked back at their brother asking in unison, "What's wrong Jarrett?"

Jarrett smiled, as tears of joy continued to stream down his cheeks and he whispered; "Now I understand so many things. Just as the Lord spoke in I Corinthians 13:12:

> *"For now we see through a glass, darkly; but then face to face: now I know in part; but then shall I know even as also I am known."*

As Jarrett quoted the scripture, his face began to glow with the presence of God. His happy brothers watched as Jarrett was taken completely into the presence of God. Their brother, who had fought against God for so long and who had struggled with his faith right up to the very end, was now seeing God as He is.

Chad turned to Joshua and said, "Josh, if only more souls had listened and had accepted Jesus as their Savior, they would..." The brothers were silent. For a moment they could again hear the mournful pleas of the damned souls, for whom it was too late.

Joshua whispered, "Yes, Chad! If they had only listened, while there was still some time to act!"

To obtain additional copies of this or other Covenant books:

A Darkness Over Covenant
The Demon Slayer

Visit your local Christian book retailer

or

On the Internet:
www.covenant-ministries.com

or

Send your request to:
A&L Enterprises
1531 Hwy 151
Ava, IL 62907